THE SECOND CHANCE CAFÉ

The Second Chance Café

A Hope Springs Novel

Alison Kent

The characters and events portrayed in this book are fictitious. Any similarity to real persons, living or dead, is coincidental and not intended by the author.

Printed in the United States of America.

Published by Montlake Romance
P.O. Box 400818
Las Vegas, NV 89140

ISBN-13: 9781611097894
ISBN-10: 1611097894

To Robyn Carr, for *Virgin River,* and to Barbara O'Neal, for *The Lost Recipe for Happiness.* These two books took me back to my roots and the stories I've longed to tell. Thank you for making this happen.

CHAPTER ONE

It was done.

The papers signed. The money transferred. The holding tight to the other shoe a thing of the past.

After weeks of waiting to hear on her offer, Kaylie Flynn was the proud owner of the three-story Victorian nestled on an oak-shaded acre and painted Van Gogh's *Starry Night* blue.

It was the house where she'd spent the best years of her life. It was the house that had saved her. She wrapped her hand around the keys, the tiny teeth like a smile in her palm, and glanced up at the windows taking her in.

The shutters would be the first thing she replaced. Several slats were broken, some dangling, others gone. They'd once been white, but the paint had since chipped and faded. A soft dove gray would suit much better. Or maybe the pale butter-yellow of Van Gogh's stars.

"You've got the keys, your copies of the pertinent documents, and my number if we've missed anything. All the utilities were turned on this morning. You'll need to transfer them into your name, but you should be set. Can you think of anything else before I go?"

The real estate agent. Carolyn Parker. The other woman had remembered Kaylie from high school, but the memories from Kaylie's past had yet to be puzzled into place. "Sorry. I was lost picturing new shutters, but yes. I should have everything."

"Ah, not quite. For new shutters, you need a contractor."

"Actually, I'm going to need a contractor for a whole lot more than that."

"Then you're in luck, because I know just the man. I'm pretty sure I have his card here somewhere," Carolyn said, her voice lost in the depths of the quilted tote hooked over her shoulder.

Kaylie was used to professional women accessorizing with designer labels. The quilted tote's paisley and pink elephant print reminded her how far Hope Springs, Texas, was from Austin—a distance that had little to do with miles, but everything to do with Kaylie's return.

"Here you go," Carolyn said, coming up with the card. "Anything you need repaired or replaced, Ten's your man. He's the best, and runs a crew that knows what they're doing, even if they're a bit unconventional."

Tennessee Keller. Two words and a phone number. The whole of the information imparted by black ink on white stock. She filed away the "unconventional" remark, preferring to make that judgment for herself. "He's here? In Hope Springs?"

Carolyn nodded, blowing at an unruly brown curl dangling between her eyes. Carolyn, Kaylie had come to notice, was always blowing, pushing, adjusting, as if she was so used to doing the same for her two-year-old twins, she couldn't stop setting things to right.

"For about seven years, I guess? Eight maybe? He did some work on Wade's back porch the summer we started dating, so that would've been...wow, more like ten."

Ten years ago, Kaylie had left Hope Springs for Austin, her departure a ship in the night to Tennessee Keller's arrival. A decade of work in the area should mean he'd have plenty of references. She tucked that thought away, too, sliding the card into the back pocket of her jeans.

"Thanks. I guess that'll do it, then. At least for now." She moved her keys from her right hand to her left to shake Carolyn's. "I really appreciate you going to bat for me with the Colemans."

"Oh, please. How could they say no? In this economy? And you paying cash? I mean, really, it's not my business, but cash?"

Kaylie's financial advisor had been of the same incredulous mind, but Kaylie would not be swayed. Cash meant the house was hers. The lawn, the trees, the memories. The bedroom. The kitchen. Most of all the kitchen.

She slipped her fingertips into the pocket with the card and toyed with the edge. She had big plans for the kitchen. Even better, now she had the funds to see them through. "I know how crazy it sounds, but it was the right thing to do."

"Well, it's your money. I guess you're the one who would know best where to put it. Listen." Carolyn was speaking into her tote again. "We rarely have any problems with vagrants or break-ins, but the Colemans got so caught up caring for Bob's parents in Wichita Falls that the place kinda took a backseat. The police have had to run off squatters a time or two."

She handed over another card from what Kaylie guessed was her collection belonging to local businesses. This one was imprinted with the official seal of the Hope Springs Police Department. "You can always call 911, but this is the direct line to Alva Bean in dispatch. If you need an officer, he'll have someone here pronto."

"Great. I really appreciate it." The card joined the one for the contractor. "Oh, wait. There is something. Would you know what time the newspaper office closes today?"

Carolyn brought up a hand to shield her eyes from the sun as it cut through the limbs of the street-side oaks. "Since it's Friday, that makes me want to say three. We've got a high school girl at the office who takes care of our listings there, so I can't be sure."

"Thanks." Kaylie wanted to put an ad in the next weekly edition, but before she did anything, she needed to get Magoo from her Jeep. "Maybe we can have lunch sometime soon? My treat?"

"Wow. A meal eaten without twenty grubby fingers reaching for everything on my plate? It's a date." With a wave, Carolyn turned to go, her sensible flats smacking against the sidewalk as she made her way to her minivan, parallel parked at the curb.

Kaylie waited until the other woman had pulled safely onto Second Street, then headed through the overgrown grass to the driveway on the Chances Avenue side of the lot. "Hey, Goo. Ready to check out the new digs?"

Tongue lolling, the two-year-old shepherd mix placed his paws on the doorframe and boosted himself halfway through the window. Kaylie slapped her hand to her thigh, and ninety pounds of dog sailed through the air to land at her feet.

She scratched between his ears, then circled the vehicle to grab his water bowl from the passenger floorboard. He trotted beside her to the breezeway connecting the garage to the house. The door there opened into a mudroom that opened into the kitchen she'd dreamed of for ten years. She filled the bowl at the sink, setting it near the back door before allowing herself to take everything in.

She didn't know where to start. The six-foot island with a stove top, cutting board, and second sink for food prep. The walk-in pantry with shelves deep enough and tall enough to stock with a platoon's worth of supplies. The linoleum that had suffered skid marks from rubber-soled shoes, and gouges from dropped mixer beaters, and stains from food coloring intended for a red velvet cake.

Kaylie wrapped her arms around her middle and remembered the klutz she'd been at twelve. All those tiny squeeze bottles, the mess on her fingers and the toes of her shoes, the droplets flung like blood from a knife to the floor. She'd ruined a brand-new sponge, wasted half a roll of paper towels, and still not wiped away all traces of the spill. She'd wanted so badly to surprise May Wise, but her foster mother had been less concerned about her birthday—or the shambles of the kitchen—than to hear through a sobbing confession that Kaylie knew about knife wounds.

As much as Kaylie would love to install hardwood or Italian marble, her plans required commercial flooring—durable; slip-, fire-, and stain-resistant; easy to maintain. The menu for her daily ten-to-two lunch would be simple, self-serve, and self-pay. Salad, bread, entrée, dessert. Payment in cash dropped in a cigar box at the dining-room door.

Kaylie's specialty was business—and brownies—not reproducing the breads baked in this kitchen the eight years she'd lived here. Or putting together the hearty main dishes she would serve others as May Wise had served those in her care. Making a success of Two Owls Café meant a cook who knew red leaf from romaine, Gouda from feta from *Parmigiano* from Swiss. Egg noodles from rice noodles from semolina spaghetti. Hiring the right woman, or man, was a priority.

She hadn't come to her plan lightly. Malina's Diner was the only true restaurant in Hope Springs proper. Max Malina did a booming breakfast business, but closed at ten once the rush was done. He reopened at four for dinner, leaving a six-hour window where anyone wanting a meal had to cook or leave town. The fast-food franchises on the interstate, Kaylie had learned, boomed at lunch like Max's place did at first light.

Two Owls Café would offer an alternative to soup and sandwiches, burgers and fries. But more than that, it would offer a place for friends to gather, and over a meal discuss crafts and child rearing, music and books and movies, favorite recipes and gardening tips. Kaylie saw her place as an oasis, one with a limited menu, yes, but then this house had always been about nurturing with things other than food.

She glanced at Magoo as he huffed and snorted his way around the room's baseboards, his tail up, his ears up, his nose hard at work. "Whaddaya think, Goo? 'Wanted. A butcher, a baker, a candlestick maker'?"

Magoo gave a single distracted wag of his tail in answer, then moved into the dining room, leaving Kaylie on her own in the kitchen. It was this room, more than any other, where she'd come to terms with the life she'd lost and the one she'd been gifted in return.

What she hadn't been able to do, however, was reconcile the images, the ones stamped on her five-year-old mind's eye: Her mother lying bloody on the floor of another kitchen. Their neighbor, Ernest, holding her tiny, shivering body and crying when the authorities had whisked her away. Her father like dust in the wind.

She needed to know the whole story. And only from the harbor of this house that had saved her would she be strong enough for the truth.

~

After carting the few belongings she'd brought with her to the third-floor bedroom, Kaylie called for Magoo and loaded both of them into her Jeep. It was almost three, and if Carolyn was right, the *Hope Springs Courant* was closing soon. Before she lost herself for hours in the house—no, not *the* house, *her* house—measuring the windows and rooms, sketching possible furniture placement, noting the most obvious of the needed repairs, she had to make the trip into town.

She found the small square building squatting on Fifth Street, the post office to its left, the Dollar General finishing off the block, and eased forward into one of the angled parking places. Giving Magoo orders to stay put, she tugged open the paper's front door and stepped into the low-ceilinged room that spoke less of urgent deadlines and more of garage sales and grocery specials.

"Good afternoon. May I help you?"

Kaylie turned to the woman who'd appeared from the closest cubicle, its walls decorated with school photos and family snapshots pushpinned into place. "I wanted to place an ad in your classifieds."

"Sure thing, hon. Let me find you a form." One hand on the counter, she bent to shuffle through the supplies stored beneath. Her nails tapping against the surface were short and painted a bright orange-pink to match her lipstick. The color was the only makeup on her face and shockingly bright, but somehow it suited her perfectly. "Here's a pencil. And here's the form. Name, address, phone number, then the ad worded exactly as you'd like it to appear. It's best if you print. Makes for fewer mistakes in data entry."

While Kaylie got started, the other woman explained the cost, the circulation numbers, and the distribution schedule. "You can pay for up to four weeks at a time, or pay for one and let us know by the next week's deadline if you want to run it again."

"I'll start with two weeks, if that's okay. See where I am with responses, and go from there."

"Put a check mark right here, then," the woman said, pointing to a box in the *For Office Use Only* section, and frowning as she began to read through. "Your address. The corner of Second and Chances? You bought the Coleman place?"

"It was the Wise place when I knew it, but yes. That's the house."

"The Wise place." The frown deepened, dredging a vee between the other woman's thick eyebrows. "You knew May and Winton Wise? Were you one of their kids? I mean, it's none of my business, but it's mostly local folks who remember the Wises."

Kaylie nodded, extending her hand. "Kaylie Flynn. I came to live with them when I was ten, though I would've been Kaylie Bridges then."

"Kaylie Bridges. Oh my God! I'm Jessa Little!" Jessa pumped Kaylie's hand as if priming a water well, her plump bosom bouncing. "Well, I'm Jessa Breeze now. I married Rick Breeze after graduation. Oh, did I ever love your brownies. I think eighth grade was when I fell in love with chocolate, thanks to you. There wasn't a weekend I wasn't baking something. And then Rick magically fell in love with me."

Kaylie laughed, glad to hear her baking had benefited others as well as herself. "Happy to do my part for true romance."

Jessa leaned closer to whisper, "I hope the name change means you've got an amazing man in your life."

"Of a sort." Kaylie glanced outside to see Magoo draped out the Jeep's passenger-side window, watching her. His tongue hung over his chin as he panted. His big paws dangled down the door. "That guy out there keeps me company."

"Huh. Looks like the type to scare off any other company you might want."

"He knows his place. He wouldn't leave the Jeep even if you waved a sirloin in front of him."

"Ah, but let someone look at you the wrong way…"

"It's definitely been an unanticipated benefit of pet ownership," Kaylie admitted, opening the Baggallini wallet attached to her belt. “Is cash okay, or do you prefer a credit card?”

“Either one,” Jessa said, then took the bills Kaylie counted out and handed her. “I’ll be right back with your change.”

While waiting, Kaylie returned her attention to her dog. Magoo had been her constant companion since an emotional, spur-of-the-moment decision had sent her into the parking lot of the animal shelter, where he’d been left with his littermates days before. She’d been sad, alone, and desperate for a friend. May Wise’s funeral had broken her.

Who was she going to call when she wanted to brainstorm new brownie recipes? Who would remind her to pick up shards of broken glass with a balled-up slice of bread? Or to clean the grease from the blades of her garbage disposal with ice cubes?

Who would answer the phone in the middle of the night and listen to her breathe when she woke from the dream that left her gasping?

“Here’s your receipt and change.” Jessa was holding out both when, perspiration pasting her bra to her breasts, Kaylie pulled herself out of the nightmare. “Not that it’s any of my business, but I read through the ad. You’re opening a restaurant?”

Kaylie cleared her throat. “I am, yes. A café. On the first floor of the house.”

Jessa toyed with a puff of a curl cupping her ear. “Do you mind if I mention this to Rick’s mother? And give her your number? The woman puts those Food Network chefs to shame.”

"Not at all. I'd love for you to. And if there's anyone else you can think of, please have them call or come by. I'm anticipating it'll be just shy of three months before the café's open, but I want to involve whoever I hire with the planning."

"Have you already moved in?"

"It's more like I'm camping in. I need a couple of walls knocked out, some painting done, an overhaul of the kitchen." Not to mention all the upgrades and improvements. "I'll be staying there while that's going on, but won't move my furniture in until the construction's finished." Another thing that couldn't wait. "Speaking of construction, do you know of Tennessee Keller?"

"Oh, sure. Everyone knows Ten. Are you looking to hire him to do the work?"

"I'd like to go with a local contractor if possible."

"Then Ten's who you want. No one's better. Ask anyone in town and they'll be able to point you to a job he's done."

"Carolyn Parker told me he'd done some work for Wade."

"For Rick's mother, too. Ten's helped her out a lot since Rick's dad died. He's a good man." Jessa paused, smiled, then pressed her hands to her cheeks as if doing so would hide her blush. "He's also quite a man, if you know what I mean."

Kaylie had never had girlfriends. She'd had classmates and coworkers; then she'd had employees. She'd also had neighbors, but no one to talk to about men. Not the confident roll of their hips as they walked. Not the fit of their clothes, the strength of their hands, their opinions. Not the zeal in their eyes when they had something on their minds.

She gave Jessa what she hoped passed for a look that said she knew exactly, when in reality she was more interested in the work he did than in the man. As busy as she was going to be over the weekend, talking to him now would make for one less chore on her list. “I’d love to see him while I’m out, but I only have a phone number. Does he have a shop? Or an office? Though I guess I could call for directions…”

“Do you know where Grath Avenue is?”

“I’m sure my GPS does.”

“He’s at the end. A big barn where he works, and a couple of other buildings. His house is at the very back of the bunch. You can’t miss it.”

“Thanks, Jessa. It’s good to see you again.”

“You too. I can’t wait to tell Rick you’re back.”

Climbing into her Jeep and rubbing her cheek against Magoo’s, Kaylie was certain more people today than Rick Breeze would be hearing that particular news.

CHAPTER TWO

Hello?"

At the sound of the female voice, all soft and southern syrup, Tennessee Keller froze. Dolly Breeze ran his front office and handled any visitors who dropped in without calling. But Dolly had cut out early—something about getting ready for a weekend craft fair—leaving Ten alone in the shop.

He really should've locked the barn door, but the horse already being gone and all that had him heading toward the front to see who'd decided a phone call wouldn't get them what they wanted.

It was a dog. Well, a woman and a dog and the red Jeep Wrangler they'd arrived in, but the big loping shepherd caught his eye before the long legs striding toward him. Yeah, some sorry state he was in when a dog got his pulse racing, and a woman was more afterthought than anything.

"I'm looking for Tennessee Keller?"

That voice again. "You found him."

"Hi. I wanted to talk to you about some construction work I need done. Jessa Breeze and Carolyn Parker both said you're the man I want." She came closer. So did the dog. She held out her hand. "I'm Kaylie Flynn."

"Ten Keller." He shook it quickly, smelled fields of sun-soaked flowers when she leaned in, and then lowered his palm for the dog, waiting until he'd been sniffed and licked before scratching the spot of soft hair behind the stiff ears. "What's his name?"

"Magoo."

"As in Mister?"

Strands of copper-blonde hair escaped her ponytail to blow in her face. She snatched them away and nodded, and he smelled the flowers again. "When I got him, he had this tiny scrunched-up face. Mister Magoo was the first thing that came to mind."

"He's got more in him than German shepherd."

"The shelter thought rottweiler."

"Good-looking dog."

"Thanks. I think so."

Good-looking owner, too, though he kept that P.S. to himself. She wore a white T-shirt caught loosely around her hips. Not Hanes or Fruit of the Loom, but something classy, rich, like the russet leather of her boots, buttery and worn to fit.

Her clothes said she wasn't from around here. They also said she wasn't looking to stand out. Interesting. He finally said, "It's been a while since I had one."

"A dog?"

"My folks were big on animal rescue." And rain forest rescue and Arctic ice rescue and closing the hole in the ozone. "We usually had half a dozen at any time. Cats and dogs both. All shapes and sizes and temperaments."

She gave a groaning laugh, as if she couldn't decide between sympathy and pity and rolled the dice. "I hope you had a big house. And an even bigger yard."

He liked her laugh, the watermelon burst of it, liked the shape of her mouth, the width. It fit her face without taking it over. The bow of her lip pointed to the spatter of freckles dotting her nose, pale chestnut flung from a paintbrush.

Motioning Kaylie Flynn out of the sun and into the barn, he perched on a drafting stool, offered her another, watched what her thighs did to the denim of her jeans when she sat. Magoo plopped to the cement floor between them, making sure the hand that had scratched his ears behaved.

"What kind of work are you looking to have done?" Ten asked, behaving. "And where?"

She tilted her head to the side. "Do you know the Coleman place? Used to be the Wise place? On the corner of Second Street where it crosses Chances Avenue?"

"Big Victorian. Blue. Lots of trees." It was one fine house. His crew had replaced the roof a few years back after hurricane-force winds stripped half the shingles away. At the end of the job, he'd made the Wises an offer, but they'd stayed until Winton had died. Then May had gone to live with her sister in Dallas, selling it before he could bite. "You handling things for the Colemans now?"

"I bought it from them. Closed this morning. It's all mine."

She said it with relish, as if she'd landed herself the deal of the century. And knowing the albatross the property had become to Bob Coleman, she probably had. Ten just wished he'd known they'd decided to unload it. He'd really wanted that house.

It was solid, sturdy. Built to stand up to the elements. Built to be used. "I didn't know they were selling."

Her smile was sly. "I didn't give anyone else a chance to find out."

"Been keeping an eye on it, have you?"

"Like you wouldn't believe."

"Mind if I ask why?"

This time she wasn't quite as quick to answer, and the slyness slid from her smile. "It was the house I lived in from the time I was ten till I was eighteen."

Huh. Interesting. He guessed her age, then did a rough calculation backward through time. "Are you related to May and Winton? Or…were you one of their foster kids?"

The questions hung between them longer than he liked. And then her response, while not exactly an answer, told him exactly what he wanted to know.

"Does it matter? To you doing the renovations, I mean?"

"Not a bit." He reached for a pencil to have something to do with his hands. "That answers the where. Now give me an idea of the what."

"I need a couple of walls knocked out, and definitely new shutters. I'm sure I'll have a longer list once I go through all the rooms and decide how to use them, but the biggest thing will be the kitchen. Unless you can work magic with what's there, I'll need to have it completely redone."

He was stuck on knocking out walls. The house had stood intact for a hundred-plus years; for some reason, he'd assumed she'd come to him knowing he'd appreciate its historic value. That he'd respect it. Not undermine it for the sake of convenience and the ego of interior design.

He rocked his pencil so the eraser end bounced off the drafting board, a gust of wind ruffling the blueprint held in place there by a two-by-four block. "You're looking to remodel rather than restore, then."

"Actually, I'm looking to renovate. I'll be living on the top two floors and using the first for my business. That requires a small commercial kitchen, and better traffic flow than the doorways allow for now." She paused, taking him in, her eyes a light green that set off her hair and broadcasting frustration. "I can explain more, or you can come by and take a look, or you can tell me I'm barking up the wrong tree and save us both the time."

He wanted to say he wasn't the man for the job, but knew he was. He wouldn't take shortcuts, or compromise the structure's integrity, or suggest additional destruction to pad his bill. He didn't want to do the job, and so he would. "I can stop by tomorrow. Noon or so?"

"That would be great. I'm roughing it until the place is ready to be lived in, so I'll be there all day." She slid from the stool and reached into the tiny purse belted at her waist for a card. "Here's my cell number. If I don't hear you knock, you might need to call. Or you could just come in and yell," she added with a soft laugh. "The place is empty, so I shouldn't have any problem hearing you."

Her card mirrored his, a name and a number, though her ink was raised, her paper an upgrade, just like her T-shirt and boots. "The dog won't sound a warning?"

Bending, she mussed Magoo's ruff until he shuddered, pleasure rolling off of him along with a cloud of coarse black and tan hair. "I have a feeling this guy will be out making friends with the local wildlife. Or at least letting them know there's a new boss in town."

Ten took in her affection for the dog, took in the fall of her hair and the dancer's arch of her back as she bent. Took in the curve of her triceps that told him a lot about the body beneath her clothes. He bounced his pencil harder, pulled his gaze away, and stared out the barn door at the trees standing sentry on either side of his road.

A lot of good they'd done him, allowing this woman and her dog to leave footprints all over, no warning or so much as a by-your-leave for the breach. He'd never indulged in the volatile mix of business with pleasure.

But what was he supposed to do now, her number and invitation in hand, the house he wanted belonging to her, and lust a monster complication growling at his feet?

He stood when she stood, and followed her to her Jeep. "Tomorrow, then. Noon sharp."

CHAPTER THREE

It wasn't the dream that woke Kaylie that night but the guttural rumble at the base of Magoo's throat rattling around like ice cubes. He'd left his sleeping bag and was standing on his hind legs at the window. Something on the lawn below had disturbed him, and as the beam of a flashlight crossed the glass, Kaylie found herself disturbed, too.

She shoved out of her sleeping bag and, heart racing, into her jeans and boots. Grabbing her flashlight, her phone, and her eight-inch bowie knife, she headed for the stairs with Magoo on her heels. She had her dog to rely on, but she knew better than anyone the truth of a stainless-steel blade.

She was halfway through the kitchen, having punched 9-1-1 on her phone's keypad, her thumb hovering over Send, when she realized Magoo's growl was gone. He was pawing at the screen door, whimpering to be let out, as if whatever danger he'd sensed from the third floor had turned out to be a friendly on the first.

Kaylie barely had the screen unlocked before the dog pushed it open and bounded through. She switched on her flashlight and followed, holding it with three fingers of her left hand, her index finger and thumb wrapped around her phone and ready to dial for help. In her other hand, she clutched the knife in a hammer grip in case Magoo had made a mistake. He rarely did, though lacking his nose, she was going to need more evidence.

She got it as she turned the corner into the front yard to see him sitting at Ten Keller's side. Not a squatter or a vagrant or a burglar or a thief, but Ten Keller. Here with no warning. Checking out her house as if the day's business hours hadn't passed. And her looking like she'd just crawled out of a cardboard box on the street. Nice. She wasn't sure if she was aggravated at him for showing up unannounced, or at herself for caring about her appearance.

"Fickle, traitorous dog," she muttered, taking it out on Magoo, who would never know, though the words were lost in the dark. Ignoring the wild mess of her hair, she doused her torch, guided toward man and beast by the light of the moon and the beam of Ten's Maglite playing off the flower beds edging the house.

By day, the fallow dirt was depressing. By night, the bleak landscape brought to mind sunken graves, forgotten, abandoned, last winter's leaves gone to compost on top. A good thing, actually. Very soon, after the threat of frost passed, azaleas. Soft pink and fuchsia and white, a crazy quilt of colors against the blue of the house.

As she drew near him, Ten looked up, looked her over, caught her eye, and nodded toward her right hand. "You planning on woodworking? Or hunting small game?"

He was the one trespassing, and he wanted answers? Good thing both Jessa and Carolyn had vouched for him, though Magoo was the best judge of character she'd ever known. "I was going to throw it at you." She balanced the knife on her palm. The handle was the perfect size for her fingers, the weight a precise match for her skill and strength. She knew that because she'd tried others when she'd decided to make the weapon her friend. "Well, not at you, but if Magoo had given the word…"

"Target practice?"

"Something like that."

He returned his attention to Magoo, squatting in front of the dog to shake. Magoo lifted a paw, his big mouth smiling as Ten ruffled a hand over the top of his head. "Sorry about waking you."

She hadn't yet decided if she was. She liked seeing him with her dog. Liked that he knew what to do, that he wasn't scared away—a contradiction that made her wonder why she had a guard dog in the first place. Sigh. "I don't think I've ever known any contractor to make midnight house calls."

"I was on my way home. Thought I'd swing by and take a quick look at the shutters." He waved the flashlight in a pass over the worst. "I didn't know you were here."

She'd parked her Jeep in the garage. She'd left no lights burning; she'd had no need. The windows in the bedroom were bare and the moon full. "I just got the keys this morning. My first night in my house."

"On the floor?"

"I've got a sleeping bag." She gestured toward Magoo. "We both do."

He scratched Magoo behind his ears one more time and then straightened, an effortlessly synced motion of hips, thighs, and abs as he gained his feet.

Kaylie swallowed. "I'm sure I told you I was staying here."

"You did, but I thought maybe you'd changed your mind at the reality of roughing it."

If only he knew what this house meant to her, how many nights she'd been unable to sleep for thoughts of this roof, and not the one in her Austin condo, over her head.

"Not a chance," she said. It was dark, but his expression seemed doubtful. "Didn't you ever take a new toy to bed with you Christmas night? Something you'd been waiting for and wanting so long you couldn't bear to let it out of your sight?"

A humorless grin tugged at one side of his mouth. "This is a toy?"

"A gift, then," she offered. "A pair of red cowboy boots or a sparkly pink plush puppy."

This time his smile was true. "I slept with a BB gun once."

Oh, good. He was human. "See? Same thing."

He looked from her face to the three stories looming in front of him. "So you've been waiting for and wanting this house a long time?"

"I have."

"But you're still set on knocking out walls."

"I am."

"No way around it, huh?"

Did he not want the work? Did he think she was blithely tearing apart a perfectly sound structure, giving no thought to the life breathed into it by those who'd called it home? Or was he so ready to start he'd been unable to put off getting a closer look?

Whatever, this conversation could wait until tomorrow. She was tired, and it was too late for arguing philosophical differences. "Nope, sorry. They've gotta go."

He made a sound, a snort, a huff, and the flashlight beam played over her shutters once more before he switched off the light to leave. “Okay then. I’ll see you tomorrow at noon.”

“Goodnight, Mr. Keller.”

He came closer, stopped in front of her, met her gaze. It was too dark to see the color of his eyes, but she remembered well their shade, honey gold and incandescent. The moon shone off his hair and brought to mind sun tea, caramel brownies, red Anjou pears.

He made her hungry, and that wouldn’t do.

“Ten,” he told her, patting Magoo’s head where the dog sat between them. “Everyone calls me Ten.”

She nodded, pressing the hand holding her knife to her belly, a sharp cutting reminder that she wasn’t here for whatever this was he had her feeling. “Good night, Ten.”

~

While Magoo took three turns and was out like a light, Kaylie lay staring at the ceiling for hours. Food. Ten Keller had her thinking of food. Of appetites. Of desire. Of brownies.

After five years in three urban foster homes with playtime corralled inside fences, she’d come to Hope Springs, and at ten years old, found a family with Winton and May Wise. The moment she’d set eyes on their densely wooded acre, she’d sworn to climb every tree.

While in grade school, she’d monkeyed her way to the top of most. In middle school, volleyball became her physical outlet of choice. In high school, she’d gone on to play soccer. Staying active had offset the obvious downside to her obsessive love for brownies.

Baking brownies had been only one of the things May Wise had given her, but it had turned into her greatest success. Varying cooking times and temperatures as well as ingredients produced a world of textures and tastes, and Kaylie had never tired of experimenting. Toffee and cream cheese and walnuts. Dark cherries and even darker cacao nibs and the darkest of espresso.

Fortunately, the Wises, their friends and her classmates, and the other kids living in the blue Victorian had been happy to gobble up her therapy projects. Because that's what the brownies had been.

She'd baked when stressed over finals or tournaments. She'd baked when overwhelmed with options for colleges and careers. She'd baked when blue, when teen love went unrequited, when zits popped up at the worst possible times. When school forms required names for her parents and she had nothing to say.

So, yes. She understood the tug-of-war played out between food and emotions. Whether baking or buying or bingeing, she'd done her share of all three.

What she did not understand, however, was Tennessee Keller bringing brownies to mind, or how she was going to work with him now that he had.

Two Owls' Signature Chocolate Brownie

oh, chocolate, our chocolate

1¼ cups cake flour
½ teaspoon salt
¾ teaspoon baking powder
6 ounces unsweetened chocolate
¾ cup unsalted butter
2¼ cups sugar
4 large eggs
1 tablespoon vanilla

Preheat oven to 325°F. Grease or spray with cooking oil and flour (or line with aluminum foil) a 9 x 13–inch baking pan.

Sift the flour, the salt, and the baking powder into a bowl and set aside. Melt the chocolate and the butter in a double boiler (or in a microwave), stirring often so as not to burn the chocolate. Mix the sugar into the smooth chocolate mixture. Add the eggs one at a time, whisking after each. Stir in the vanilla. Add the flour mixture, folding in with a rubber spatula.

Pour the batter into the prepared baking pan. Bake 30–35 minutes, or until an inserted tester comes out mostly clean. Cool completely before cutting.

CHAPTER FOUR

Settled by German farmers along the Guadalupe River in 1872, Gruene, Texas, thrived for years as a commercial cotton hub, only to be decimated by a 1920s boll-weevil blight and doomed by the Great Depression. A half century later, the community was annexed by New Braunfels, having found new footing as a center for tourism and art. One of the town's most famous landmarks, Gruene Hall, opened in 1878, and in 2001 made *Forbes* magazine's "50 of America's Best" list as Best Country Honky-Tonk.

Luna Meadows had waited tables at Gruene's Gristmill Restaurant while in high school. As a young man, her father had worked at Gruene Hall. It was there where he'd met her mother, and though Luna was born a year later, it wasn't until her fifth birthday that her parents tied the knot in a celebration of her birth, their joining, and the purchase of Meadows Land—the farm in nearby Hope Springs where they raised Delaine Merino sheep for wool.

Today, the street outside the dance hall was barricaded, and big white tents were set up for a craft fair sponsored by one of the area guilds. The early-March sky was cloudless and blue, the sun warming air cooled by what was no doubt one of spring's last cold weather fronts. In the Meadows Land booth, Luna's mother, Julietta, demonstrated spinning and weaving while her father, Harry, hawked their wares.

Wares which included Luna's scarves.

Cameron Diaz had been the first celebrity to wear them, picking up several in the tony Austin boutique that sold Luna's Patchwork Moon collection of uniquely textured and colored creations, each of which told its own story. Soon after, paparazzi shots of the scarves around the necks of Katie Holmes, Emma Watson—even Brad Pitt—popped up in entertainment rags.

Though she'd grown up watching her mother throw the shuttle of weft yarn through the shed of the warp, it wasn't until Luna was confined to bed after a car accident as a teen, her broken hip keeping her from the funeral of her best friend, that her mother brought her a portable loom, along with hand-spun-and-dyed woolen and worsted.

Even burying her nose in big books with big stories had not kept Luna's mind off her loss. Somehow, her mother had known weaving would do what reading hadn't been able to, and Luna had lost herself in the colors of harems and spices and exotic flowers. Violet that burst like crushed grapes. The sunshine of saffron and topaz. Joyous persimmon and cool, moody jade.

She loved what she did, loved being able to pay her own way and to contribute to the family coffers, but she did not love the notoriety. The attention screwed with her process, and so she let those who wore her scarves do her advertising for her, agreeing to an occasional interview as long as accompanying photos were of her work and not her.

The locals who knew her got a kick out of keeping her secret. Their doing so allowed her the freedom she was enjoying today, roaming the streets, where impatiens bloomed in sidewalk whiskey barrels, browsing the wares in the guild members' booths, breathing deeply of the smells spilling from the food vendors' carts, cotton candy and funnel cakes and sausage-on-a-stick, and blending in, unnoticed, just a regular girl having fun.

Recognizing Dolly Breeze's quilts folded on frames beneath the Hope Springs Crafts Club tent, Luna headed that way. Working with a sixteen-inch hoop, Dolly sat in a rocking chair, the fabric of a crib-sized quilt like a waterfall over her lap. She gave Luna a quick wink, then returned her attention to the two seamstresses who sat with her. Both had their own small projects—one a needlepoint Christmas stocking, the other what looked like a crocheted place mat—well under way.

Luna listened to their chatter about old bundles of lace found in sewing baskets, and guild members who couldn't whip a stitch to save a life, and pattern thieves who deserved to have their thumbs cut off, all the while admiring the craftsmanship of the items on display. The cards of old buttons amused her, as did those of antique braid trim.

"Oh, I meant to tell you," Dolly said, speaking to the woman working on the place mat as Luna picked up a vintage roll of glass-head straight pins. "One of the foster children who used to live with May and Winton Wise? She bought that old Victorian of theirs from the Colemans."

"You're kidding."

"And this is the best part. She's going to open a café. Jessa called me yesterday and told me to go by and talk to her because she's looking for a cook."

"Which girl is it?"

"She's Kaylie Flynn now, Jessa says, but she used to be Kaylie Bridges."

Luna's head came up, her nape tingling, her stomach tumbling to her feet. She squeezed the paper roll, the pinheads gouging her palm, the cardboard buckling from the same pressure crushing the air from her chest.

"Kaylie Bridges. The one who used to bake all those brownies?"

Dolly nodded and leaned closer, but still spoke loudly enough to be heard outside the booth. "And whose mother went to prison for child endangerment and distribution of illegal narcotics."

Luna knew the story better than most, knew details these women as outsiders couldn't. She'd been told them all in confidence, told them by a family friend. Told them by a man who'd come home from his Gulf War deployment to tales of violence and drug abuse and a child at risk.

A man who'd been looking for his daughter ever since.

CHAPTER FIVE

Saturday morning, Ten was just out of the shower when the phone on his nightstand rang. Dripping water on the hardwood floor, he crossed the room to pick up the handset—though when he saw the caller's name on the display, he winced.

It was a reaction he'd yet to tame even after all these years, expecting bad news that never came. "Manny. How goes it?"

Manuel Balleza responded with a weighty sigh. "Same as always. Wondering when the good guys will catch a break. Hoping there's still time to make a difference with all that's wrong in the world when they do."

Always the optimist, that Manny. "What have I told you about taking the latest crime stats personally?"

The other man bit off several choice words. "You can't be surprised why I'm calling."

Manny had been Ten's older brother's parole officer, and since Ten had set up shop in Hope Springs, he'd put several of Manny's parolees on the payroll. Most had worked out just fine. Hardly a surprise, since none were career criminals, just men who'd made a life-altering bad choice, like Dakota.

So, no. Ten wasn't surprised at all. "What's his name and when's he getting out?"

"Will Bowman. He's being released first thing Monday. Wired a little tight, but overall a good kid."

Weren't they all? Good kids, tightly wired? "I've got a job to look at this afternoon, so Monday evening would work."

"Sounds good. He's done construction. Tucked away two years of an engineering degree before screwing things up."

And how many others had been there, done the same stupid stuff? "As long as he's not afraid of heights. This job comes through, I'll have shutters on a three-story Victorian at the top of the work order."

"Doesn't seem to be afraid of much of anything, which is pretty much the problem with most of these yahoos."

Ten laughed. "Watch who you're calling a yahoo. Dakota's a productive member of society these days. Or he was last I heard."

And that had been, what? Six years ago? Seven? Ten had no idea where his brother had gone once cut free from Manny and the state. Then again, he didn't know much of what was up in his sister's life, aside from what he heard secondhand. And he was completely out of the loop with his parents. As much as he liked the peace and quiet of the status quo, he wasn't exactly proud of it, a conundrum he supposed he'd have to work on one of these days. Once he figured out how to let go of the emotions strangling him—shame that he hadn't been there for Indy or Dakota, anger that his parents hadn't been there for any of them.

"Doesn't make him any less of a yahoo," Manny said, clicking off after promising to call Monday and set a time for Will's visit. Punctuality was a big deal for Manny. He made sure his charges knew his straight and narrow was as much of a sentence as the one on the inside that the parole board had seen fit to cut short. Grown men, yet like kids in kindergarten they still had to toe Manny's line.

Ten's brother had done just that, abided by the conditions set for his release and served his term sans a single violation. While under Manny's thumb, he'd done grunt work for another contractor in the area, the five-year road to his master's in architecture halted by the two spent in prison for aggravated assault. Ten had been the one to reach out, to stay in touch, at least until Dakota made it clear he wasn't interested in brotherly love.

If Dakota had a particular reason for not going back to school, he'd never mentioned it to Ten. Neither had he shared any regrets he might've had about swinging that baseball bat instead of calling the law. One reckless moment, and the blueprint they'd designed for Keller Brothers Construction was good for nothing but the bottom of a birdcage, and Ten left to establish the business on his own.

He'd tried to bring his brother in after his release, but Dakota was having none of it. Whether because he was sore over Ten moving forward without him, or raw over his time behind bars, Ten didn't know. Dakota wouldn't talk about either, or about his life on the outside being changed forever. Ten had finally let it go. His brother was a free man, going it alone his choice. That didn't keep Ten from feeling he had never done enough to help.

And because of that, he gave parolees a paycheck and a boost onto their feet. He knew what it meant for a man to lose his mind for a single moment, and to have that single moment screw up the rest of his life. Dakota couldn't vote. Couldn't own a gun. Couldn't run for office. To Ten's way of thinking, the last two weren't a big deal but the first, yeah. That ate at him. A street-corner dealer. A gangbanger. Bernie Madoff in the day. Those thugs had a say in the way the country was run.

But because at eighteen his brother had hunted down the worthless prick who'd tried to rape their sister, and premeditatedly swung a bat at the back of his head, Dakota could no longer make his voice heard. Offering hope to others who'd been just as rash and impulsive allowed Ten to make a statement the only way he could, while making amends for what felt like letting his brother down.

His folks, on the other hand...They'd coddled kids whose own families were more demanding, loving the attention that came with being cool. The same way they loved looking good for rescuing animals and saving the planet. The teens they'd spoiled, many his and his siblings' friends, hadn't been fooled, and more than a few had taken advantage. Two whom his parents had sworn to save from neglect had required enough of their money—court costs, attorney fees, forfeited bail—that Ten's paying his own way through college had been less about independence than it was a necessity.

He wondered what Kaylie Flynn had been like as a kid. Then he wondered what had happened to make her a ward of the state. He'd never known a foster to go to the lengths she had, claiming for her own the home that wouldn't have been hers if not for fate and social services. There had to be a reason, and he was curious enough to want to knock down her walls and find it.

CHAPTER SIX

It was long past lunchtime, was closer to the middle of the afternoon, in fact, before Kaylie thought to check the time. Her day had been taken up with fabric swatches, a tape measure, and the windows on her new home's first floor. Since the construction wouldn't affect the exterior walls, she felt safe doing the calculations now, but she wouldn't order her window coverings until her contractor gave her the all clear.

She knew she wanted lace panels, and had in mind a gorgeous Nottingham lace, but had also decided on natural-wood blinds, rather than drapes, to counter the heat of the sun. She remembered the nearly suffocating summer warmth in the rooms with west-facing glass. Unchecked, the temperature would not make for pleasant dining.

She was on all fours figuring yardage with the calculator on her cell phone when she realized she was no longer alone. Magoo, smelling of turned earth and pine needles and happy sun-heated dog, scrabbled across the dining room's worn floor to let her know Ten was waiting. How long he'd been standing there, Kaylie didn't know, but she was pretty sure he'd beaten Magoo inside.

Hands on her thighs, she sat back and took him in where he leaned against the doorframe. He wore khaki pants and deck shoes, his white work shirt rumpled in a freshly washed-and-dried casual way. His hair was damp and combed back, curling beneath his ears, his jaw smooth and clean. She inhaled deeply, smelling…goodness, and rain on grass, and a faint woodsy spice, and she had to measure her breaths, not wanting to indulge in his scents when so many others lingered in this room.

The others…they were the ones deserving her regard, and she smiled, filling her lungs as they surfaced. Sage and brown gravy and marshmallows melted on yams. The memories overwhelmed her, and for no reason she could put a name to, she found herself pushed to share one of the best. "I ate my first real Thanksgiving dinner in here. I started fifth grade in Hope Springs and didn't know a soul. I was the only one living with the Wises then. Other kids came in time for the holidays, but those first few weeks it was just me, and May spoiled me insanely."

She picked up her phone, her pencil, her legal pad, and got to her feet, staring at her notes as her smile began to fade. "She packed lunches that made my classmates beg to trade. Homemade cookies. Homemade bread with her own jam and butter. Not exactly the most nutritious of meals, now that I look back, but they gave me what I needed."

And why was she telling him all of this? Why weren't they looking at the walls she wanted gone? Why wasn't he saying something instead of standing and listening as she remembered being ten years old and drowning?

She turned for the window, leaned her forehead against the glass, and conjured pictures from this place and the autumns she'd spent here. The zing of pine and damp cedar and Rio Grande Valley grapefruits, of yeast bread and nutmeg and cloves in cider. Tiny white lights draped in uneven ribbons from the porch roof's edge, twinkling like strings of holiday fireflies.

Kaylie was going to have lights year-round. She'd hang them before Two Owls opened and leave them burning long after the doors closed for the last time. She hoped to be eighty by then. She planned to live here forever.

"Tell me about Thanksgiving dinner."

Ten. He was still here, and she…she was drifting off as if he had all the time in the world to wait on her. As if he cared about the years she'd spent in this house. As if his knowing who she'd been then would make a difference now.

Don't look to where you've come from. Look to where you're going. How many times through the years had Kaylie thought back on May's words? She'd known returning to Hope Springs would be as difficult as it was essential, but she had to get a grip. This house was her anchor, her island. From here she could safely face the past.

And so she took a tentative step. "I doubt it was much different than yours. Turkey, gravy. Cornbread dressing with all the sides."

He came into the room then, walked toward her. She heard his footsteps on the hardwood, saw his reflection in the glass, found her nose lifting, scenting. He moved to the window's other side and leaned a shoulder against the wall.

"No," he said, looking out at the porch instead of at her. "Tell me about that first Thanksgiving dinner in this room."

Too late she wondered if she had the words, or if this intimacy was a good idea at all. But something told her he wouldn't laugh or judge or think her crazy. That, like May, he knew how to listen. That he was willing to listen. That for whatever reason, he wanted to know about that day.

Absently, she brought her fingers to the base of her neck, felt her pulse there, racing. "I was pretty sure it was the best meal I would ever eat in my life. And it wasn't just the food, though I'd never seen so much on one table. There was another girl here with me by then, Cindy, and a boy who was five named Tim, and you've got to know the money the Wises were paid by the state was not why they volunteered to be foster parents. They truly wanted to make a difference.

"Anyway, we had turkey and all the trimmings, but also homemade rolls the size of softballs. Winton would wind up like a pitcher and toss them to us. I think as many landed on the floor as we caught, and Cindy was horrified every time she missed one. Tears started streaming from her eyes, but she never made a sound. May finally realized what was happening. I guess she knew about Cindy's home life, that she was afraid she'd be whipped for wasting good food, and for the mess."

"And you?"

"I'd lived in some heinous conditions, so food on the floor was nothing. It was May trying to make Cindy feel better that nearly did me in." Kaylie turned around, curled her palms over the lip of the windowsill, and sat. "May had baked pies. Like dozens of pies. Pumpkin, cherry, chocolate, lemon, apple...imagine a pie and it was there. Most would go to friends over that weekend, but she made sure we knew we could have whatever we wanted.

"Cindy cried without making any noise, and all May could think to do was feed her. So there were all these slices of pie, and the smells were crazy amazing, spicy and sweet and hot sugar, and Cindy just sat there, like a statue, rivers running down her face. May's eyes puffed up and she started crying, feeling helpless, I guess, or guilty for traumatizing a girl who'd been through so much, and I couldn't stand it. I started shaking, then sobbing.

"The five of us, me, Cindy, Tim, and the Wises ended up on the dining-room floor, all of us crying, then laughing. Cindy was the first one to pick up a roll and throw it back at Winton. It was a free-for-all after that. The biggest food fight you can imagine. The floors, the walls. Our clothes. Our hair. We were rolling in mashed potatoes, dripping with gravy. May ground an entire coconut cream pie in Winton's face. And finally, *finally* Cindy stopped crying."

A shoulder still propped on the wall by the window, Ten—who had turned out to be a very good listener—waited until he was sure she was done, then grinned. It was the kind of grin that took over a face, and it hit her like a hot roll to the head that Jessa Breeze had been right. Separate from the way he made her itch, he was really nice to look at, and even more so when he smiled. His hair had started to dry and was falling over his ears and forehead and almost into his eyes. And his eyes were sharp and attentive and that beautiful shade of honey brown.

"Sorry about all of that," Kaylie said, because never in a million years would she have told that story to a stranger, and she couldn't figure out what it was about Ten Keller that had her sharing it with him. "It's just this house. It…takes me back."

"I'm guessing you've got hundreds of memories to go with every room in the place."

"At the very least." But it was time to get down to business and leave him with just the one. "Okay, the way I'm picturing the café, I need to be able to set up tables of different sizes to fit different sizes of groups. I'm thinking friends will come for lunch while the kids are in school. Maybe some will have book club meetings, birthday celebrations. Things like that."

"And you want walls knocked out to make this room larger?"

She breathed in, out, smoothed the hair bound into a tail at her nape. Back on track. This was good. He was her contractor, not a confidant, and why things felt otherwise… "I don't see how else I'll manage the seating."

"Hmm. What if…" Ten left the question incomplete, and stepped from the dining room into the hallway that ran down the center of the house.

Kaylie followed him as far as the dining-room door, then waited as he walked into the adjoining parlor before reversing course and checking out what had been Winton's den. The next door opened into a large bedroom May had used for sewing. Ten spent a couple of minutes in all of them, the rap of his knuckles on the walls echoing like woodpeckers hammering at the chinaberry trees.

Her hands stacked on the door facing behind her, Kaylie leaned back, wondering what he saw, what the sound of his knocking told him about the walls. Was he figuring out which ones bore weight and had to stay? Or deciding they'd been here so long, done their job well, and all deserved a pardon?

She got his respect for the century-old workmanship, understood he wouldn't be who he was if he didn't weigh the integrity of the structure against the client's demands. But this was her house, and she had specific plans, ones she'd spent months fine-tuning. If she had to go through the hassle of interviewing multiple contractors, instead of using the one the locals swore was the best, she would.

"Are you married to the idea of one big dining area?" he asked as he exited May's old sewing room and came back to where Kaylie waited.

"Well…I'm married to the idea of not shunting people off to eat in small spaces. For romantic dinners, maybe, but that's not what I'm planning to serve, and the acoustics would be terrible in cramped quarters. Not to mention navigating in and around the tables—"

"That's not what I was thinking." He walked to the center of the dining room and stopped. "What if you got rid of the door from this room into the hallway, did the same to the ones on either side, and widened the entries to allow better access? Then instead of taking down the walls, cut similar openings between the rooms. The arches can be designed to match the ones on the porch, keeping your Queen Anne look.

"It would give you the space you want," he said, walking toward her, his hands shoved in the pockets of his khakis, his shoulders hunched like a boy hoping to get his way. "But it would also keep my preservationist heart from breaking."

"A compromise."

"Something like that."

Winton's den, where Kaylie had curled into the corner of his huge leather sofa and listened to him read *Moby Dick* and *Gone with the Wind.* May's sewing room, where Kaylie had sat cross-legged on the tufted top of a pink storage ottoman and counted knitted-and-purled stitches. The dining room, where Kaylie had been filled to the brim with good food and good fun and been encouraged to throw hot rolls like softballs.

She wasn't concerned about Ten Keller's preservationist heart, but his solution meant keeping most of each wall intact, and that made her happy. What made her even happier was the idea of using all three rooms, rooms where she'd emerged from the cocoon that had kept her from breaking, and grown into her own skin.

Her smile came easily, as did her words. "Let's do it."

~

When Kaylie was twelve years old, May Wise introduced her to brownies, starting her off with boxed mixes rather than batter made from scratch. Boxed mixes were nearly impossible to mess up, and even batches left in the oven too long were softened when topped with ice cream.

Kaylie took to brownies like a butterfly to new wings, and she quickly worked up to May's family recipes. Oh, the bounty she found in the collection of handwritten and creased sheets of stationery. Growing confident, she'd added chocolate frosting with pecans, then feeling adventurous, swirled in cream cheese and thick melted caramel and marshmallow crème. She'd even tried her hand at blondies, but always came back to her true love.

She'd baked after school once a week, then handed out the goodies at school. The other kids made for perfect market research, willing to try anything and full of teenage opinions. She'd listened to the good, the bad, the worst, more interested in what her taste-testers had to say than in who was doing the saying—probably why she'd hadn't remembered Carolyn Parker and Jessa Breeze. Or maybe leaving Hope Springs so soon after graduation was the culprit behind her faulty recall.

On that day in June when she'd turned eighteen, she'd packed eight years of her life in cardboard boxes, tucked the memories that didn't fit into the back of her mind, and left town. She didn't want to miss what she no longer had. She didn't want to depend too much on her old life to get her through her new one. She was on her own, a legal adult. The time had come to put away childish things.

For the most part, she'd done a good job. The scene with her mother in the kitchen, or the one of Ernest handing her over to social services, rarely surfaced. She sent cards and gifts to Winton and May on the appropriate holidays, but May was the one to initiate most of their sharing-the-latest phone calls, to drop by for catching-up visits while in Austin.

Kaylie loved seeing the older woman, but it took her hours to get over the calls, days to move beyond the visits. The state and her caseworker said she was all grown up, her connection to the Wises severed. The same state that had incarcerated her mother, that had no idea who, much less where, her father was.

And though the state had provided her college tuition, her two bakery jobs had covered the rest of her expenses as well as funded her savings. One had her up at three a.m. making doughnuts, but it was the other that she'd loved. The other that had taken her from brownies to places even

May Wise hadn't tried. Tarts and tissue-thin phyllo and tiered cakes with fondant. Desserts that required hours to assemble, commanded high dollars, garnered the bakery the notice of Zagat.

There Kaylie learned about royal icing and meringues, about candied nuts and custards and gold leaf. It took her six years to finish her business degree, but those same six years gave her a hands-on education that was even more valuable, and at twenty-four she opened the doors to the Sweet Spot.

For the next four and a half years, the bakeshop had been Kaylie's bread and butter, her creations in demand by event planners and brides-to-be and small eateries who offered her desserts off menu. Customers would find an extra brownie added to their order and become regulars, just as Kaylie had planned. And now she had new plans, ones designed to take the place of the old.

Strange as it was, she trusted implicitly that Tennessee Keller would do right by her. His honesty was at the root of her trust; he hadn't agreed to knock down her walls to land the job and an easy paycheck. He'd negotiated terms that worked better for them both and, more important, preserved the house's integrity. She liked that. She liked it a lot. Plus, Magoo approved.

But the curious fluttering in her belly when he was around...it bothered her. She hadn't come here for this. She hadn't expected it. She wasn't sure what to do with the things he made her feel. But she was bothered even more by the desire she had to let him take over. A weekend into their working relationship, and she had a notepad full of his ideas—*his,* not hers—designed to streamline her project, giving her more time to spend on the personal reasons behind her return to Hope Springs.

He was a professional. She knew nothing about tearing apart a house and putting it back together. She should be happy for the help. But leaning too heavily seemed a weakling's way out, and she prided herself on her strength. She had to be here, up-to-her-neck involved, digging in the emotional muck waiting to take her down, because how else would she find her answers? That was what mattered, right?

Learning why her degree, her independence, the success of the Sweet Spot had never given her what this house had. Finding out what had happened to bring her to the Wises in the first place. Discovering the truth of what she'd done to cause her mother to want to leave her. And most of all—what about her four-year-old self had driven her father away.

CHAPTER SEVEN

On Tuesday, Kaylie was up at first light to let Magoo outside. The dog had a schedule, and her job was to stick to it, but that didn't mean she had to go with him while he did his thing. Her closest neighbor in the unzoned and most bucolic section of Hope Springs was a half mile down Second Street. The adjoining lot on Chances Avenue was undeveloped and overgrown. Magoo had quickly learned the boundaries of his yard. That left Kaylie free to brew her morning coffee and bolster herself to see Ten.

Strange that she felt the need to do that. She shouldn't feel the need to do that. She'd hired him to do a job, but their synergy on Saturday as they'd discussed her plans had left her rather weak in the knees. It wasn't an uncomfortable feeling; not in the least. But her schedule didn't have time for it; her life didn't have room for it. Once the renovations were complete, he'd no longer be part of her day-to-day life. As long as they stuck strictly to business, she wouldn't be left to deal with the complications that came with even temporary emotional bonds.

Coffee poured, creamed, and sweetened, she crossed to the kitchen window to check on Magoo, bringing her mug to her mouth and seeing as she did that she had company.

The woman standing at the end of Kaylie's driveway could only be described as exotic. Her hair was waist length, as straight as a needle, as black as onyx. A headband pulled it away from her face, and Kaylie couldn't even imagine the weight of it against the woman's back.

Along with skinny jeans and a coral linen tee, she wore a colorful scarf looped like a necklace of fringe. Rather than continuing the T-shirt's color scheme, however, it served as an accent, the colors of indigo and ocean green and deep violet woven like an undersea current. And she wore the most gorgeous pair of suede boots in the same purple shade.

Magoo, the friendliest guard dog on the planet, having introduced himself and received a nose rub in return, now led her toward the back door. Kaylie pushed it open to meet them.

"Hi," the woman said, her voice no more accented than Kaylie's, which came as a surprise. "I'm Luna. I'm looking for Kaylie Flynn."

"You've found her. What can I do—" Kaylie took in the colors in the scarf, the pattern, the story they told. She'd fondled a similar one in an Austin boutique that carried the Patchwork Moon collection, the label's design including the artist's signature, but decided she couldn't justify such an extravagant purchase when she wore chef whites all day and pajamas all night. "You're not Luna Meadows, are you?"

Luna nodded, her smile momentarily stiff before softening. "I am, though most people don't know me from Eve."

And Kaylie, drawn to the other woman's honesty the way she'd been drawn to Ten's, could tell she liked it that way. "Then mum's the word, and I'll make sure Magoo there keeps quiet, too."

"He's a beautiful dog."

"Thanks, I think so." She gestured toward the kitchen, curious as to why Luna Meadows would be looking for her. "Would you like to come in? I only have bar stools to sit on, and nothing to offer you but coffee or water."

"Water is fine, and I'd love to see the place. I understand you're doing some renovations."

So word was getting around. "I am, yes, with plans to open a café."

"The café is actually why I'm here." The screen door bounced closed behind both women and the dog. Luna perched on the stool Kaylie offered. "I was at a craft show in Gruene over the weekend. That's where I heard the news. I used to work there at the Gristmill Restaurant, and if it's true that you're interviewing for a cook..."

"Oh, definitely," Kaylie said, handing Luna a bottle of water, amazed that not only was word spreading, it was leaving Hope Springs—even if Gruene was only a few miles east.

"Good. I know someone who might be perfect."

"Would it happen to be Dolly Breeze? Because her daughter-in-law sang me her praises last week."

"Dolly would be an excellent choice, but no. This is someone else."

Topping off her coffee, Kaylie glanced toward the other woman. "Why don't you have her, or him, come by and talk to me?"

"I will, but could I ask first about your plans? Your hours, your menu." Luna toyed with a nick in the bottle's label. "I hate to be pushy, but I don't want to waste your time or his if things don't sound like a good fit."

"Sure." That made sense. "I'll be open for weekday lunches only. At least to start. If there's a demand, I may add weekends and dinners down the road." She took a sip of her coffee, then took the bar stool across from Luna's at the island. "As far as the menu goes, each day there'll be a single entrée, along with salad and bread. For dessert, brownies. I'll handle those. And I have a wonderful recipe for hot rolls the size of your head," she said, and thought of the Thanksgiving story she'd told Ten. "Those I'd prefer *not* to handle, though I can."

Luna nodded, her expression thoughtful. "What about your main dishes? You said there'll just be one?"

"For now," Kaylie replied. "The café service will be set up buffet style, so I'll have to see how it's all received. The entrées will be…hearty and nurturing, as well as nourishing. I'm competing with fast-food burgers and fries and taco trucks and buckets of chicken with potatoes and gravy. I'll never win over the Lean Cuisine crowd, but that's the beauty of self-serve and bushels of salad."

"Let your conscience fill your plate."

"Exactly."

"And your entrées?"

"Casseroles, primarily. Lasagna. Baked ziti. King Ranch Chicken. Stacked spinach enchiladas." Kaylie found herself smiling, her stomach rumbling. She needed breakfast before she skipped it and went straight for lunch. "Things that aren't all Italian or Tex-Mex, which is why I need the cook, because that's where my mind wants to go."

A dimple in her cheek, Luna lifted a brow. "Are you sure it's your mind in charge?"

"When it comes to food? Never."

For the next half hour, and much to Kaylie's surprised delight, the two women talked about everything under the sun. After explaining the workings of Two Owls, Kaylie learned her guest had grown up in the area and still lived on her parents' farm. It was there, at Meadows Land, on the far edge of Hope Springs, where her father raised the sheep that produced the wool her mother spun and dyed, and Luna then wove into scarves.

"Why scarves? Why not shawls, or rugs?"

"Because I have a short attention span? A need for instant gratification?" Luna laughed. "A scarf can be done fairly quickly, as long as I have inspiration and the right yarn. And not a lot of other things going on. Like shopping. Or sleeping. Or tubing down the Guadalupe. A shawl would probably take me the rest of my life."

Kaylie shared the other woman's love of shopping and sleeping, though she had never done so much as dip a toe into the Guadalupe or the Comal. She'd been busy with school, then busy with work, and without close girlfriends—or guy friends—she'd been on her own. Luna made her promise to join her for a rafting trip, and without giving it a second thought, Kaylie agreed, hungry for the society this new relationship offered, though she did extract a return promise from Luna to show her the workings of a loom.

It was girl talk, punctuated with waved hands and wide eyes and nodded understanding. It was comfortable, natural, familiar when familiarity made no sense. Yet as their bond blossomed, Kaylie opened up, as if a door shut tight for years had flung wide. "Depending on how *much* news is getting out, you may not know that I used to live here."

"In Hope Springs?"

"In this house. I came here when I was ten."

"You must've lived with the Wises," Luna said.

"Did you know them? Would I have known you? We're about the same age, I think, but I've forgotten most of the kids I grew up with."

But the other woman was already shaking her head. "I went to a private school. And I only know of the Wises from hearing their names come up in conversation."

"Do they come up a lot?" Kaylie asked, wondering why they would, in what context. Wondering if anyone ever talked about her, about what had happened. Who might know more than she did and could answer questions, or point her to where she could find them.

"No, but they were very well thought of. I know Dolly Breeze was good friends with May, and Dolly's heavily involved in the local craft scene. She's the one I heard talking about your café."

"May Wise is the best thing that ever happened to me. I don't know where I'd be today if my caseworker hadn't sent me here." She wrapped both hands around her coffee mug and stared down into her drink. "My first few foster homes didn't exactly work out. Most of that was my fault, I'm sure. I was confused and angry and I missed my parents terribly. And I'm sorry. I don't know why I'm telling you this."

"Don't worry about it. You must've entered the system fairly young, if you came here when you were ten. I can't imagine much of anything being your fault."

Kaylie shrugged. Her logical side knew Luna was right, but her logical side wasn't the one that woke up with nightmares. "Part of coming back here is about finding out what happened with my parents to send me into foster care."

"You don't know?" Luna asked, having gone still, her gaze caught on Kaylie's.

"I remember enough of the specifics." She wasn't going to talk about the knife, or the body on the kitchen floor, or the blood on her toes. "But I don't know where either of my parents are. Why they never came to get me."

"You haven't heard from either of them?"

She shook her head. "Not in twenty-three years."

"So you're taking matters into your own hands."

And hoping her hands were big enough. "Something like that."

"I feel like I should wish you luck," Luna said, with just enough hesitation for Kaylie to sense her discomfort, as if she didn't want to cause more pain than Kaylie had already endured. "I'd be more of a basket case than I already am if I hadn't had my parents to keep me sane."

"I had May and Winton. Only for eight years, but those eight years were everything. And please don't feel bad telling me how close you are to your parents. You should be. You're supposed to be. And I'm glad for anyone who has that."

After that, the conversation returned to her plans for the café. While talking about the casseroles May had served in an effort to stretch a dollar, Luna told her about Dolly Breeze losing her husband, and that to make ends meet, the older woman had gone to work for a local contractor, Ten Keller.

"Word has it that she keeps him on his toes," Luna said.

"Did I tell you he's doing my renovations?"

"No, but I assumed he would be."

That gave Kaylie pause. "Why the assumption?"

"Ten Keller is pretty much the local go-to guy for such things."

"What do you know about him?"

"You mean personally?"

Kaylie nodded.

"He's single. He's hot." She said it with a grin. "He takes care of those around him. Why he hasn't been snatched up is always a topic of gossip. At least in the circles where people do that sort of speculating," she said and added a wink.

Circles and hot topics and gossip about men. Things Kaylie had little experience with. The fact that she found talking about them to Luna so comfortable caught her off guard. Since when did she have conversations that weren't about work?

Was it Luna who made it so easy, or was this more of the magic of the house? As she got up to set her coffee mug in the sink, she gave the other woman an interested "Hmm," because she didn't know what else to say. And then a knock on the door saved her.

"Good morning."

She hadn't heard his truck arrive, and Magoo had apparently decided Ten didn't need to be announced. That dog, making his own rules. Kaylie turned. Behind her, Luna murmured something, but she had room for nothing but Ten and the way her kitchen warmed.

Stepping from the breezeway into the mudroom, he reached down to scratch the top of Magoo's head, his gaze caught on Kaylie's, asking...for permission to enter? To forgive him for being so bold with *his* plans for *her* house, and for the unsettling look in his eyes? Not to hold his preservationist heart against him?

He held up a white bag with the Butters Bakery logo. "I come bearing breakfast."

Oh, good. A distraction. She waved him all the way in. "And I happen to have a fresh pot of coffee."

"Sugar and cream?"

"Coming up," she said, noticing as she turned to serve him that Ten wasn't alone.

He followed the direction of her gaze. "This is Will Bowman. I'm putting him to work on your shutters. Will, Kaylie Flynn, and Luna Meadows."

"Good to see you again, Ten," Luna said, skimming him with a smile before settling on Will and staying there. "Hello, Will."

Kaylie didn't blame her. Will was tall, lanky, his limbs almost too long, like those of a swimmer meant for speed. His hair was black and cut short except where it fell forward over his eyes. Rock-star hair. And rock-star eyes, sapphires sparkling beneath coal lashes.

"Nice to meet both of you," Will said in a voice too civilized for someone decked out in biker boots, dark jeans, and a long-sleeved T-shirt the color of his hair. His gaze traveled the kitchen, avoiding Luna's, and even Kaylie could see by the tic in his jaw what it cost him.

"Coffee, Will?" she asked, setting Ten's cup in front of him on the island where he'd pulled up a bar stool to break open the bakery bag.

"Sure, thanks, just black." He took the stool next to Ten's, then took the doughnut Ten handed him, biting off a hunk as if he were a lion and the doughnut fresh meat.

"Will here's been out of pocket for a while," Ten said, and the side of Will's mouth clicked up to reveal a dangerously deep dimple. Kaylie swore she heard Luna sigh. "Figure a week on a ladder will help him find his balance."

Or cause him to fall flat on his face.

Will must've seen Kaylie's flicker of doubt. "Keller here's a big believer in on-the-job training."

"Hasn't let me down yet."

Kaylie had hired him. She had to trust him. "As long as the job gets done and no one gets hurt, I'm staying out of this one."

"I'm sorry to interrupt," Luna said to Ten, laying a hand on his arm before turning to Kaylie. "I've got an appointment I've got to get to, so I need to go. But we'll talk more soon?"

"Yes, and thank you for everything."

"How about lunch next week?"

"Absolutely."

"Great. We should go to the Gristmill. I can show you my old restaurant stomping grounds."

"I'd love it."

"I'll get out of your way then. Again, nice to meet you, Will. And, Ten, I can't wait to see what you do with the house."

"Well, you won't have to wait long," Kaylie said, loving it when both Ten and Will looked her way. "Did I not mention that I want to open Memorial Day weekend?"

"That's just under three months," Ten said, frowning.

"And I'll be paying a very nice bonus if you can get it done."

"A bonus, huh?" He narrowed his eyes, holding her gaze while he popped a bite of doughnut into his mouth.

"I think that's my cue to get busy." Will hopped down off his stool, dusted the doughnut crumbs from his hands, and then finished his coffee, his gaze on Luna as she left, as if giving her a good head start before following.

"That was...interesting," Kaylie said, though it hardly seemed an encompassing enough word for the tension Will and Luna left like smoke in their wake.

Once the screen door bounced shut, Ten said, "As long as she knows I can only vouch for him as a new hire. She's on her own for the rest."

Good to know she wasn't imagining things. "What did you mean about his being out of pocket for a while?"

"Nothing to worry about. Just that he's been out of work," he said, dunking the last of his doughnut into his coffee. "His people skills are kinda rusty, but a friend I'd trust with my life sent him my way, so I thought I'd give him a leg up."

Kaylie watched him cock his head to the side and bite into the soggy cake pastry. She wondered what he would think to learn the gossips loved him. Then she wondered if he already knew. "Luna mentioned you take care of people."

His brow came up as he lifted his mug to his mouth. "I didn't know you and Luna were friends."

"We just met this morning," she said, toying with the crumbs from her Danish, uncertain what to make of his look. "She came by to talk about the café."

"You two didn't waste any time, did you?"

"Getting to know each other?"

"Getting around to men."

Was he teasing? Accusing? Just making conversation, or wanting to know? "We were talking about my plans for the house, and your name came up as my contractor. That's all."

"Me taking care of people doesn't sound like my name coming up as your contractor," he said, and sipped his coffee again.

"Is that why you came by the other night?" she asked without meaning to. Having him aware of her curious nature seemed a bad idea for some reason.

"You think I was taking care of you?" he asked after a long moment of doing nothing but looking her over, her hair, her nose, the freckles that dusted her chest above her very modest décolletage.

Yeah. A bad idea. She wished she hadn't rinsed out her cup. She needed something to do with her hands. "Or Magoo, at least."

At the sound of his name, the dog wagged his tail, the *thump-thump* against the floor the only sound in the suddenly still room, bringing a smile to Ten's face. "No, Kaylie. I didn't come to check on Magoo."

She hadn't wanted to hear him say that. She didn't know how the implication that he'd come because of her made her feel. She looked after herself. She had for the last ten years. The idea of a man, this man, Tennessee Keller, thinking her knife and her dog and a life spent braced for bad news wasn't enough…

What was she supposed to do now? "That's good, because he's perfectly capable of taking care of himself."

"I'm sure he is."

"Anyway." She sat straighter, brushed back her hair, hoped an escape route would fall into her lap, and found one in a box on the kitchen counter. "I picked up several flooring samples yesterday, so we should probably look at those."

Ten laughed and started gathering up the detritus of their impromptu meal. "Then let me get Will set up taking down the old shutters, and we'll do just that."

CHAPTER EIGHT

Hands at her hips, Luna leaned against the back bumper of her car, staring at the wooded lot across the street from Kaylie's house. She wanted to walk into the thick stands of trees and let them close around her, to lose herself along with this big truth only she knew.

Was she really going to do this? Tell Kaylie's father where she was? Upset his life and his daughter's, too? Did she even have that right? Both seemed to be making their way, and happily so, but what if they would be happier together?

What if Kaylie could share with Mitch the sort of relationship Luna had with *her* father? She counted on him for so much. His support had allowed her to make her own way, to learn from her mistakes as well as her success. How could she keep Mitch and Kaylie from the same, knowing what she did about the hole in both of their lives?

She surged away from her car, balled her hands into fists, and groaned, because taking off into the woods would ruin her new suede boots. And tramping through the trees wouldn't do anyone any good anyway. "To tell or not to tell. That is the question."

"I'm happy to offer an ear if you need one. Unless you find it nobler to suffer the slings and arrows of outrageous fortune on your own."

At the sound of Will Bowman's voice, Luna turned. He'd come up behind her silently, headed, she supposed, for Ten's truck, parked at the edge of the street. He was wearing sunglasses that covered his beautiful blue eyes, and she wanted to ask him to take them off, but kept herself from being that obvious by biting down on her tongue.

His black hair, stirred by the breeze, had fallen forward. He reached up to rake it back, lifting his chin as he did, and she was caught again, as in the kitchen, by the shape of his hands, his fingers long, his palm large and square. Dark hair feathered along his wrist from his forearm hidden beneath the long sleeve of his black pullover tee. Her fingers itched to touch him there, and she didn't know why.

"Sorry. Didn't mean to startle you," he said when she took her time answering.

She looked back to his face. "You didn't. Not really. I'm more embarrassed to be caught talking to myself."

"I do it all the time, so it makes perfect sense to me."

"Good," she said. "Because I'm not making any at all."

"The offer of an ear is still open," he said, and cocked his head. "Though I understand the slings and arrows thing if you'd rather not."

She didn't even know him, and yet, almost as much as the volcano of frustration rising inside of her, his sincerity, when he stuffed his hands in his pockets and shrugged, made her want to tell him everything. About Mitch. About

Kaylie. About her own accident from so long ago. About losing her best friend and still being burdened with keeping Sierra's secrets safe.

"Are you close to your parents?" was what finally came out of her mouth, and she wanted to grab it back, to apologize for being so forward, until she took in his expression.

His mouth pulled into a smile. Dimples appeared in both cheeks, crow's-feet at both temples, which told her his eyes were smiling, too. And that he was older than she'd originally thought. That had her wondering what in his life had gone so wrong that he was working for Ten. And then he answered and she lost what she'd thought a fairly stable balance.

"Who said I have parents? Maybe I was hatched from an egg sprinkled with fairy dust. Or brought up by wolves."

Something led her to believe in the possibility. Something about him that brought to mind magic. And, boy, wouldn't magic come in handy right about now. Because magic was the only thing that would've tamed the volcano. She had to tell someone or explode into ash and flames. "I have a friend, a man I used to work with. He had a child years ago with a woman he never married. While he was overseas in the service, his child's mother got in trouble with the law. The child went into the foster care system. He didn't know about any of this until long after the fact."

"Are you the child?" he asked when she finally stopped to take a breath. "And you don't know if you should tell your father who you are?"

"Why would you think that?" she asked, finding it strange that he'd go there before anywhere else.

"When someone has a friend with a problem, a lot of the time it's not a friend at all."

True enough, she thought, and smiled. "No. I'm not the child. In this case, it really is about a friend."

"You know both parties?"

"I do."

"And you don't know if you should stir up the past and put them together."

"I don't. The past is…messy. Very messy."

"Are you asking for my opinion?"

She found herself nodding. "I guess I am."

He turned to lean against the car beside her, arms crossed as he glanced over. "Are you close to your parents?"

Her smile widened. She felt it in the muscles of her cheeks. "They're my very best friends. I don't know what I'd do without them."

Which was why this conversation was one she should be having with them—not with a man she didn't know. Except her parents were aware of Mitch Pepper's story and couldn't be any more impartial than she was.

Will looked away, his gaze focused somewhere in front of him. "If you're trying to re-create what you have with your family for your friend, don't."

"Why not? Isn't that a perfect reason?"

"Perfect for you, sure. But it's not about you. It's about two people who've made their own way for a lot of years. What's the impact to their lives going to be if you upset the status quo?"

It sounded so obvious when put like that. "So I shouldn't tell either of them? Even if I know they're looking for each other?"

"Are they? Actively? Or are they just giving lip service to wanting to find the other because it's what society expects?"

This had been such a bad idea. She was more confused than ever. "You're saying what they claim to want might not be what they want at all?"

"You're the one who knows them," he said, and shrugged. "You're going to have to be the one to figure that out. I'm just a boy who was raised by wolves."

"You're pretty intuitive for a boy raised by wolves."

"Intuition is everything. Animals wouldn't survive without it."

"Even human animals?" she asked, wondering again about this one's crimes. He had that lean, wary look of someone who'd spent time wishing for eyes in the back of his head. Ten didn't take on hard cases. And Manny didn't send him anyone but those ready to return to the lives they'd left behind. Lives they'd screwed up with a single mistake—something Luna was too familiar with.

"We let a lot of things get in our way. An animal's intuition is about survival, not ego."

"Did ego get you in trouble?" she asked, because she wanted to know. She'd never been as curious about Ten's other ex-con hires, but this one…

He laughed then, a deep, clear rumble full of things to tempt her. "That, Miss Meadows, is for me to know. And for you to wonder about."

"Fair enough." After all, she didn't want him asking about her secrets. Her stupidity. A condition she still struggled with, it seemed, when out of the blue she next heard herself asking, "Would you like to get coffee later? Or dinner sometime?"

"Do you cook?"

Did he want her to? Did he want her to for him? Did he want to get her alone? *What in the world was wrong with her?* "Not if I can help it. I'm a big fan of takeout."

"In Hope Springs?"

Should she tell him? "I live a ways out of town, so it's an easy drive to New Braunfels."

"I do."

"Cook? Or live in Hope Springs?"

"Both. For now, with the living part. Since Manny set me up with Ten. But I've always cooked."

Was he offering to cook for her? Because she really didn't know where this conversation was going. "Kaylie's looking for someone for her café." And why was she telling him that when she wanted the job for Mitch? Unless what Will had said was already at work on her subconscious, making up her mind for her, keeping trouble at bay.

But he shook his head. "Gotta see through this construction gig. And I don't think I'd like cooking on a large scale. It's just something I enjoy for fun. And with friends."

She looked at him, wondering if he'd served time for something as petty as aggravating someone, or not answering questions. "Is that a yes or a no, then? To coffee. Or dinner."

"It's my way of asking if you'd let me cook for you."

"It really is easier if you just come out and say what's on your mind."

That laugh again, intimate and melodic. "I may not be good with invitations, but I definitely know not to speak my mind."

That was novel. Most men had no trouble coming on to her. And that incongruity allowed her a boldness she didn't often give into. "Do you have a cell?"

"I do," he said, and gave her his number as she pulled hers from her pocket and typed out a text.

She hit send and his phone beeped seconds later. His eyes on hers, he reached for it, finally dropping his gaze to the screen.

"Saturday would be good for me, too," he said, looking up as he did. "And now that I have your number, I'll be in touch."

"I look forward to it."

"And maybe you can text and let me know what you decide. About putting your friend in touch with his kid. Because I could be way off base. It's been known to happen."

In the past, perhaps, but she had a feeling whatever mistakes in judgment he'd once made were ones he'd remember before making more. "I could text you. Or I could tell you about it while watching you cook. Unless having someone watch makes you nervous."

"I've had someone, many someones, watching my every move the last three years. There's very little that makes me nervous." He took her in slowly, his gaze moving from her chin to her nose to her forehead. "Then again, none of them had eyes like yours."

That made her blush. She'd always thought herself too worldly to blush. She gestured toward her car. "I need to get going."

"And I need to get to work."

"Thank you for the advice, boy who was raised by wolves."

"Thank you for letting me cook for you, moon girl."

Moon girl. So strange to hear someone besides Mitch use the term of endearment, though considering the origin of her name, it wasn't surprising Will had gone there. "Until Saturday, then," she said, reaching to open her door.

He beat her to it, lifting the handle, so tall beside her, so unlike the men in her life and others she'd known. None of them had been the wolf this one was. None of them had made her want to share all the things she kept close. None, save for another who could never be hers because of the things she hadn't been brave enough to tell him.

Will stood in the road behind her as she drove away, his black jeans and black shirt and black hair filling her rearview mirror, and leaving her wishing she'd had a night free before Saturday. She wanted to see him sooner, to talk to him in greater depth. She thought he might have a lot of interesting things to say—though she needed to decide what to do about Mitch and Kaylie before she spent time getting to know a wolf.

CHAPTER NINE

By Wednesday, Ten had submitted paperwork for all the building permits needed for Kaylie's renovations. Hope Springs had very little in the way of bureaucratic red tape, but enough to foul up his mood. Kaylie had settled on the commercial flooring, but that was it. There were fixtures and cabinets and countertops to decide on, not to mention appliances. And that only took care of the kitchen.

But since that room would take his crew of two the longest to rewire and replumb, it was the room he wanted to tackle first. And with Kaylie's mind set on a Memorial Day opening, he thought he'd run by her place and give her a status update. Yeah, he could do the same thing with a phone call, but he wanted to see her even more than he needed to talk to her, and since he was already out…

It had been a long time since he'd found a woman intriguing. Granted, he didn't get out much these days, so he saw mostly women he knew. Wives of other men. Female friends. When he needed more than conversation, he had a favorite bar outside of Austin and a waitress there who knew what he liked.

Kaylie Flynn intrigued him in ways few women did. He couldn't figure her out, and that made him want to try that much harder. It also frustrated him because whether he figured her out or not didn't matter. She was a customer and, for now, off-limits. He knew better than to mix business with pleasure. He couldn't risk losing a job and failing the men he employed. Dakota had found his own way, but these men…Ten had been charged with their futures, with providing them stability as they returned to society. That responsibility outweighed any desire he might have for a woman's—for Kaylie's—company.

At the ring of his phone through his truck's cab, he activated the hands-free button on his steering wheel and said simply, "Keller."

"Ten. It's Manny. Thought I'd check in with you on the Bowman kid."

Will Bowman was hardly a kid. "It hasn't even been a week. You expecting that much trouble out of him that you can't even give me a week?"

Manny snorted. "Someone take a piss in your oatmeal this morning?"

Ten huffed. "Just dealing with a new client who I'm pretty sure is gonna cause me a lot of grief." No need to expound on the type of grief, or that it was his response to said client at fault. Kaylie couldn't be blamed for making him want her.

There. He'd admitted it. He was attracted to her and off his game because of it.

"That might not be the best environment for Bowman. Tension like that." Manny paused, and Ten could hear computer keys clicking in the background. "Maybe you've got another job he could work? Though I'm only assuming you've got him on this one due to timing and all. Set my mind at ease, Keller, would you?"

What was going on here? "You're kidding me, right? I can't remember you ever sending me someone as laid-back as Will."

Manny laughed. "Don't let the boy fool you. And don't let him take up with anyone he might meet on the job."

Now the other man was out of line. Working for Keller Construction wasn't an anonymous program with steps best taken alone. If Will wanted to date, that was on him. "I'm not his daddy. Or a therapist. Or a nanny. His personal time's his business. And if it's not, that's between the two of you."

For a long moment Manny went silent; then he cleared his throat and said, "Maybe we should have this conversation tomorrow. Over a plate of breakfast tacos at Malina's."

"We can," Ten said, pulling to a stop behind Kaylie's Jeep in her driveway, shifting into park and watching her toss a ball across the yard for Magoo. "Eight good for you?"

"Make it seven. I've got an appointment in Austin at nine thirty."

"Seven it is. See you then." Ten disconnected the call, shut off his truck, and climbed from the cab as Kaylie walked toward him. He'd been wrong about her hair. Unless it was the shade from the yard's trees turning it more red than blonde. She wore her boots and her jeans, but today's top was thigh-length and sleeveless. A cool white number that made him think of summer, and the flowers he'd smelled that first day on her skin.

"Checking up on us again?" she asked as she reached him, then leaned down to pick up the ball Magoo had dropped at her feet. She scratched his head, said, "Good dog," and threw it.

Ten watched it sail across the yard, watched the dog race after it. "That's some kind of arm you've got there."

She laughed. "I was a total jock in school."

"Really."

"Does that surprise you?"

He knew so little about her that everything he learned came as one. "Jock's not the first thing I'd think about you, but that's probably because I had a sister who was and spent more time wearing jerseys and kneepads than anything else. That's the association my mind makes. Not boots and jeans."

"You have a sister." It wasn't a question, but a statement, as if she was turning the information over in her mind.

"And a brother." Though he didn't know why he'd brought them up. He wasn't in touch with either. His fault, at least when it came to Indiana. And to his parents. Unlike Dakota, they still lived close.

"That must've been fun. Growing up. Having them around."

Because she'd been in foster care, away from what family she'd had. "Do you have siblings? Or is that something you might not know, growing up like you did? And maybe I should just shut up now. Sorry."

She shook her head, tucking back strands of hair that fell forward. "It's okay. I don't mind you asking."

"It's not my business."

She reached out, touched his wrist. "It's fine, Ten. Really. I don't know if I have siblings, no. I was my mother's only child, at least at the time. When I was taken away from her, I was only five. I never saw her again."

He didn't know a lot about foster care, but that seemed strange. "Did the court deny her visitation or something?"

"It's a long story," she said as Magoo returned, having abandoned his ball to sniff the trail of something more interesting than rubber. "Want to walk? I need to fetch this one's ball, since he forgot that's his job."

"Sure," he said, stuffing his hands in his pockets because he didn't trust himself not to return her touch. The pressure from her fingertips still lingered on his wrist like trouble he didn't need.

He was beginning to think this might've been a mistake, taking on a job for a woman who stirred him the way this one did. He couldn't risk the involvement, risk things not working out, risk losing this job when Will was depending on it. But he was here, and he was human, and he wanted to know why she'd had to learn to wield a wicked knife. She baked brownies for a living—she didn't skin wild game.

"Listen. Kaylie. I didn't come here to dig into your personal life. Or to check up on you. I just wanted to let you know I'll have the permits next week, and I'll get the kitchen started before dealing with the other walls."

She bent for a stick while walking, swiped it through the tall grass at her side. "You could've called to tell me that."

"I was in the neighborhood..." He was such a bad liar, and shrugged, thinking of his earlier conversation with Manny. "You know how it is. Sometimes a phone call goes places best explored in person. Questions come up. That sort of thing."

She slowed her steps, raising a hand to shade her eyes as she watched Magoo chase after a squirrel. "Then to answer your question, the court didn't have to deny my mother visitation. I mean, I guess they did, officially, but since she went to prison, it really didn't matter."

"Prison?" He'd assumed unfit parent, but he hadn't assumed criminal.

"Child endangerment. Possession with intent to distribute. She was coming down off a crystal-meth high and bleeding on the floor when they took me from her."

Without thinking, he pulled his hand from his pocket and reached for her, but checked himself before taking hold of her arm. "Kaylie?"

She stopped walking but continued to chop at the grass with her stick, the smells of the dew and the turned earth heavy in the air. "I love this house, this property. Everything good that I know started here. And I cannot *wait* to open my café. But I came back here, to Hope Springs, because of my parents."

"They're here?"

"I have no idea where they are," she said, looking at Magoo as he ran toward her. "Either of them. I came back here so I could find out."

Now he was really confused. And worried. If her mother had been sent to prison, how was Kaylie going to feel about Will being an ex-con? "You don't know where they are, but you came back here to find them?"

"It's not about where they are. It's about me needing to be here." She turned then, her attention on the house shaded by the trees, the blue darker than Ten would've chosen, but one that for some reason fit Kaylie to a T. "I can't even tell you what it was like to come here after all the places I'd been before."

"You were moved a lot?"

"I was. I don't know why. The system, I guess. Too many kids and not enough parents, good parents, anyway, to foster. I don't think I was that much trouble." She stopped to laugh, to ruffle a hand through Magoo's thick coat before he bolted away. "Coming here saved me. I wouldn't be who I am today had it not been for May and Winton. Here I can do anything. Open a café. Start over. Face the past. Sleep. And I have no idea why I'm telling you all this. You didn't come here for my life story."

Start over. Face the past. Sleep. *With a knife at her side?* He thought back to her telling him she'd lived in heinous conditions. "Do you not sleep now?"

"Not well," she said, kicking into the grass and dislodging Magoo's ball. "I've been running on empty most of my life. Early on, it was not knowing if I was going to wake up the next day and find someone packing my things."

"Even once you were here?"

"It got worse once I was here." She bent for the ball, her back arching and drawing Ten's gaze. "I wasn't attached to the previous families I'd lived with, so leaving was more uncertainty than anything. Here I was afraid because I never wanted to leave and feared I'd have to. It got better over time, but then there was school and sports and all the things that keep teens from getting enough sleep. Then college and three a.m. doughnuts for the bakery where I worked. Then my own doughnuts, my own bakery. And now my house and my café."

Amazing, a life laid out in a matter of words. "I'd say you need a vacation, but if you're anything like me, getting away wouldn't make it any better. You'd still be calling back to check on things."

"Why do we do this to ourselves?" she asked, the shake of her head acknowledging the trait they shared. "I really hope I can find a cook who I can rely on as a manager, too, but I doubt my control-freak nature would let me take full advantage."

"When does your ad come out?"

"Next week. Oh, while I was at the *Courant*'s office, I ran into a girl I used to go to school with. Jessa Little. Jessa Breeze now. She said she was going to tell her mother-in-law about the position, that she was an amazing cook. Do you know her? Dolly Breeze?"

Perfect, he mused with a snort. "I do. And I'd really rather you not hire her."

She looked up at him, frowning. "Why's that?"

"She works for me."

"Oh, that's right. Luna told me." Her eyes went wide as if he'd truly surprised her, and she loved the jolt of being surprised. And then she was laughing, the burst of sound spilling over him, infectious. "I'm so sorry," she finally managed to say. "I guess this is one of those let-the-best-man-win situations or something."

He hoped not, because he didn't stand a chance. "Or a sign that I should be the one putting an ad in the paper."

"Wouldn't that be jumping the gun? Such an easy admission of defeat?"

She was laughing again. Ten could only shake his head. "I know for a fact Dolly would rather spend her time in a kitchen or behind a sewing machine than at a desk making sense of my paperwork."

She cocked her head, the bow of her mouth so very tempting. "You're not doing yourself any favors here, you know."

"I know a lost cause when I trip over one."

"Then I look forward to meeting her. And I appreciate the recommendation, though I hope I have several applicants to consider. That's actually why Luna stopped by yesterday. She wanted to know about the position for a friend of hers."

"How'd she hear about it?"

"At a craft show over the weekend."

Figured. "No doubt from Dolly, if Jessa told her."

"I have a feeling Jessa was dialing before I'd pulled away from the building," Kaylie said with a grin that had Ten nodding.

"That sounds about right."

"You know," she said, considering him. "The way word of mouth works here, I could've saved the cost of the ad."

"Guess you were too young to have known that when you lived here before."

"Too young, too involved with school." She chopped her stick through the grass again. "Too busy making sure not to do anything to cause the Wises to want to send me away."

"From what you've said, I doubt doing so crossed their minds."

"That doesn't mean it didn't cross mine."

Fair enough. "Maybe you could ask some of the people who knew you back then about your parents."

"I don't think they'd know them. I wasn't living here when I was taken from my mother."

"What about your father?"

"I don't have a clue where to start looking for him. I don't even know his name."

"It's not on your birth certificate?"

She shook her head. "I've thought back, trying to remember what my mother called him, but all I knew him as was Daddy. Even Ernest called him Daddy."

"Ernest?"

"He lived across the hall from us. He was a widower, well into his seventies I'm sure, with a grizzled white beard that always fascinated me, since his skin was so black. Ernest Flynn."

"You took your last name from him."

Magoo came running up then as if remembering his ball. Kaylie cocked her arm and threw it, this time toward the house, canting her head for Ten to walk back with her. "I knew in high school that as soon as I was old enough I was going to change my name. I thought about asking May and Winton if they'd mind me taking theirs, but decided against it. They'd given me so much already. Then I thought about Ernest. I was five the last time I saw him. While the police and paramedics dealt with my mother, he held me in his lap on the apartment building's stairs. He was crying as loud as I was when the social worker took me from his arms. I remember that moment as clearly as if it were yesterday."

And she laid it all out as if describing a day at the zoo. "Sounds like he was a good friend."

"I've been lucky. I've had some of the best. Part of me says I should leave things alone, let those relationships hold me. Ernest. May and Winton. Saul Golden, the man who gave me my first bakery job. He passed on before I could go back and thank him for the time he'd taken with a curious eighteen-year-old who knew everything about brownies but little else." She reached for his forearm to stop him. "You like brownies, don't you?"

"Love 'em," he said, doing his best to ignore the warmth of her fingers.

"Good. The first batch I bake in the new kitchen will be all for you."

"That sounds even better than the bonus you put in my contract."

"Please. It's just brownies."

But it wasn't. It was Kaylie's heart and soul. It wasn't impersonal money, or a case of scotch whiskey he could buy for himself. It was Kaylie thinking of him, baking for him, putting herself into a gift for him. "Thank you. I'm a big fan of chocolate."

"Too bad you never stopped by the Sweet Spot. Chocolate was our specialty."

"Chocolate what?"

"Chocolate everything. Cookies and cakes and pies."

"And brownies."

"The very same brownies I get to bake here," she said, her gaze leaving his to return to the house.

His followed, and he took in the multitude of windows that would require hours of work to keep clean, the roof he'd replaced once already but that had suffered additional limb damage since. The flower beds were crap, though he knew she had plans to hire a landscaper, and there was an acre of wooded yard to maintain.

It was an amazing house. An amazing burden. And he was really glad he hadn't known it was for sale. He would hate to have taken it away from her.

Wake Up and Smell Two Owls' Chocolate Brownie

we got your coffee right here, joe

8 ounces unsalted butter
3 ounces unsweetened chocolate
8 ounces semisweet chocolate
3 extra large eggs
1 tablespoon espresso powder
1 tablespoons vanilla
1½ cups sugar
½ cup flour
½ tablespoon baking powder
½ tablespoon salt
1 cup chopped pecans or walnuts (optional)

Preheat oven to 350°F. Grease or spray with cooking oil and flour a 9 x 13 x 1–inch baking sheet.

Melt the butter, the unsweetened chocolate, and the semisweet chocolate in a double boiler (or in a microwave), stirring often so as not to burn the chocolate. Cool slightly. Stir together in a large bowl the eggs, the espresso powder, the vanilla, and the sugar. Add the warm chocolate mixture to the bowl and cool. Sift the flour, the baking powder, and the salt into a small bowl. Add to the cooled chocolate mixture.

Pour the batter into the prepared baking sheet. Bake 35–40 minutes, or until an inserted tester comes out with a bit of batter attached. Cool completely before cutting.

CHAPTER TEN

Since she'd waited tables at the Gristmill Restaurant in high school, Luna knew the best time to catch Mitch Pepper. He'd been a staple in the kitchen for years, acting as friend, mentor, or guilty conscience—whatever a coworker, most of them younger, might need. Having been around the block, Mitch was a straight shooter. And the particular block he'd been around had everything to do with his aim.

After her late-day meeting at the Austin boutique to talk about Patchwork Moon's spring scarf line, Luna had made the drive to Gruene and the Gristmill before she could change her mind. Yesterday's visit with Kaylie had given her a lot to think about, but she still hadn't decided if she was doing the right thing. It was her conversation with Will Bowman, however, giving her the most grief.

Did she owe the same truth to Kaylie she owed to Mitch, whom she'd known since she was a girl?

Mitch, who'd rocked her to sleep while her parents cleaned up the kitchen after dinner? Mitch, who'd talked her father into letting her keep the dog abandoned in the ditch beneath the sign at the farm's entrance? Mitch, who'd come to the hospital the morning after her accident and told her Sierra hadn't made it through the night?

Her mother had wanted to wait until she was stronger. Her father had been unable to say the words. Mitch had been the only one thinking clearly. He'd known she could handle the truth and needed it. Now another truth was eating at her, and no matter what Will Bowman said, Mitch was her priority. He would know what to do about Kaylie.

The restaurant was closed, the kitchen staff going through their nightly routine of food storage and cleanup, the smells of browned butter and cream sauces, grilled beef and fried onions hanging heavy in the air.

Having been a part of this same activity with so many of these same people, she had a lot of catching up to do on her way through the stations to Mitch. She found him sharpening his knives, and because of the thing that had brought her here, she shivered.

"Mitch?" When she had his attention, she raised a hand. "Got a second?"

He looked at her over the dark rims of his half-glasses. "Hey, moon girl. What's shaking?"

He was smiling, as always, the laugh lines fanning out from his eyes like a map of the life he'd made for himself, each groove detailing the happiness he'd found after all the years he'd spent with none. She hated taking that away from him. Thinking she might be giving him back even more was the only thing pushing her on.

"Could we talk for a minute?" She gestured over her shoulder. "On the patio maybe?"

At that, he frowned, his green eyes behind his narrow black frames so much like Kaylie's it hurt Luna's stomach to hold his gaze. He wiped his hands on the towel he pulled from his shoulder, never looking away as he slid the neck straps of his apron over his head. "Everything okay? Something wrong with Harry?"

"No, Daddy's fine. Mom too. I just need…to tell you something."

"Sounds ominous," he said, his rough laugh fooling neither of them as he locked away his knives and his whetstone before following her out the back door. She wound her way through the empty tables to the rail that fenced off the restaurant from the river. Mitch followed, leaning a shoulder into a support beam and asking, "What's up?"

She looked at the moon, a new moon, her moon, and made a wish for a happy ending. "I went to Hope Springs yesterday."

"Okay."

What to say? Where to start? "When I was here for Saturday's craft fair, I heard about a woman opening a café there and thought of you. I know she's doing her own desserts—she used to own a bakery in Austin—but she's looking for a cook."

"Ah, thanks, sweetheart," Mitch said, the relief in his words doing nothing to salve the pain to come from what she'd learned. "But I'm happy right here."

"I don't think it's full-time. She's only serving lunch," she said, and turned in time to see him shaking his head.

"Even if I wanted to, I wouldn't have time. Can't be in two places at once. Lunch-only still means a lot of prep work, and I've got to be here at noon, because this place pays the bills."

"There may not be as much prep work as you think. Just big pans of a single entrée that diners dish up themselves from a buffet."

"Huh. Cool concept. But no can do. My days are jam-packed as it is."

"Are you sure? A change of scenery might be nice. A new kitchen. No fish to fillet or steaks to grill. No sauces or desserts or sides." She should've thought this through. Painted the idea as irresistible. Made him an offer he couldn't refuse. Spun him a tale to draw him to Two Owls, one to save her from spelling out the reason she wanted him to visit the café.

But Mitch wasn't a dreamer. He got things done, wasting no time because of wasting too much already. "I can't think of a single good reason I'd want to work in Hope Springs. Which means there's a reason you want me to. So what is it?"

She shook her head, backed away. "Never mind. This whole thing was a stupid idea." She headed for the far side of the patio and the beer garden beyond. She should've talked to her father first. He was Mitch's best friend, and had an answer for everything. He would know what to do.

Mitch grabbed her arm to stop her from leaving. "You haven't had a stupid idea since I've known you. Something's up. And I'm not letting you go until you tell me what it is."

She was frustrated, near to angry, but with herself, not with Mitch. She should've listened to Will. She shouldn't have come here without a better plan, and now she was stuck because he was a pit bull. That's what she loved most about him. He cared. He worried. He didn't want those close to him to hurt.

"Luna?"

She stared at her feet, swallowed.

"Luna?"

She couldn't tell him. Not like this.

"Luna, I swear—"

She spun on him then, coming apart. "It's your daughter."

Mitch's face went beet red, the moonlight blanching the color from his goatee and his hair. He released her, took a stumbling step in reverse, hit the patio's long cracked wall. "What?"

Luna's chest grew tight, her eyes damp. "Kaylie. She's living in Hope Springs."

All Mitch seemed able to do was pound his head against the wall. Bang. Bang. Denying, disbelieving. "Kaylie? My Kaylie?" Bang. Bang. Bang.

Nodding, Luna tried to find her voice, though the words she spoke came out in a whisper. "She spent eight years there in a foster home."

"A foster home? And she went back?" Mitch asked, his face screwed in pain, his voice strangled.

"She bought the house where she lived."

He gulped down a watery breath. "Why would she go back?"

God, but his tears were going to do her in. "It's a great house. A big Victorian with an acre of trees."

"And she bought it?"

"Sold her business in Austin and paid cash, I hear."

"Wow." He scrubbed both hands up and down his face, then back over the crew cut he still wore. "Just...wow."

"Yeah. She's pretty amazing."

"Is she? Really?" he asked, begged, the words cracking and thick with emotion.

Luna had no words at all. She could barely breathe.

He sank to his heels, rocked back and forth. "Crap. What am I supposed to do?"

"Apply for the job?"

He laughed, his agony etched in the lines on his face. "Yeah, that's not going to happen."

"Why not? You wouldn't have to tell her who you are."

"I couldn't do that. No way." He got to his feet, laced his hands on top of his head, his eyes red, his sorrow keen. "I could never do that to Kaylie."

"You wouldn't have to hire on, but you could at least go see her. Go meet her. Get to know her."

But Mitch was still shaking his head. "Moon girl, I love you for this, but I lost my baby years ago. The woman in Hope Springs…she's someone else. Someone with her own life. Someone I don't deserve to have in mine."

And then he returned to the kitchen, looking a whole lot more worn than when she'd found him ten minutes ago, and breaking her heart with his slumped shoulders and dejected, old man's gait.

~

Walking from the lingering heat of the restaurant's kitchen toward the railing where the patio overlooked the Guadalupe, Mitch stopped to light the cigarette he'd bummed from a busboy when clocking out for the night. He hadn't smoked in ages. Not since returning to Texas, after four years spent in barracks around the world, to find his daughter gone, swallowed up in a system designed to keep her safe and well cared for.

Giving up cigarettes had been as much about his health as about distancing himself from the monkey riding his back. His employer knew that he'd lost Kaylie to social services. He'd told Harry Meadows, of course, so Julietta and Luna knew, too. But he didn't want to be reminded of those years, when smoking had given him something to do with his hands besides slamming his fists into faces or walls.

It was the same reason he cooked.

To come to terms with using a knife.

His daughter. Kaylie. Little Kaylie with her strawberry-blonde hair and face full of freckles and the big gap where her teeth would come in…later, when he might be deployed and unable to see if he was going to have to pay for braces.

He sucked in smoke filled with tar and nicotine and wondered what Luna had been thinking, telling him about Kaylie being so close when he'd become so good at imagining her in Seattle, or Minneapolis, or New York City.

To find out she was right here, that she'd grown up and stayed instead of getting away from the Texas Hill Country and all the crap that had ruined her life.

Then again, look at him, living within spitting distance of all he'd lost. He laughed and tossed the rest of the cigarette to the stone floor before thinking better of littering, and retrieving the smoldering butt. He stuffed it in his pocket, watched the water roll, the moon on its surface broken by the ripples, long teasing striations of light.

So his daughter shared his love of cooking. He couldn't help the smile that tugged at his mouth at the thought.

It felt strange, thinking of Kaylie and smiling. For so long thinking of Kaylie had been the worst sort of pain: Where was she? Who was taking care of her? *Were* they taking care of her, or was she stuck in a room with five other kids, sharing one big bed and fistfights over toys?

That's what had got to him the most. That's when he'd start imagining her being raised elsewhere, by folks who knew all the things kids needed. Like bedtime stories and stuffed pink puppies, lessons on tying shoelaces and help with a toothbrush and comb and piggyback rides.

He rubbed at his eyes, smearing the grit from the kitchen that was stinging them. That Luna. Such a sweetheart. He knew why she'd told him. She wanted him to have what Harry did. She adored her father, and her father thought being wrapped around her little finger was the best place to be.

It wouldn't happen. No way he and Kaylie could have the same thing. No way, no chance. The past was the past. He'd had four years to be a father and had made a mess of it. Trying to get that back was a fool's errand, and Mitch Pepper was done with being a fool.

No matter how badly he ached with the thought of being this close to his girl.

CHAPTER ELEVEN

Max Malina was a crusty Brooklynite who'd set up shop in Hope Springs the year Tennessee Keller was born. Ten had probably eaten as much of Max's cooking as he had of his own, or anyone else's. Malina's was open when he was ready for breakfast and when he called it a day. It was only at lunch that he had to fend for himself, which meant most of the time he didn't bother with more than a protein bar from the stash he kept in his truck. He could see why Kaylie had decided to do something about feeding lunch to Hope Springs. Good call on her part.

Sitting in a booth near the front door of Malina's Diner, he sipped from his second cup of coffee and wondered why he was here. To meet Manny, sure. But the rest of it? He'd been in a weird frame of mind when they'd spoken the other day, and not in the mood to hear the other man harsh on Will. That didn't mean Manny was in the wrong any more than it meant Ten's intuition about his newest hire would play out. But since he was a big part of Manny's program, he owed the other man the floor. And an explanation. Just not one that involved what he was feeling for Kaylie.

"Is it getting to be too much?" Manny asked, sliding into the opposite side of the booth.

Ten returned his coffee mug to the table and sat back. "Good morning to you, too."

Manny signaled to the waitress for his own cup, then leaned forward and scowled fiercely at Ten. "Well?"

Fine. He could get down to business, too. "What? Giving these guys a job? Why would you think that?"

"I don't think that. I'm just asking. Dakota's been off my caseload for years. And you've put in plenty trying to make up for what he did."

"That's not why I do this."

"Sure it is. You didn't go after Robby. Dakota did, and ended up behind bars. The guilt's still eating you alive. You've gotta let it go. You did what you could for your brother. I know you would've served his time, too, but the system doesn't work that way. And I need to know I'm sending my guys into a working situation that's not going to mess with their already messed-up psyches."

Ten didn't like having his head examined. Especially by a parole officer. "I'm fine. Will's fine. If you've got someone else you need put to work, send him along and he'll be fine."

"Fine."

"Fine. Now can we eat? You've got to get on the road. And I've got a job to get to."

"Sure," Manny said, taking the coffee from their waitress's hand before she could set the cup on the table. "Tell me about it."

"Because you're interested as a friend? Or because you want to know what Bowman's up to?"

"Can it be a little bit of both?" he asked, then smiled as he brought his coffee to his mouth.

"If it'll get me out of here faster, sure," Ten said, grinning as well, then giving his order to their waitress before she left.

Manny held up two fingers to signal he'd take the same. "C'mon. Tell me. You said something about an old Victorian. Wait. Do you mean Bob Coleman's place?"

"Yep. That's the one."

Work out of the way, Manny sat back, relaxed. "Wow. If I recall correctly, you were looking to buy that monster."

Ten nodded. He'd driven Manny by the house a couple of times, made the other man listen to him wax poetic about all he could do with the place. "I wanted it, but didn't think the Colemans would sell. I hadn't been watching for it to be listed."

"Who beat you to it?"

Ten hesitated, not wanting to share Kaylie's business, then realized it was all public record and nothing she was trying to hide. "One of the kids who used to live there with Winton and May Wise. Name's Kaylie Flynn."

"Huh. No kidding. I hadn't thought about the Wises for a long time. They've both passed on, I believe."

"They have. Kaylie had been keeping an eye on the place."

"Guess she wanted it more than you did."

"She's got a connection to it that I don't." He reached for the first of his three breakfast tacos the minute his plate hit the table. "She's converting the first floor into a café. I've got Will taking down the shutters, checking all the windows for damage."

"What's the tension you're throwing him into?"

"It's nothing that's going to be a problem for him, or, by extension, you."

Manny thought for a moment. Then gave a snort that had Ten rolling his eyes. "That leaves you. And her. And confirmed bachelor that you are, you don't know what to do with the idea of a woman you want living in a house you want without you living there, too."

No matter how good a friend Ten considered Manny, he was not talking about any of this until he'd figured it out for himself. "I'm pretty sure that doesn't even deserve a response. So I'm not going to give you one."

"You don't have to, man. I've known you a lotta years. You haven't said more than two words in all that time about the personal lives of any of your clients. You've only mentioned one or two by name. And you haven't dated anyone seriously since I've known you."

"I'm not dating Kaylie."

"Yet."

Ten was not having this conversation. "We're doing nothing but talking about her house." Mostly. "It's not a personal relationship. I've got too many obligations, and a lot of them thanks to you, to take time for a personal relationship."

Manny finished off his first taco and picked up his second. "More than anyone I know, you need to take time. Stop beating yourself up, or thinking you don't deserve anything good in your life. If Dakota knew you've been carrying this guilt all this time..."

Since neither one of them had seen Dakota in years, it was hard to say what he'd do. And Ten got Manny's concern. That's what friends were for. But in this case, the concern butted up a little too close to meddling. Good-natured meddling, but still. "So, what? You're moonlighting as a shrink now?"

"Could be you need one," Manny said, and when Ten lifted a hand to object, the other man continued. "Or at least a friend willing to tell you the truth from this side of that wall of yours."

"Oh, so now I've got a wall."

"Jericho-sized. Lots of hardheaded bricks. With a moat."

Ten grunted and dug back into his food. If his head was hard, it was his business. And if he'd put up walls, he had his reasons. Manny might think he knew the way of things, but he hadn't been standing in Ten's shoes when Dakota had swung that bat.

"Letting someone in," Manny went on, "say, this Kaylie… wouldn't be a bad thing. Man wasn't meant to live alone."

"I do just fine living alone. And I told you. Kaylie's business. I don't mix my work with my downtime."

"Can't say I've known you to take any downtime."

Ten thought about Kaylie's mouth, her laugh, the bow of her lip, her freckles, her eyes that said so much while appearing so sad. "Since you don't see me but every couple of weeks, there's a lot of what I do that you don't know."

"There's a lot of what you do that I don't *want* to know. But as much as you think I'm up in your business because of mine—"

"Which you are—"

"—I'm your friend and am pretty fed up with you taking the blame for everything that went down with your family. It's time to let it go, Ten. You were sixteen years old, Dakota was an adult, and your parents should've paid more attention to what the kids under their roof were doing."

And about that, Manny was right. "Enough. I came here for breakfast, and to assure you I'm not dropping Will Bowman into hot water. What I didn't come here for is an intervention, or whatever the hell this is."

"This is a friend talking to a friend. But if you say enough, then enough." Manny reached for his coffee. "I can talk about soccer instead."

Another smile pulled at Ten's mouth. "That's okay. You know how I don't feel about soccer."

"And that I've never understood."

It was on Ten's drive from Malina's back to the shop when Manny's words truly sank in. Ten didn't like thinking about his high school years, the events that had sent Dakota to prison. No matter what Manny said, it was Ten's fault. He never should've asked their parents if Robby Hunt could stay with them during spring break...

Robby and Ten had grown up together, been close friends since they'd played shortstop and second base in Little League. The other boy had come from what teenage Ten had thought to be an overly strict family. Robby wasn't permitted to do half of what Ten's parents allowed. He'd had a curfew. Ten hadn't. He'd had a restriction on how much TV he could watch each day, what music he could listen to, what movies he could see, where he could go and with whom. Ten had been a free agent, making his own decisions.

Looking back, it was easy to see whose parents had been more involved in their kids' lives. It hadn't been Drew and Tiffany Keller, that was for sure. It was a wonder Ten's sister, Indiana, hadn't given them a grandchild before her fifteenth birthday, as little instruction as they'd provided her in the ways of the world and of men.

And if not for Dakota and his baseball bat, that very well might've happened against her will.

CHAPTER TWELVE

Thursday morning found Kaylie sitting cross-legged on the kitchen counter, her coffee on the window ledge, a sketch pad in her lap. Magoo lay stretched out in the middle of the floor, snoring, a sputtering nasal sound punctuated with an occasional whine and whiffle. Kaylie shook her head, smiling. As excited as she was to get started making over the house, she would miss these quiet—or mostly quiet—mornings with only her fur baby for company.

Her love of spending the early hours in silence was one of many things she owed to May Wise. How many times had she come down to breakfast before the rest of the kids to find May packing lunches, humming softly as she slathered slices of homemade bread with thick layers of jam, loaded others with wedges of cheese? May had always known Kaylie was there, but had done no more than smile to herself, letting Kaylie be the one to speak first.

Sometimes she had, asking if it was okay to pour a bowl of cereal rather than wait for everyone else and pancakes or French toast. But sometimes it had been Winton, or Cindy or Tim, joining them and starting the conversations it took the entire morning to finish, and that Kaylie, wide-eyed, had soaked up. So, yes, she loved her quiet time, but she couldn't wait to fill this house with voices again, words tumbling over one another to be heard.

She'd missed that, living alone. The chatter at school had been too chaotic, that at work about work. But during the eight years she'd lived in this house, there'd been a constant flow of words that mattered. Winton reading aloud, May teaching her to bake, Cindy and Tim and later Joelle playing Monopoly or Scrabble. Then there were the warm spring days the family spent on the spot Winton cleared for softball, and the cheering, the screaming, the distracting cries of *batter, batter, swing!*

She'd woken up thinking about seasonal themes for the dining rooms, and had been playing with the idea since. After talking to Ten on Saturday, she'd decided she wanted to add a fourth room to the connected eating spaces, and was waiting for him to get here so they could discuss whether it was best to add the solarium or the parlor to the maze.

The parlor was her first choice, as it would expand the dining area toward the front of the house, keeping the rooms at the rear hers and private. Plus, she loved the solarium. Almost as much as the kitchen. She'd spent so much time in there doing homework or reading or napping, or staring out at the trees, lost in thought. And yet these days she was hardly ever alone, and the thoughts she would've once kept to herself she was sharing with Luna and Ten.

There had to be some reason she felt so free to disclose the details of her life to these people she'd just met. Talking about her past was not part of her plan. She wasn't a talker, a sharer. She never had been, but especially not when it came to her feelings. May had tried in that way she'd had, kind and subtle and making it seem as if she wasn't prompting at all, to get Kaylie to open up.

But that part of her had closed down the day her mother had left their apartment bandaged and handcuffed in an ambulance, and social services had taken Kaylie out of Ernest Flynn's arms. She knew she came across at times as cold, as aloof, as distant, but keeping her feelings to herself was how she'd survived. So why was she opening up now? Was it the magic of the house? Was it the people coming into her life?

Or was she in a better personal place, finally ready to shed the protective cocoon of isolation she'd spent so much time burrowed inside?

She was just reaching for her coffee when she heard the slam of a truck door. Finally. Magoo heard it, too, rousing and trotting to the mudroom. She glanced out the window at her right in time to see a man in black Dockers and a white dress shirt with cuffed sleeves step down from a truck much like Ten's.

His hair was buzzed short, and he wore a goatee, both the honest salt-and-pepper of his age, though he moved like a man much younger and she realized he was built like a younger man as well. She watched as he made his way up the driveway, slowing as he studied the house and the grounds.

She hopped down and stretched—she'd been sitting hunched over way too long—and tossed her pencil and paper to the counter behind her, making her way to the door. Giving Magoo the signal to stay at her side, she walked out and raised a hand in greeting. "Hello."

The man's head came up sharply, and he stopped in his tracks as if startled, shoving his hands into his pockets as he stared at her and frowned. She obviously wasn't who he'd been expecting, because his frown deepened and then he swallowed, his throat working as he raised a hand to scratch at one side of his jaw.

"Can I help you?" she asked. Guard dog Magoo sensed no threat and sat, his wagging tail stirring up driveway dust.

"I'm sorry," the man said, holding up a finger. "Give me one second." He returned to his truck, opened the door, rubbing at his forehead, then at his eyes, as he leaned to reach for something in the cab.

Kaylie waited, wondering if he was here to meet Ten, maybe checking to see if he had the right time or right address. Will Bowman was due later to get back to work on the shutters, but the internal construction wasn't scheduled yet. She was expecting Ten later, too.

She started to call out and tell her visitor just that, but he closed his truck door and came toward her, lifting a tentative hand.

"Hi. Sorry about that. I just…I'm looking for the owner."

"You've found her. I'm Kaylie Flynn."

"Flynn?" he asked, and gave a huff before a smile pulled at one side of his mouth.

Something tingled at the base of her spine. "Is there a problem?"

He shook his head. "No. Nothing. It's just that I once had a friend with that last name. Haven't thought of him for years."

Ah. The surprise of nostalgia. "You are?"

"Mitch Pepper," he said. "Luna Meadows told me you were looking for a cook. Told me I should come talk to you."

"It's nice to meet you, Mitch," Kaylie said, offering her hand. "And there's no need to apologize."

He laughed again, his handshake brisk and brief. "Oh, I beg to differ, but that's on me."

Strange thing to say, that. "Luna said she used to work with you, I think?"

"Sor—" He held up a hand to stop himself, came closer and started again. "I cook at the Gristmill over in Gruene. She waited tables there in high school. I got her the job, actually."

"You've known her a long time, then."

"I have. Her dad, Harry, he's one of my oldest friends. We were in the service together, and he talked me into settling here after my discharge."

He looked to be about the right age to have been deployed during the first Gulf War, maybe just this side of fifty. "Would you like a cup of coffee, Mitch? I just brewed a pot."

"Sure. That would be great," he said, as she turned for the house. "This is some place."

"It is, isn't it? I don't know if Luna told you, but I used to live here, years ago. I loved it so much that I had to buy it when it came on the market." She pulled open the screen door into the kitchen. Magoo bounded through but Mitch waited, gesturing for her to go ahead. She did, smiling to herself at the show of chivalry that had her thinking again of Ten. He was similarly kind, thoughtful. She wondered what he'd think of Mitch, frowned as she wondered why his opinion mattered.

"I guess it'll be a while before you open for business?" Mitch asked, the door bouncing shut behind him. "It looks like you just got the keys to the place."

"About a week ago, yes." She reached for a mug where they sat in a row on the countertop, filled it and handed it to him, then gestured to the raffia-handled shopping bag she was using for storage since the cabinets would be coming down soon. "I've got sugar and sweetener, and cream in the fridge."

"Black is fine, thanks," he said, and blew across the mug's surface before sipping. "When do you plan to be up and running?"

"Memorial Day weekend," she said, topping off her own mug.

"So you've got a building contractor lined up?"

"I do. He came with great references. Even Luna approved."

"Luna's got good taste. And a good sense about people."

"She seemed anxious that I consider you for the cook's position."

He gave a huff of breath as if tickled. "I got the same pressure."

"And here you are."

"Here I am."

"Even though you already have a job."

"I explained that to her. She wouldn't take no for an answer."

Kaylie canted her head, considered him. "So is there any point to our talking about the position?"

"I wouldn't have come otherwise. My time's too valuable to waste. I imagine yours is, too."

Honesty. Integrity. Respect. "If you worked with Luna when she was in high school, you must've been cooking at the Gristmill for, what? A dozen years?"

"Closer to fifteen. It's been quite a long haul."

"You know this isn't full-time, yes? Luna explained that?"

He nodded, holding her gaze, his fashionable black glasses framing eyes as green as her own. "She did. If this turns out to be something I'm interested in, I'd cut back on my hours in Gruene. Can't be in two places at one time."

Something he was interested in. Not something she thought he was right for. Not something she might want him for, or offer him. Interesting perspective. She liked that he spoke his mind. "Since Luna told you how things will work, why don't you ask me any questions you have. We'll start there."

"I've only got one right now."

"Which is?"

"Can I see where you'll be building out for the café?"

CHAPTER THIRTEEN

Mitch didn't care about seeing any of the house, only that she loved it and it meant something to her. Her. Kaylie. His daughter. His girl.

God, but she was beautiful. So sweet and so smart and her teeth so straight. He still carried a picture of her, one where she was all smiles, the big gap between her baby teeth making him wonder how her permanent ones would come in.

He'd told himself he wasn't going to come here. What he'd said to Luna was the truth. He'd lost his baby years ago. This woman was someone else. But he'd known from the moment he'd heard the news that he'd make the trip, if just to see her. He'd been looking for her more than half of his life.

How could he not come to see her?

"Did you live here a long time?" He wanted to know everything, but he was a stranger and had to be cautious in what he asked.

"For eight years. All but the elementary school ones. Those I spent…other places."

Elementary school. That would put her here at about age ten. Where had she been the years after he'd left for boot camp and she'd been whisked away from Dawn? Where were those *other places*? And why had she taken

Ernest Flynn's last name? He'd been their neighbor in Austin. Mitch couldn't imagine Kaylie remembering him, she'd been so young. But the name change explained why he'd had no luck in finding her. He'd been looking for Kaylie Bridges all this time.

"Guess it's nice to be back and catch up with old friends."

"Actually, I haven't had time to see but one yet, and that by complete accident. I ran into her working at the newspaper office when I placed my help-wanted ad."

"So I'm getting a jump on the competition, huh?"

"You are. Pays to have friends in high places," she said as she led him from the kitchen into what he supposed was the original dining room. "I'd planned to gut most of the first floor and convert it to one large eating area, but Ten talked me into a better use of the space."

"Ten?"

"My contractor, Tennessee Keller," she said, walking him out of the room into the main hallway, their footsteps echoing in the cavernous space. "He suggested using the two rooms on either side of the dining room"—she pointed to both—"just cutting entrances between them and connecting them that way."

"A sort of maze, then?"

"In a way, yes."

"Is it a better use? For you? For your business?" And then he shut his mouth because what she did here with her property was none of his. He wasn't sounding like a potential employee, but more like…an overly concerned father.

"It is, though I did have to think about it."

He stopped himself from saying *I'm sorry* before saying, "It's not my place. I had no right to ask."

"It's okay. I don't mind. If you end up being part of what I do here, I'd like your input. I want this to be a team effort. And I want it to be fun."

He couldn't be a part of it. Even wanting to, he couldn't. He had too much to atone for and she had no reason to give him that chance. He would make the most of today because he could never come here again. The deception was already knotting his gut, and this was only one hour out of one single day. He stepped away from her to look into the two rooms she'd indicated, needing to breathe, to close his eyes for a second and tighten the noose of his control.

He wanted so badly to take her in his arms, to show her the tattered photo he'd had in his wallet for twenty-three years. To tell her how often he'd taken it out while on his bunk in the desert, how he'd talked to her about his day, his mission, the friends he'd lost to enemy fire and to PTSD.

He hated her mother even more than the system for keeping her from him, when all he'd done was straighten out his life to give his family a better one.

"What do you think? Will the connected rooms work better than tearing out walls to make one big one?"

He came back to where she was waiting, her dog lying beside her, patient, its chin on its paws. Mitch pointed toward the front of the house. "Include that front room up there, too, and you'll have additional seating and no real wasted space on this floor. Unless you had something else planned for the...I guess it's a parlor?"

He looked to her again, watched as an enormous smile spread over her face, her mouth going wide and her eyes catching the light shining through the stained glass on the doors at the hallway's end. "Just this morning I decided I wanted to add the parlor to the build-out. Glad to know the idea makes sense."

"Well, I'm not your contractor." He'd feel guilty as hell if his comments pushed her to a decision that might not be the right one.

"No, but you've been in the business a long time. I'm just starting out."

"What did you do before this?" he asked, though he knew. He'd hung on Luna's every word, replayed them over and over in his mind.

"I owned a bakery in Austin. The Sweet Spot. Brownies were our specialty. My specialty. I actually learned to bake them while living here. It's a wonder the other kids and my foster parents didn't each weigh a thousand pounds."

This wasn't his business. Not any of it. Yet it was so hard to hear her say these things, to have her share them so openly and not want to ask for more. She owed him nothing. He owed her everything. But none of that was able to stop him from asking, "Foster parents?"

"Winton and May Wise. They took me in when I was ten, and I only left at eighteen because I had to. I mean, I could've stayed, I guess, gotten a job here. But since the state paid my tuition and a big chunk of my expenses, I moved to Austin for school. And I worked to put away money for the future."

"Austin. You went to UT?"

She nodded. "Took me six years to get my degree, but that's what happens when you have to make doughnuts and bear claws at three a.m."

He wanted to tell her how proud he was of her, what an accomplishment it was to work one's way through school, but he couldn't tell her that. Just like he couldn't pull her close and breathe the scent of her hair. Just like he couldn't take this job.

"It wasn't easy, but it's been *so* worth it."

He shouldn't have come here. He should've stayed in Gruene where he belonged. He should've left well enough alone; he had a good life. But it was a life with a big fat hole in it. Something he'd been ready to live with until the day he died. Or so he'd thought. Because looking now at his beautiful girl, his smart, ambitious, green-eyed girl, he felt the hole deepen to expose the core of who he was.

He cleared his throat. "So you'll be open for lunch, what? Five, six days a week?"

"I'll start out at five, then add to that if Two Owls demands it."

"Two Owls?"

"After Winton and May. Just seems fitting. They were two of the wisest people I've ever known."

Were. "Then they're..."

She nodded. "Winton passed on a few years ago. May more recently. I was actually able to come back here and buy this place because of them. They took care of a lot of kids over the years, but May stayed in touch even after I'd graduated. She told me once that I was the daughter she would've wanted if she could've had children of her own."

"Sounds like they were as lucky to have you as you were to have them," he said, his heart crumbling in his chest like crushed bread crumbs. He should've been the one to make all of this happen for her. Him, not strangers. Even though they'd loved her, they couldn't have loved her as much as he did.

"I know. I was lucky."

"They left you this place?"

"No, but they named me in their will, or May did, since Winton was gone. The inheritance made it possible for me to buy it. She'd had to sell it after he was gone, so I bought it from the current owners, and...I don't know why I'm telling you all this. You didn't come here to hear about my life."

That was the only thing he'd come here for. "Don't think a thing about it. It gives me an idea of who I'd be working with." But he wouldn't be working with her. It was just a truth that needed to be said.

"Well, good. Because I think we'd be a good fit. If you were in the market for a job. And could put together casseroles that weren't all Italian or Tex-Mex," she said, adding a self-deprecating laugh and a questioning arch of her brow.

"I cooked in the service and did a short stint in a hospital cafeteria. I can make a one-dish meal out of anything."

"Do you have a résumé? Not that you're looking for a job."

He found himself smiling. "If I were applying for the position, I'd be happy to e-mail it to you."

She reached into the back pocket of her jeans and handed him her card. "My e-mail's not on here, but my number is. If you decide you're interested, call me. Or—wait. I've got a pen in the kitchen. I'll write down my address. Make it that much easier for you."

He followed her through the house, flicking the card with his thumb, giving it back to her when she picked up the pen she'd left on a pad on the counter. While she jotted her address, he glanced at the sketches she'd made.

"What do you think?" she asked moments later.

He looked up as she returned the card, tucking it into his shirt pocket and grinning. "Sorry about that. I'm not usually a snoop."

She waved away his comment. "I was working on this earlier. The layout of the eating areas. It's rough, because I won't know if my measurements will need adjusting after the construction is done."

"Can I borrow your pen?"

"Sure," she said, handing it to him.

Flipping to a new sheet, he quickly drew a rough floor plan of the rooms he'd walked through. He'd seen houses similarly converted into restaurants and had a good idea of what she was going for. But having a self-serve buffet line instead of a waitstaff delivering orders required a different traffic flow.

He pointed to an area on the sketch representing the front door and foyer. "You'll use the door as it is now for your entrance, yes? And you'll put in a parking lot of some sort off to the side of your driveway, I imagine. People will come down the main hall to what? The original dining room? Is that where the buffet will be?"

He looked up, saw her studying his design, her brows knitted, eyes darting from the top of his drawing to the bottom. "You're right. I need a better space for the buffet table. I'll have to rethink the seating in that room."

"Or you build out your kitchen, taking over the room here," he said, using her pen as a pointer to indicate what he thought might've been a solarium. "Use that space for the food service. You wouldn't want it open into the main prep area, so maybe just cut an entrance there," he said, slashing two lines over the one for the wall. "Limit access with swinging saloon doors. Staff can easily get in and out with the pans, but it won't invite customers into the kitchen itself."

She crossed her arms, her gaze going to the window over the sink as a truck pulled to a stop on the street beside her driveway and a tall kid in black got out and began unhitching a ladder from the rack in the bed. She looked back to the pad. "If I did that, there would also be less disruption to those sitting in the original dining room from those making their way down the buffet line."

"And the heat from the braziers and the warming lights will be contained in the smaller space. Vented properly, it won't be an issue for the diners walking through." He added the last as the ladder banged against the side of the house next to the kitchen window. "Sounds like your contractor's not wasting any time."

"The shutters are a mess. And that's Will, one of Ten's crew." She raised her gaze to his. "You secretly want a new job, don't you? Or a second job. I know you do. C'mon. You can tell me."

Oh, she made him want to laugh, to grab her up and swing her around the way he'd done when she was a toddler. But all he could do now was smile, and hope he could keep holding it together until he was out of her sight. "What I can tell you is that I need to get going or I'll never get back in time for my shift tonight."

"Okay then. You have my card. You've heard my sales pitch. I want to say hello to Will, so I'll walk you to your truck. Just let me know if between here and there you change your mind."

Mitch smiled, happy he'd have another five minutes to spend with this girl he loved, because they would have to be his last. He wanted to ask her so many things: Why had she taken Ernest's name? How many homes had she lived in? What did she remember of that day their lives had changed? Had she ever wondered about him? Did she hate him?

He reached his truck before she was finished talking to Will. They were friendly together, but he didn't pick up on anything more and was glad. The kid had an edge to him, something that raised Mitch's hackles when he didn't have a right to judge whom Kaylie kept company with, did business with. Slept with, he added, and cringed. He'd given up his rights when he hadn't insisted Dawn marry him, or at least name him as father on their baby girl's birth certificate. That's probably why this Will was making him itch. Mitch saw too much of his cocky younger self and recognized trouble.

He opened his door, reached for the sunglasses he'd set on his dash, and fished his keys from his pocket, waiting. Kaylie finished up and headed toward him, her dog tagging along, his smile as wide as hers. Mitch dropped his gaze to the ground and gripped his keys in a fist. "I never asked," he said as she reached him. "What's your dog's name?"

"Magoo." She scratched the top of his head. "He's my best friend. And he's supposed to be my security system, but I'm not sure his tongue qualifies as a deadly weapon."

"He's got the teeth for it. I'll bet he'd use them if you were threatened."

"I try not to advertise that fact, but yeah. I feel pretty safe with him around."

"You'll still get an alarm system?" He had to ask. He couldn't leave her like this, unprotected, and never see her again without asking.

"Of course. And sooner rather than later. I had a bit of a scare the other night. Turned out to be nothing, and Magoo was there, but since there've been vagrants—"

"You're staying here? The place is empty." He didn't like the sound of this. He didn't like it at all.

"I'm only roughing it until the construction's done. I'll move in my furniture at the same time as that for the café. I'm thinking of it as an adventure."

And all he'd be thinking about was her here alone. A second truck arrived then, nosing to a stop in front of Will's. The sign on the door said *Keller Construction.* Kaylie waved at the man climbing down from the cab, then held out her hand to Mitch. "A pleasure meeting you, Mitch. My help-wanted ad is running in this week's *Courant.* If you want to talk more about the position, you know how to reach me."

He hated letting her go. Her hand was so small in his, making him think of the way she used to reach for him, raising both arms, wiggling her fingers until he'd lift her and toss her over his head and catch her as she'd giggled and screamed.

Clearing his throat, he gave her a nod. "Appreciate your time. And best of luck, not that you'll need it. You've got a great place here. The perfect location. A fairly unique concept."

"Thank you, but I'm sensing a lack of enthusiasm."

"I just hope you don't get taken advantage of."

"By all these men, or by my customers?"

"I was thinking customers, but now that you mention it…"

She laughed. "Thanks again for stopping by, Mitch. If you decide against applying for the job, I hope we can stay in touch."

CHAPTER FOURTEEN

Who was that?" Ten asked, his gaze following the progress of Mitch Pepper's truck as the other man drove away.

More than his gaze. His *frowning* gaze. Strange, because he hadn't even met the man, and she hadn't thought him the type to jump to conclusions based on...what? The way Mitch looked? The way he dressed? "A friend of Luna's. She sent him about the cook's position. I told you the other day he was coming, when we talked about Dolly Breeze."

"Huh," he grunted, his gaze still pinched as it followed Mitch's progress down the narrow road. "He from around here?"

Now she was the one frowning. "I'm not sure where he lives, but he works at the Gristmill in Gruene."

"I see."

"Really?" She was pretty sure he wasn't seeing anything but red for some unfathomable reason. "What exactly is it that you see?"

"You're not sure where he lives? Did he apply for the job? Fill out an application?"

Okay. This was getting ridiculous. She turned to him, arms crossed, wondering what had made him decide she needed a keeper—or worse, that she was a poor judge of people. "If I decide I'm interested in hiring him, I'll get all the information I need…though, now that I think about it, I didn't ask for much when I hired you, did I?"

"That's different." He bit off the words, looking toward the house, away from her, fighting some internal battle.

"Is it? Tell me how you doing one job for me is any different from him doing another one. Or how Carolyn and Jessa vouching for you is any different from Luna vouching for Mitch."

"He'll be in your house, working alone with you…" And then he stopped, letting the sentence trail as if realizing the absurdity of what he was saying.

But just to be sure… "Sounds to me like what's been going on this past week. Except it hasn't been Mitch I've been working alone with." She didn't want to alienate Ten, not after the work they'd already put in as a team, but she had to clear the air. "Word of mouth, trust, handshakes. Those are the things I've looked forward to, coming back here. Having you second-guess my business decisions, well…it's just not going to work. You know that, right?"

"Sorry." He raised a hand, then ran it back through his hair. "I have somewhat of a suspicious nature."

"Somewhat. Is that how you describe it?" She needed to let it go. He'd apologized, and she wasn't one for harping, but she was curious…about Ten, about what had brought on his overreaction, about the things he stirred in her each time they were together, things that had nothing to do with his renovating her house.

"Ignore me," he said, shading his eyes as he watched Will come down his ladder. "I was snakebit in the past, a onetime thing, or so logic tells me, but that filter's hard to get rid of."

She could understand that. "Logic doesn't take intuition into consideration."

"No, it doesn't, but since I didn't meet your Mitch, I don't think intuition's at fault here. It's just me and my issues with trust. I had a good friend, and he hurt my family, and I've had trouble kicking the rush-to-judgment habit."

"If he hurt your family, he wasn't a good friend," she said when he drifted off, but his admission pushed her further. "Were you suspicious of Will? When you took him on? You said he was a new hire. Did he get the prying eye of your microscope, too?" She let that sink in, added, "Did I?"

He laughed, breaking the tension binding the moment. "You came to me with money. You get a pass. And Will was recommended to me by a friend, and yeah. I see the hypocrisy. Guilty as charged."

"That's how this works. Will, Mitch, you. A sort of six degrees of professional separation." She followed the direction of his gaze, watched Will take a scraper of some kind to the frame of the shutter he'd brought down with him. "And sometimes the professional becomes personal."

"Like with you and Luna," he said. "Or maybe even Luna and Will."

"Yes," she came back with, though she'd wanted him to say *you and me, me and you.* She just wished she knew why. But since he wasn't here for that any more than she was, she got back to business. "Mitch did mention something I've been thinking about. Especially since Carolyn told me the police have had to deal with vagrants. I need to see about an alarm system."

"An alarm system." He repeated her words, and when he looked back to her he was frowning, but this time with concern. "You mean besides the dog and the knife?"

She glanced away, remembering the night she'd come downstairs with said dog and said knife to find Ten shining a light at her shutters. His being there was one thing. Her reaction to him as they'd talked another. She'd been having trouble with that part ever since. She was having trouble with it now. And no matter how many times she told herself to stay focused on why he was here, her mind rebelled.

He was standing too close, as close as he'd been when she'd had only moonlight to show her the way. Today she had blue skies and the dew in the grass and Ten within touching distance. Breathing deeply to settle her nerves, she thought it might not be vagrants she needed an alarm to protect herself from, and she wasn't sure how to fit that realization into her plans or her life.

"I can take care of myself," she finally said. "But I'd prefer law enforcement take care of the bad guys."

"Then how about I hook you up with a guy I know who sells security systems. He does commercial installations, but you're running a business, so that's close enough."

"Sounds good." Though she'd check his guy's references, as she'd checked Ten's. Not that she'd done as thorough a job as she should have, making up her mind to hire him when he'd stopped at midnight to check on her shutters. "See? The six degrees of professional separation at work."

"Okay, okay," he said, holding up both hands as he laughed. "I give."

"Don't give yet. I want to mine your local connections for one more thing."

"You keep mining, I'm going to have to start charging."

"Funny. I want to put in a vegetable garden. And I need to do it ASAP or it's going to be too late. Who do you know who could help me with that?"

His expression clouded over again. "You want someone to do all the work? Or just advise you?"

"I want someone to do the initial work, but I should be able to take it from there, watering, feeding, whatever else needs to be done. I want fresh tomatoes and cucumbers and such for my salads, and then maybe have someone can or freeze what I can't use now for casseroles later in the year."

"You hire Dolly, she can take care of that for you."

"The canning, or the whole shebang?"

"The canning. But I do know someone who should be able to help with the rest." He dropped his gaze to the ground, shoved his hands to his hips, and scuffed the toe of his boot over the driveway's gravel. "I'll just have to look her up. We haven't talked in a while."

Why did she get the feeling he wasn't thrilled at the thought of doing so? "Someone you know well?"

"My sister. Indiana."

The one who'd been a jock. He'd mentioned her before. But before Kaylie could ask any of the questions bubbling to the surface, Will's shout of "Ten!" had both of them turning his direction. They made their way back to the house. Will had laid the shutter across two sawhorses and was still poking and picking at the frame.

Without saying a word, Ten joined him. Kaylie stood back, her hands in her pockets as she watched them, both men frowning, Will pointing to another section of the wood and Ten using the tip of his pocketknife to peel back a split section, jumping back when a stream of winged insects rose from the exit he'd made.

Kaylie lifted her gaze as they formed a cloud, then looked back at the two men. "Don't tell me. Termites."

"Yep," he said, drawing out the one word until it sounded like two.

"Why wasn't this discovered during the home inspection?"

"I'm going to guess whoever did it didn't bring a tall enough ladder, and only checked the shutters he could reach."

"That sounds highly unethical." Not to mention like a possible construction delay should the infestation be widespread.

"Could be whoever you hired wasn't qualified to look for insect damage. A home inspection's pretty noninvasive. A visual going-over wouldn't necessarily have turned up these little buggers. Will had to pull the shutter and dig."

"Guess I need to get an exterminator in here to take care of this."

"Good thing I know someone," Ten said, jamming his knife point down in the wood.

All Kaylie could do was groan.

CHAPTER FIFTEEN

The dream came that night, creeping in as if sensing Kaylie had let down her guard. Magoo belly-crawled closer, whimpering and wary, the blade of the bowie knife glinting in the light from the moon. It was heavy in her hand, pinning her knuckles and wrist to the floor. The hardwood was cold to her fingers, the bare window damp with the chill of the mid-March air.

On the other floor she was seeing, blood pooled around the body lying there, spreading like spilled milk in slow motion, reaching for the legs of the chair where she sat curled into the tightest ball she could manage. Her nightgown was soft and worn where she pulled it over her knees to her feet, a faded Strawberry Shortcake smiling up at her and telling her to be brave.

She nodded quickly, swiping at her eyes and trying not to look down to where the other face seemed to be smiling as well, looking at her, waiting for her to be brave and use the knife, too. She hadn't meant to hurt anyone. She'd only wanted some soup, and had tried to open the can. That was all. She hadn't meant to hurt anyone else. She missed her daddy so much.

She curled her toes because of the blood, wiggling them to shake off the spatter. But the droplets stayed, clinging, too thick and heavy to drip from her skin to the vinyl chair seat. The liquid was warm, yet still she shivered, and when it wouldn't go away, she screamed.

There was a man, then loud footsteps racing, louder voices yelling, the loudest sirens of all screeching like she did when her mother pulled a brush too hard through her hair.

Sweating, she jerked up, Magoo's head on her knee, his dark eyes wide with worry, the whites crazy bright. She pulled in a deep breath, shaking, catching back a sob as she leaned forward to bury her face against her dog's. He licked her arm where she'd wrapped it around his neck, licked it again as if letting her know everything was going to be okay.

"Kaylie? Are you there? Kaylie?"

That voice. It sounded like Ten's. Why was she hearing Ten? And then she realized she was holding her phone, the display lighting up the room. "Ten?" she asked, as she brought the device to her ear. "Is that you?"

"Yes. Crap. Are you okay? It sounds like you're crying. And it's the middle of the night."

"I had a bad dream. I don't know why I called you. I'm sorry. I'm so, so sorry."

"Do you need me to come over?"

"No. I'm fine. I'll let you..." She started to hang up but stopped herself. She didn't want to be alone, not yet. And Magoo, as much as she loved him, couldn't say the words she needed, even if she didn't know what they were. "It's a nightmare I've had most of my life." She took a deep breath, rubbed at her forehead. Magoo crawled closer to rest his chin in her lap. "After I moved to Austin, I used to call May. I didn't even have to say anything. She would just pick up the phone and start talking."

She heard him blow out a heavy breath. Then he asked, "What did she say?"

"I don't even know. She just talked. Her voice was enough, I guess." She gave a little laugh. "I think she talked about recipes. Changes she'd made to ones she'd never been happy with. New ones she'd tried. What the children in the house thought about them."

"How long after you left did the Wises continue to take in kids?"

She leaned her forehead against Magoo's, kissing him to let him know she was fine. He rolled onto his back, his tongue lolling as he panted his joy and waited for her to rub his belly. "About five years, I think. I know by the time I graduated from UT May and Winton were the only two in the house. Winton had a heart attack not long after."

"That was when May sold to Bob Coleman?"

She nodded, forgetting for a minute that Ten wasn't in the room with her. "Yeah. She went to live with her sister in Dallas."

"Did you stay in touch?"

"She was good about it. I was terrible because it always hurt so much after seeing her." And then, without understanding why Ten made it so easy for her to open up, or why with him she felt safe doing so, she told him something she'd never told another living soul. "I felt abandoned when I left Hope Springs. It was stupid. I was in school and lots of my classmates were on their own. And it wasn't like the Wises had kicked me out..."

"It was your home. From what you've said, the only one you'd ever really had. What you felt is pretty normal, I'd think."

"Thank you, but I still feel terribly selfish. I want to apologize to them for even thinking it," she said, tears welling again as she remembered May so often telling her, "Don't look to where you've come from. Look to where you're going."

"Did you ever tell them you felt that way?"

"No."

"Maybe you should have. Not placed blame, but explained. Been honest."

She had been honest. At least in her actions. Staying away. Never being the one to touch base except when *she* needed something. She buried her face in her free hand. "I'm a horrible person."

"Don't say that."

"A not-horrible person would've come back to visit." She pulled in a shaky breath. "I was too caught up in what I was feeling to realize they weren't the ones to abandon me. I'd abandoned them."

"Kaylie—"

"It's true. I did. I walked out of this house and never looked back."

"That's *not* true. If you hadn't looked back, or thought back, you wouldn't have been so dead set on owning the place. On returning to what you'd known here."

"But I didn't tell them that." Why hadn't she told them that? "They never knew."

"You might be surprised what they knew."

"How could they?"

"Because they knew you."

She closed her eyes and tucked her chin to her chest, still unable to believe that she'd called him. And more than a little bit embarrassed that she'd spilled her insecurities as easily as she might a glass of water. "You're a nice man, Tennessee Keller. Thank you."

"So maybe I can count on you doubling my bonus, huh? Since I'm so nice and all?"

She grinned. A full-on pulling at her cheeks that left no room for the sadness she'd let take over the room. "We'll have to see if you earn the first one, won't we? Before I can think about doubling it."

"Are you okay now? Think you can get back to sleep?"

She pulled her phone away from her face to check the time. "It's almost four thirty. I might as well get up."

"Malina's opens for breakfast at five. How 'bout I buy you a waffle?"

"Mmm. Waffles. How 'bout you buy me three?"

CHAPTER SIXTEEN

Knowing the truth of Will's situation, Luna expected his loft to be small, one room even, with a sofa that folded into a bed and a kitchen tucked up against one wall. But it wasn't anything like that. In fact, his apartment was almost as large as her suite of rooms in the house where she lived with her parents.

She'd often thought about moving out, living on her own. And, in a way, she did live on her own. She just did it under their roof, sharing the house's big kitchen, but having her own apartment in a wing her father had decided to add just for her, one for which he refused to take payment.

Will had been in prison for three years. He hadn't told her why, but she knew Tennessee Keller never hired career criminals, or those who sold or used drugs, or anyone who might present a threat to the community in which he worked. He hired men who'd made mistakes, who'd paid for what they'd done, earned and deserved a second chance.

His philosophy had been born of personal experience, that much she knew, but she'd never asked for details. Ten's business wasn't any of hers, and because of the tragedy in her own past, she knew more than most people should about speculation. But her refusal to gossip didn't mean she wasn't curious. About Ten.

And about Will. Especially his living conditions. She'd had no idea the old textile warehouse on the outskirts of Hope Springs had been converted into living quarters, though from what she could tell, Will had the entire top floor. She handed him a bottle of Tempranillo Cabernet. "I like your place."

"Thanks." He read the label with an appreciative look. "I had a lot nicer one before the whole prison thing."

Nicer? Really? Though she supposed he wasn't talking about the size. "You've got to have twelve hundred square feet here."

"Fifteen, actually. Hard to tell when it's empty of what used to be all my worldly possessions."

"Used to be? You don't have them anymore? Or you haven't had a chance yet to get them out of storage?"

"This is all that's left," he said, waving an arm toward the stools at the kitchen bar, the big-screen TV, and the bed with the black iron headboard. It looked like it belonged in a New Orleans brothel, with its exquisitely rumpled white sheets and duvet. "My girl stored what mattered before getting rid of the rest of my stuff. Then she got rid of me."

So he'd been in a relationship. And now he wasn't. "You're making me curious, you know."

"I like curious women."

"As much as you like keeping them in the dark?"

"I like *you,* Luna Meadows. You're a bright girl."

So he liked curious women, but he thought of her and his ex as girls. Time for a change of subject, she decided, breathing in and finding one. "Smells like Italian."

"Spaghetti. From scratch. Well, a can of crushed tomatoes as the base of the sauce, but my sauce. And my bread. Had to work half a day for Ten, or we would've had my pasta, too."

He thought of her as a girl, yet he'd gone all out to cook for her? His signals were dizzying. She didn't know where to turn next, but followed him toward the kitchen anyway. "I'm impressed. A wolf boy who cooks."

Using a wooden spoon, he stirred the sauce slowly. "Not as impressive as a moon girl who dresses celebrities."

So he knew who she was. "I don't dress celebrities. I just weave scarves."

"A spider, collecting her flies."

Luna wasn't sure she liked the analogy. Being a spider. Creating traps. Lying in wait. Devious. It was too close to the truth. But she didn't have time to respond. Will was spooning up a bite of sauce for her to taste.

She leaned forward, holding his gaze, his hand beneath the spoon to catch any drips. She took the spoon, the flavors bursting in her mouth, Will's fingertips grazing the skin beneath her chin as he took the spoon away.

"Good?" he asked, and she nodded, too choked by his touch to speak. "Can you grab a couple of plates from the cabinet there?" He canted his head to the left, nodding when she pointed. His dishes were heavy stoneware, and she only just stopped herself from flipping the plate to look at the manufacturer's mark on the back.

She set the plates side by side on the bar, choosing two wineglasses from another shelf as Will strained the spaghetti and dished it onto the plates. He spooned sauce onto both and then retrieved the bread from the oven. Luna found forks and napkins and a corkscrew for the wine. Will did the honors, handing her the first glass. Luna had just taken a sip when he spoke.

"Did you decide what to do?"

The way he came out of nowhere with things amused her. "About?"

"Your two friends who are looking for each other."

She didn't want to answer. She didn't know why except for some reason he made her feel that whatever she decided to do would be the wrong thing. She reached for her fork, twirled it through the spaghetti, but stopped with it halfway to her mouth when he started shaking his head.

"You did, didn't you? You told them."

"I told one of them."

"Which one? Father or child?"

That part he didn't need to know. "The one I've known the longest, that I'm closest to."

"Why? Wouldn't that be the harder friendship to lose?"

"I don't want to lose either, but I owe this friend the truth."

"So you don't owe it to all your friends?"

"That's not what I meant," she said, thinking again of Sierra, and the whole Caffey family, but especially Angelo. He'd lost his sister when Luna had lost her best friend. It was a shared loss that should've brought them closer, but she was too tangled in the truth she'd kept from him to know where to cut through the knot. "Do you not believe in degrees of friendship?"

"Sure, but I don't believe in being dishonest to anyone I call a friend."

"Would you expect me to tell you the same things I tell Ten Keller? When I've known you less than a week and known him for years?"

"You and Ten good friends?"

"Are you changing the subject?"

"Just wandering a tangent. But no, I wouldn't expect you to tell me the same things you might tell Ten. If," he added quickly, holding up an index finger, "it wasn't something that involved us equally. In that case, yeah. I probably would because I wouldn't care that you'd known him longer. Not if what you knew was just as important to me."

And what she'd told Mitch mattered deeply to Kaylie, too. She frowned, staring down at her plate. "That's not fair. You're generalizing, not taking the individuals, their situations, into consideration."

"And you're rationalizing the decision you've already made about who gets to know the truth and who doesn't."

"I don't want to talk about this anymore."

"Because it makes you uncomfortable?"

"No, because…" She sighed. "Okay, yes. It makes me uncomfortable, though it's the whole situation, not just talking about it. Thinking about it's just as bad, and I've done nothing else now for a week."

"Why a week? What happened?"

"That was when I found out about the child my friend's been looking for."

"It's hard keeping secrets."

"It is. They…hurt."

"Do you think it's going to get better? With time?"

She thought again about Sierra and Angelo. "It won't. I know that for a fact."

"More secrets?"

"Maybe. Maybe not. Maybe I want to talk about you now."

He looked away. "There's nothing about me worth talking about."

"No secrets of your own? No rationalizations making you uncomfortable? No choices to regret?"

"Regrets? You're asking me if I have regrets? Knowing where I've been the last three years?" He shook his head, laughed, and dug into his spaghetti.

"But I don't know why you were there. It's possible whatever sent you to prison is something you had to do. A situation you had to fix because no one else would. An ongoing wrong you couldn't live with yourself without righting."

He snorted as he reached for his wine. "I leave those things to better men than me. Party leaders. Movie stars. Action heroes."

What in the world had he done? And why couldn't she let it go, give him the same privacy she valued? "If you don't want to tell me, just say so."

"I don't want to tell you."

"That's fine."

"But you still want to know."

She shrugged, toyed with her fork. "It's human nature to be curious."

"I thought that was the nature of felines."

"Are you sure your girl didn't dump you because you were so horribly frustrating?"

He laughed again. "Now that's a real possibility. She said that about me a lot. And I don't think she meant in bed."

Heat spread over Luna's chest and rose up her neck. "I'm sure that's too much information."

"I'm sure it's not."

"What are you doing for Easter?" The question was out of her mouth before she could think better of it. Did she really want to spend more time with him when he was so confrontational? When he pushed so aggressively for answers she didn't want to give? And did she really want him meeting Mitch when he already knew Kaylie?

"Easter, huh?" He finished his wine and sat back. "Boiling bunnies?"

"That's not funny."

"Boiling eggs?"

That was her job. "I'm being serious."

"Why are you being serious?"

Oh, good grief. "My family has a huge Easter barbecue every year at the farm. I was seriously thinking of inviting you. But now I'm seriously not."

"Aw, c'mon," he said, full of petulance and charm. "I love barbecue."

"Who are you, Will Bowman?" *And what am I getting myself into with you?*

"Just a boy—"

"—raised by wolves. I got it. You invite me into a loft you shouldn't be able to afford with what Ten Keller is paying you. You cook me spaghetti from scratch. You don't make a pass at me. You challenge me at a deeply personal level when you know nothing about me." She took a deep breath. "That was some kind of wolf pack."

He stared at her for a long moment, his gaze sharp, almost cutting. "Do you want me to make a pass at you?"

That's what he'd pulled from her speech? Over everything else, that's what he'd heard? "That's not what I said."

"Do you want me to make a pass at you, Luna? Because I can," he said, going still.

"That's not how this works, asking if I want you to." He was frustrating her. He was heating her up. He was so aggravating. So gorgeous.

"You like rules, don't you? Conventions. Laws."

"Unlike you?"

"I have a lot of questions. And I don't need someone else doing my thinking for me. But I try not to cross any lines without very good reasons. Or invitations."

"Like a vampire waiting to be asked into someone's home?"

"Some rules can't be broken. Consequences." He shook his head, made a tsk with his tongue. "Consequences can be a bitch."

Never in her life had she had dinner with a man and fallen into a conversation that felt more like an inquisition. Or therapy. Her head hurt, and she knew it wasn't from the wine. But she also knew she wasn't going to get any of the answers she wanted tonight. And she might be a lot better off without them. She was safe. If he answered all the questions she had…

"I want you to make a pass at me," she said, wondering how she would respond if he did. Wondering, too, if she was only wanting him to in order to see if he actually would.

He'd been twirling the spaghetti dangling from his fork into the bowl of the large spoon in his other hand. He stopped, and his head came up, his dark hair falling forward over one eye. The other shone bright enough for two, blue like a gas flame, blue like the Caribbean Sea, stealing what breath she hadn't pulled in to hold.

He reached across the bar, took her headband from her hair. The heavy strands closed like a curtain to hide much of her face, her ears and her jaw and her cheekbones. She leaned on one elbow, using the fingers of that hand like a rake to clear her field of vision.

"Why do you wear it so long?"

Except to trim the ends, she hadn't cut it since high school, since the accident, since losing Sierra. "I just do."

"There must be a reason. Convenience. Fashion. To use like Mary Magdalene."

At that, she sat straighter. No challenge was worth this one's aggravation. "I take it back. I don't want you to make a pass at me."

"You do. But not tonight."

So now he was a mind reader? She placed her napkin on the bar next to her plate, slid from the bar stool, and found her purse and her keys. "Thank you for dinner. The spaghetti was wonderful. And the bread."

"And the company?"

"The company has been…interesting." Intoxicating. Insufferable.

"Just not what you expected." He came around the bar, his body long and controlled, and loomed over her. "Or wanted."

"Unexpected, yes. But since I obviously don't know what I want—"

"Don't go away mad."

"I'm not mad. I'm—"

"Frustrated?" He came closer. "Wet?"

This was when another man would have reached for her. This was when she would have made it easy for him to, and gone willingly. Not Will. Another man. One who was less of an enigma. And less…worthy. Even thinking such a thing left her feeling like she needed to pull her nose out of the air, and yet it was the most authentic thing she'd felt in ages. He made this happen. This self-reflection. This honesty.

"Good night, Will."

"Good night, Luna. I'll see you on bunny day."

CHAPTER SEVENTEEN

Kaylie stared at the framed permits hanging on the kitchen wall. Ten had picked them up from the city this morning and displayed them as required by ordinance. Though he and Will had been around the last week, their work had been confined to taking down the shutters and dealing with the unexpected insect damage.

She wasn't surprised it was taking them so much time; the house had been empty and left to the elements longer than she'd realized when it came up for sale. She just hoped the Colemans' neglect wouldn't cause Ten to have to repeatedly revisit his schedule. She didn't want to push back her Memorial Day opening.

It wasn't like she couldn't make use of the downtime should Ten have to deal with additional unknowns. She'd been here a week and had done nothing toward finding her parents. Even after the Internet service had been installed on Friday, she'd done little more than respond to what e-mail she hadn't already taken care of from her phone.

She had plenty of time, she told herself. She'd waited this long; what did another month or two matter? She was here now, and she was safe; surely her earlier desperation to find them was an exaggerated memory, her anxiousness fueled by May's passing and the reality of being alone.

But none of that was the truth.

She didn't want to face the truth—the fear that she would never find what she was looking for. Or that she would, and hate her discovery. She wasn't sure which idea depressed her the most, but both weighed her down so that she wasn't sleeping; she was barely eating. She was going to have to take that first frightening step and jump.

Hearing the click of Magoo's nails on the floor, she turned around, her gaze going from her dog to the two men standing in her dining room, talking. She couldn't hear what they were saying; Ten's voice was pitched low, his hands animated as he used the canvas of the air to illustrate his words for Will.

Will nodded, did some drawing of his own, and then gestured overhead, at which point he and Ten walked out of the room. Moments later, she heard knocking against the far wall of the kitchen. Though Ten had initially seemed suspicious of Mitch, he'd agreed it was a good idea to move the buffet line. That left Kaylie to mourn the loss of her solarium, but since Two Owls would benefit, she hadn't pouted long.

Men. She wished she understood them better, how they thought, what drove them, where they went when they stopped listening. She'd worked with men, knew them as employers and employees, and she'd had lab and study partners in college. But she'd never had the emotional intimacy that opened the doors to her answers. Which left the questions to pile up and get in her way.

Winton Wise had been the best male role model she'd had, and he'd spoiled her for anything less. She'd learned so much from him, and oodles of that when he wasn't looking. She'd watched him with May, how he would hand her a knife or a stick of butter or a cup of coffee before she could ask.

She'd seen him with the other children she'd lived with, how kind he'd been to Cindy, who'd suffered unfathomable abuse, how patient he'd been with Joelle, whose development had been halted by complete neglect. How eager he'd been to answer every question Tim had asked about what he was reading.

The men who'd been charged with her care before did little more than drop her off at school on their way to collect their monthly check from the state. None of them read to her from Jack London and Victor Hugo, even when she was too young to understand much of *Les Misérables.* None of them played Scrabble with her and the other kids in the house and refused to go easy on them.

None of them had showed her how to run a lawn mower or change a flat tire. Granted, she'd been too young to do more than fold laundry and wash dishes before coming to live in Hope Springs, but she'd been old enough to know what little guidance or true parenting her previous families had provided.

She'd wanted badly during those years to find her real father. The only thing she could think to do was ask her caseworker, but those visits were few and far between and only rarely made by the same person. They'd promised to look into finding him, to let her know what they learned, but nothing had ever come of those promises, and all she'd learned was to deal with the disappointment.

Looking back, it was a wonder with the turnover she wasn't the one who'd gone missing. Or maybe she had.

She'd always wondered about that. Had her father ever returned to that apartment and realized what his absence had cost him? Had he searched out her mother, learned what had happened? Or had he felt a huge relief at having escaped the burden of a kid?

She'd had Winton. She didn't need a father now. But just like she wanted to know what had happened to the woman who'd given birth to her, she wanted to know where the man who had fathered her had ended up. What had happened to him. Where he had gone and why.

She'd spent too much time wondering and she needed to tie up the loose ends of her past. They'd been dragging behind her too long, tripping her and tangling up in the threads of her present life, an umbilical cord binding her to a place she would never return to.

"Enough," she said, pushing her hair from her face, startling as Ten appeared in her peripheral vision. "How long have you been there?"

"Just came in," he said, and stopped beside her. "Though you've been standing in that same spot for a while."

Embarrassingly, she had. "And how would you know that? Have you been spying on me?"

"No. I haven't been spying on you." He gestured over his shoulder. "I saw you from the dining room when I was talking to Will." Then he nodded toward the wall. "I can't imagine those permits are what's holding your interest."

Ah, but he was wrong. "Are you kidding? I love the permits. They mean we're really moving forward."

"You thought I was kidding about making that happen?"

She heard the frown in his question and looked over. "You're not the one I doubted."

His frown deepened, and he crossed his arms as he looked at her. "Why would you doubt yourself?"

"Doubt's probably not the right word," she said, heading for the coffeepot and her empty mug. "It's more that I didn't believe everything would fall into place."

"You knew what you wanted. You made plans and followed through. That's how dreams become reality."

"I've never been much of a dreamer. I've had to be practical." She filled her mug, asked with a lift of the pot if he wanted any.

He raised a hand, shook his head. "I'm pretty sure you can be both."

"Is that how you got to where you are?" she asked, stirring in sweetener and cream. "Being a practical dreamer?"

"My case was more about having decided early on what I wanted," he said, coming closer and boosting up onto one of the bar stools at the island. "So I guess I was a practical planner. And then just practical when my original plans fell through."

"Really? What happened?" she asked, holding her mug in both hands and bringing it to her mouth.

"Keller Construction was supposed to be Keller Brothers Construction. But Dakota, my brother, his life took an unexpected turn and I ended up going it alone." He picked up the pen she'd left with her legal pad, clicked it on, clicked it off. "It worked out, so I can't complain, but I know some of what you're going through. Wanting something. Planning for it."

He had a brother and he had a sister, but he wasn't close to or in touch with either. Who was Tennessee Keller? What had happened in his life to alienate him from those he should love? And why did it surprise her that his background wasn't any more all-American than hers?

Strange that she'd made up her mind that such was the case before getting to know him at all. "I've thought about that. What I'll do if Two Owls isn't the success I'm hoping for."

"And?"

"Most likely I'd go back into the bakery business. I know it, and even when things are tough people want desserts. There are still weddings and holidays and office birthday parties. Plus, between working for Saul and for myself, I made a lot of contacts. I could almost pick up where I left off."

"Where would you go?"

Go? "Nowhere. This is home."

"I'm not sure Hope Springs can support another bakery."

She hadn't yet visited Butters Bakery, but loved the irony in their slogan: *Heavy on the Butt.* She needed to go by and introduce herself, start off on the right foot. Not leave Peggy Butters to wonder if she was here to put her out of business.

She wasn't. Not at all. "Then I'll wash dishes for Max Malina. Or flip burgers at one of the fast-food joints on the interstate. Or see if Peggy Butters might want a partner. I intend to take my last breath in this house."

He gave her a wry grin. "And you don't think you're a dreamer."

"That's not a dream."

"So if I want it, I'll have to pry this house out of your cold, dead hands."

"Something like that," she said with a laugh. Then what he'd said registered. "Do you want this house?"

"I did some work for the Colemans and pretty much fell in love with it. Told Bob to let me know if he ever decided to sell and I'd see about taking it off his hands. Either he forgot or didn't think I was serious."

"But you were."

"Yeah. It's a good house."

"I'm sorry. Well, I'm not sorry you didn't get it, but I am sorry for your disappointment. Though I have a feeling mine would've been worse."

"Red cowboy boots. A sparkly pink plush puppy."

She couldn't believe her middle-of-the-night confession of what this house meant to her had stuck with him. "You remembered."

"I pay attention. And, yes, sometimes I jump to conclusions. I'm working on that," he said, his smile a devastating revelation of dimples. "Thanks to you."

Her skin heated, her throat, her chest, the palms of her hands, and she blamed the coffee in her mug. "You're welcome. Though it wasn't my intent to change you."

"Wasn't it?"

"Of course not." She thought back to their conversation earlier in the week. "I only wanted you to give Mitch a chance, rather than assume he was going to take advantage of me." When he didn't respond, she added, "That's what you were thinking, wasn't it? That's why you were so suspicious of him. Or maybe wary is a better word."

"No, suspicious is fine. I've got this…thing about looking out for people I care for. I didn't pay attention one time when I should have, and things for my family went south. I've tried to make up for it since, and I go overboard sometimes."

"Does that mean you care about me?" she asked, wishing as the words left her mouth that she could grab them back and swallow them whole. "I'm sorry. That was forward of me." When all he did was smile, she asked, "What?"

"I don't think I've ever heard anyone apologize for being forward."

This. She didn't know how to deal with this. With him. What he made her feel. The things that came out of her mouth because she wondered what he was thinking, what he thought of her. "May taught me better. That's all."

"Don't apologize for asking what's on your mind. And to answer—"

"No. Don't answer. I shouldn't have asked. You were talking about your parents. Your brother and sister. I shouldn't have said anything." She fluttered a hand. "I blame the house."

"Are you still not sleeping?"

She'd said that to him, too. That she'd come here to sleep, to start over. "I'm sleeping. And I'm starting over. It's the facing the past I'm having trouble with."

"How so?"

Big confession time. "I haven't done anything toward finding my parents."

"How can I help?"

She looked at him, stared at him, confusion a tilt-a-whirl in her head. "You want to help."

"I can. I've got crazy Google-fu."

"I can do it on my own. I don't need help." She had her house and her knife and her dog. She had her memories. She had her nightmares. But she also had May's words: *Don't look to where you've come from. Look to where you're going.* And that advice, more than any of her fears, left her conflicted. "I mean, thank you for offering. But I need to do it."

He got to his feet, shoved his hands in his pockets, and shrugged. "I never did answer your question, you know. Yes. I care about you. And I'm offering to help because of that. It's what friends do."

Friends. Yes, they were friends. She was the one who kept imagining more. "I'll be fine. Thank you."

"But you'll take me up on the offer if you need to?"

"So you can show off your…Google-fu?" And there she went again, teasing, even flirting, making the tension between them uncomfortable instead of keeping to the business of Two Owls that had brought them together.

"It's a man thing," he said, doing a quick flex of his pecs. "Flaunting our mad problem-solving skills."

But wasn't that about attracting a mate? The male of the species proving himself with his flashy feathers? Was that what was happening here? Was he preening? Or was her limited experience with men at fault, causing her to read more into his offer than was there?

He backed away before she could respond, saying, "I should probably get back to work. Leave you alone with your…staring."

And then she laughed. He made her laugh. And if nothing else, there was that.

CHAPTER EIGHTEEN

What did you do with Magoo?" Luna asked once she and Kaylie had been seated at their table on the Gristmill's deck. Beneath them, the Guadalupe River drifted lazily, bubbling over rocks and fallen logs.

"He's in the house with Will and Ten. I told them to lock him up in the mudroom if he gets in the way." Their server arrived with water and menus, taking their order for iced tea and then leaving them alone.

"We've got two Great Pyrs on the farm, but they're shepherds more than they are pets. I did have a dog when I was younger. She'd been dumped in the ditch in front of the farm. Sweet little Maya. She was part Chinese crested and part Jack Russell. I miss her." Luna reached for her water and sipped. "I'd love a Magoo of my own. Though maybe a smaller one. Like Maya's size. She fit on my lap. Magoo would probably smother me."

Kaylie laughed. "He was so small when I got him. I had no idea what his food bill was going to eventually be."

"I can imagine. But I'm sure he's worth it."

"He'd be worth double," Kaylie said, opening her menu. "And he's a lot less maintenance than a relationship." Though where that had come from she didn't know. She'd never had a serious relationship. What did she know about what it took to maintain one?

"I'm spoiled by the single life. I do what I want when I want."

"Do you date?" Kaylie asked, Ten coming to mind as she did. Her stomach tightened and she wanted to blame the response on hunger. The items on the menu had her mouth watering, but the pull in her belly was about Ten's hands and his smile and the early sprinkling of coconut-colored strands in the *dulce de leche* of his hair.

Coconut brownies. With sweet Mexican caramel. She pulled her phone from her pocket and sent herself a text so she wouldn't forget. Pecans, too. And a hint of cayenne. Yes. Absolutely cayenne. Done, she glanced up to find Luna staring, a sly I-know-where-you-went grin on her mouth.

"Hazard of the job," she said, gesturing with her phone. "I have to catch the ideas before they slip through the sieve of my mind."

"What was it? Something about the house? The menu?"

"Brownies. *Dulce de leche* and coconut and pecans, I think. And cayenne."

Luna sat with her elbows on the table, her chin cradled in her palms. Her eyes twinkled. "I like the way you think. I could see the same colors in a scarf. Coconut for the primary, then accents of the other colors. Maybe blood orange, too."

"Ooh. I wonder how the orange would taste," Kaylie mused, typing out another text. "Sorry. One second, then I promise no more work talk."

"Are you kidding? I'm fascinated by work talk. It's better than dating talk any day, though I'm still trying to figure out how you went from men to food."

Luna's comment had Kaylie biting her tongue rather than admitting the idea for the brownie had been born of her thoughts of Ten. If the recipe turned out as wonderfully as she anticipated, she'd have to think of an appropriately cryptic name.

She would enjoy remembering the flavor's genesis, but she didn't want anyone else to know. Which brought her back to her original question. "So? Do you? Date?"

"I actually had a man cook dinner for me on Saturday."

"Ooh, nice," Kaylie said as their server returned with their tea and to take their orders. They both splurged on the bronze catfish topped with tequila butter and lime, and loaded baked potatoes. Kaylie's stomach rumbled again as she handed her menu to the young man. "I haven't eaten a decent meal in days. And I've never had a man cook for me that I can remember."

"This one surprised me, though I'm not sure why. I don't know him well enough to have had any expectations."

"A new guy?"

"You met him at the same time I did. Will Bowman."

Kaylie thought back to the tension the two of them had stirred in her kitchen and decided her immediate attraction to Ten might not be as unusual in the broader scheme as it was in her own experience. "He seemed…I don't know. Nice sounds so lame, but he was. Maybe a little bit intense."

"He's definitely that. He's also very smart and very sweet. And a very good cook. And very—"

"Hot. He's very hot."

Luna tossed back her head and laughed. "Oh yeah. Unfortunately, or maybe very fortunately, I can't tell you if he's good in bed, or even a good kisser. He does smell good, though. I hugged him when I left and got close enough to learn that at least."

Did that mean Luna had wanted to kiss him? To sleep with him? Without knowing more about him than she did? Kaylie's thoughts turned to Ten as if his direction was the only one they knew. They'd been close enough to touch several times as they'd passed in the house, as they'd studied blueprints spread out on the kitchen island. She hadn't even noticed a cologne, but fresh air and laundered clothes and clean sweat. The light spice of aftershave. The pitch of pine sawdust clinging to his skin.

She reached for her tea, perspiration dotting her nape and the valley between her breasts. It was warm out, but nicely so, not enough for her to blame the weather for her sweat. She so wanted to blame the weather for her sweat. This talking men and sex and thinking of how Ten smelled…

"Hello, ladies," said a familiar voice behind her, a welcome interruption to her disturbing thoughts. As Luna looked up, Kaylie turned in time to see Mitch Pepper stop at their table, his smile hesitant and not quite reaching his eyes. "I hope you ordered the catfish. I filleted it fresh this morning."

"We did," Luna said as Kaylie nodded. "Did you two already meet?"

"Mitch came by the house last week."

"About the job?"

"Yes and no," Mitch answered, hedging. "I love what Kaylie's got planned, but this place is my home. I just don't think two part-time gigs will pay the bills."

Kaylie said to Luna, "I think he came by because you wanted him to. Not to see about the job."

"She sees right through me," Mitch said. "Actually, both of you do."

"It's our job as women," Luna replied, her gaze flicking from Kaylie to Mitch and back. "Did he have ideas for more casseroles than you've come up with?"

"We didn't talk specifics, but he swore he had all sorts of secrets up his sleeve." Kaylie glanced up at Mitch, watched the slow shake of his head.

"I've seen him in the kitchen," Luna, laughing, leaned forward to say. "He does. Trust me."

"And before one of you manages to worm them out of me, I'd better get back and make sure your orders are being taken care of." He lifted a hand in farewell. "Kaylie, good to see you again. And Luna, I'll see you Sunday at the farm."

"Oh, that's right. Easter dinner. Kaylie, you have to come," Luna said.

Was it Easter already? "I'll have to check my calendar and see what's going on with the house."

"It's Easter. It's a holiday. Nothing is going on with the house. I already invited Will, and Ten will be coming, too. It'll be great. My parents' Easter dinners are not to be missed."

"She's right about that," Mitch said, strangely wistful, even reserved. Then he shook it off and waved as he walked away. "You two enjoy your lunch."

Kaylie turned and watched him navigate the series of connected steps, greeting customers and staff alike. "He seems like a great guy."

"I'm glad you think so. He's been a wonderful friend to our family. My father especially."

"He told me they served together in the military."

"My dad talked him into settling here after their discharge. I don't think he could stand the idea of not having Mitch near. They'd been together since boot camp. My parents had been having some problems and Daddy enlisted so they could have the space to see if they could work things out."

"That must've been tough on your mother. Having the responsibility of you and the farm without him there."

"It was. I'm pretty sure his enlisting took their problems to a new level, but the separation also made them closer than ever. Her two brothers and their wives came up from Mexico and helped out, so it was all good in the end. Funny enough, things didn't get rough until they got married." Luna stopped to let their server place their plates on the table. "It's one reason Daddy and Mitch are so close. Their service had a huge impact on both of their home lives, though in completely different ways."

"How so?"

"Mitch enlisted to make a better life for his child and the woman he lived with, but came home to find them gone."

Kaylie's heart jumped in her chest. "Gone? What do you mean?"

Luna picked up her fork, her gaze on her plate as if she was gathering her thoughts. Kaylie reached for her napkin and spread it over her lap. "You don't have to answer that. It's none of my business, and having some ugly events in my past, I totally understand the importance of keeping private things private. I shouldn't have asked." She felt terrible for doing so, but the words had been there before she could stop them.

Luna finished with a bite of her potato. “He wouldn’t mind you knowing, I’m sure. But yeah. It’s not my place to share all of what he went through. Maybe if he comes to work for you, he’ll tell you about it one day.”

“It’s pretty apparent he’s not coming to work for me. He’s got a good thing going here. I wouldn’t give up a comfortable life for the unknown.”

Luna’s expression softened. “But isn’t that exactly what you’ve done?”

Kaylie laughed at the contradiction of her words and her actions. “You’re right. But it would be different for Mitch. I’m only offering *him* part-time employment, while I’m starting over with a new business. He’d be crazy to make that kind of change.”

“A full-time change, sure, but I could see him doing both. It would be a matter of balance, but he could make it work.”

“You seem awfully invested in him coming to work for me.”

“Is it that obvious?” Luna asked, her laugh almost nervous.

“It is. And I’m dying to know why.”

“I’m not sure I can explain it, to be honest. It’s an intuition thing, I guess. I see him in a rut. I want him to have more.”

“But he seems happy in what you call a rut. He may not think of it that way at all.”

“Oh, I’m sure he doesn’t.”

“But you do.”

Another laugh, another strange show of nerves. “I just know how good he is at what he does, and how happy it makes me when I have a new project on the horizon. Like my brownie scarf. I think the change would spice things up for him. Give him a new challenge. Something to look forward to."

There was something Luna wasn't saying. Kaylie was sure of it. But she wasn't sure if she wanted to press or leave it alone. "I gave him my card and he knew my ad was coming out last week. I've got one interview tomorrow and another Friday. I really want someone on board for planning before I open."

"Well, like you said, he's got your card. And he's got to want it for himself."

"And who knows. He may decide that he does," Kaylie said, driven to appease the other woman because Luna seemed genuinely disappointed. "But even if he doesn't, a very good thing has come out of you sending him to me."

"It has, hasn't it? I would hate to have missed out on meeting you."

"And I you," Kaylie said, certain she and the other woman were seeing the beginning of what was going to be a beautiful friendship.

Two Owls' Number Ten Brownie Special

richly textured and full of the unexpected and sure to please

1½ cups unsalted butter
1¼ cups unsweetened Dutch-processed cocoa powder
2¾ cups sugar
½ teaspoon salt
¼ teaspoon cayenne pepper
2 teaspoons grated orange zest
5 eggs
1⅔ cups flour
½ cup sweetened coconut flakes
½ cup chopped pecans
½ cup *dulce de leche*

Preheat oven to 325°F. Grease or spray with cooking oil and flour (or line with aluminum foil) a 9 x 13–inch baking pan.

Melt the butter over low heat in a large saucepan. Remove from heat and whisk in the cocoa powder until smooth. Stir in the sugar and the salt until blended. Whisk in the cayenne pepper and the orange zest, followed by the eggs one at a time, blending after each. Add the flour to the saucepan, and fold in lightly with a spatula or spoon. Mix in the coconut and the pecans.

Pour the batter into the prepared baking pan and spread evenly. Warm the *dulce de leche* (in a double boiler, or microwave on low) enough to drizzle over the top. Bake for 40–45 minutes, or until an inserted tester comes out with a bit of batter attached. Cool completely before cutting.

CHAPTER NINETEEN

Having unloaded her Jeep, walked the acre of her lot with Magoo, fed him, watered him, and then spent twenty minutes under the spray of her shower, Kaylie came downstairs feeling somewhat less exhausted to find Ten in the kitchen finishing up for the day.

He'd been outside with Will when she'd returned from her trip to Gruene, and she'd thought it best to unwind a bit before seeing him. She was still turning over the girl talk she'd shared with Luna. But mostly she was still working through her thoughts of Ten.

She'd never had a man inspire her to create a brownie before. Yet Tennessee Keller had sent her mind turning to food since the midnight he'd stopped by to look at her shutters.

She'd been forever getting back to sleep, thinking about the color of his hair, the texture…continuing as the days passed to think things she didn't need to be thinking about the way he might look beneath his clothes. She especially did not need to be thinking that now, when he was in front of her, moving fluidly from one chore to the next, his body not overly muscled but so very strong.

She hadn't expected to enjoy hearing him as he worked inside her house. The constant whine of his saw, and his and Will's nail guns, and his stereo playing Amos Lee and the Avett Brothers and the occasional Led Zeppelin and Johnny Cash. She wasn't sure which man chose which music, and she had no plans to ask. She liked the mystery as much as the companionship.

It was all strangely comfortable, knowing she wasn't alone when she'd been alone so much of her life. Much of that was the house. Much, but not all. Ten's noise wasn't the intrusion she usually found such racket to be. The question was why, but she wasn't sure if knowing the answer would solve anything, and so she looked up—only to realize Ten had stopped moving and was staring at her.

"Sorry about that. Lost in thought."

He nodded as if he'd grown used to her doing that. "You had a good time with Luna today?"

"I did, yes." She paused, thought of the things she and Luna had talked about, families, friends. Men. "And I saw Mitch again."

"Mitch?"

"The applicant for the cook's position? Luna's friend?"

"Oh, that guy," he said, his tone of voice like a string of nasty adjectives tacked on the end.

If he'd known the other man, this attitude he had might make sense. But it didn't, and so she asked, "What is it with you and him? Or with you? I get that you let down your guard in the past and someone got hurt because of it, but that has nothing to do with Mitch. Did he wrong you in another life or something?"

"Sorry." He tugged the plug of an extension cord from the wall and wound the long orange snake using his palm and his elbow. "It's none of my business who you interview or hire."

"Thank you," she said, but was then struck with a thought. "I know that you're looking out for me, and I appreciate that, but you're inching up on going overboard again."

He snorted, tossed the extension cord into the pantry with his jigsaw. "I don't know him. He's not from around here."

"Luna knows him. So does her father. He and Mitch did their military service together." Ten arched a brow at that, and Kaylie went on. "Besides, I'm not from around here either. Not really."

"You lived here with the Wises for eight years. I think that qualifies you as a local."

She'd always felt she belonged here, but that didn't necessarily hold to his definition. "What about you? When did you come here?"

"I lived in Round Rock growing up, so we were close."

That had her remembering Carolyn Parker saying he'd been here ten years. "Why Hope Springs? Is this where you and your brother had planned to open up shop?"

"We didn't get that far in the planning stage. I came here...for some of the same reasons you did. Starting over. Getting some sleep."

"Looking for your family?"

"Looking to get out from beneath mine."

Except he hadn't. He carried what had happened, whatever it was he blamed himself for, to this day. And obviously he realized that or he wouldn't have told her about his habit of rushing to judgment. "Did it work?"

He was quiet for a moment, looking at the drill bit he held, then bit off a brusque "No."

"Have you talked to your sister yet? About my garden?"

"No."

If he wanted to look out for her, focusing on her garden instead of Mitch was a good place to start. "I need to get it in—"

"I know that."

Crabby, wasn't he? "If you don't want to talk to her, I'll get someone else."

"You asked me to help. I'll help."

"On my schedule or yours? Because time is something I don't have."

His jaw tightened. "Fine. I'll try to touch base with her tomorrow."

"She's still nearby?"

He nodded. "She's also busy. Or was last time I talked to her. I can't guarantee when she'll be able to get away."

What was it about his family? He didn't know what was going on with his sister. He didn't know when he'd last talked to his brother. "I didn't ask you to guarantee anything. She might not be able to fit me in, or she might be outside of my budget."

"Hey, I'm just the yellow pages. It's your business who you hire."

"Thank you."

"Oh, that was sneaky."

She smiled.

"Fine. Hire your Mitch Pepper. Just don't expect me to run interference if he steps out of line."

Seriously? He thought *Mitch* might step out of line? "All I expect from you is to have this job done well and on time."

"Oh, really," he said, shoving his hands to his oh-so-lean hips, his too-long hair catching in his collar and making her want to lift it away. "So you don't expect me to talk to Indy? You don't expect me to hook you up with an exterminator who'll get the job done right, or a security guy who won't put in an extra camera or two you don't know about?"

"I'm sure I can get recommendations from Carolyn or Jessa. Or even Luna." Which she should've done in the first place. She was relying on him too much. "Really, Ten. I don't need you thinking you know what's best for me." And then she took a deep breath and let go of the thought that had been building. "Whatever happened with you failing your family, I'm not a token charity case or whatever for you to use to make up for that."

"Wait a second," he said, reaching for her arm as she turned away, and stopping her.

She wanted to go. She wanted to stay. She wanted the choice taken from her because she was in a place she didn't recognize or know how to navigate. And yet she'd been thinking since lunch about being here, wanting things from Ten she couldn't name, she didn't understand, she longed for without knowing why.

"You can't say something like that and not expect me to respond."

"Then respond." She was baiting him. She was pushing him. She didn't know why. But she knew why exactly. She wanted this. She wanted him. She wanted.

He backed her into the wall beside the door, against the space where the refrigerator would go. The big commercial refrigerator, with half-glass doors and shelves for industrial casserole pans and bushels of lettuce and crates of tomatoes.

The spot was tall and wide and there was plenty of room for both of them to fit. He laced their fingers and raised her hands to her shoulders, anchoring her with his body, his feet on either side of hers, his thighs, too, as he lowered his head, his eyes bright, his nostrils flaring as he breathed.

She was frightened, but not of him as much as herself and the things she didn't know. She'd been here before with boys who thought themselves men, but not with these feelings, her belly, her heart, and not with Tennessee Keller. He smelled of a day's work and sawdust and worn cotton and a woodsy spice she'd noticed before in passing. It was subtle and she wanted to close her eyes and savor it, to remember it later when he wasn't so near. But closing them meant not seeing him and she wanted that most of all.

His lashes were long, the same turned-earth brown as the stubble of his beard. She wondered about the hair on his chest, on his legs, in private places. His lips parted, smiling, inviting, she didn't know. Before she could figure it out, time jumped forward and his mouth was there covering hers. He moved gently against her, soft and persuasive, the pressure of his lips imploring more than demanding, and at odds with the shackles of his hands.

The heels of his palms pushed against her, pushed her wrists against the drywall, pushed her knuckles, too. But his mouth didn't push. It begged, and she breathed deeply and parted her lips the way she knew he wanted. The way she instinctively wanted as well.

He slipped his tongue into her mouth, softly at first, then more boldly, going deeper, then sweeping harder as he learned her, coaxing her to follow his lead, to mate her tongue with his, to come with him into his mouth, to stay.

She curled her fingers around his, her nails digging into his skin with her need to hold him, to grip his shoulders, to cup his nape and thread her hands through his hair.

She wanted more than this, and her chest ached and her eyes, closed now, grew heavy with tears because she had no other outlet for the feelings bursting inside of her. Ten was here, touching her, his hands, his thighs, his chest when he leaned into her, his tongue and his lips as he loved her mouth with his.

Reality fell away, leaving magic, Ten's magic, here in her kitchen, the only sounds in the room their breathing, the tiny moans of the house, the wind through the breezeway stirring the bamboo chimes, a clutch of a whimper in her throat when he rubbed his thumbs over the heels of her palms.

He caught at her bottom lip, holding it, slicking it with his tongue, then finding hers and slicking it, too. He tasted of the coffee he'd last drunk, and he tasted of salt, and he was warm, hot even, his lips softer than she'd thought they would be, the stubble of his beard as it rasped over her chin arousing. Her nipples pebbled, and the whimper in her throat clawed loose in desperation. The sound, barely audible, was enough.

Ten stopped, his mouth a hair's width from hers, his breathing ragged, the brush of air as he exhaled like a furnace at her cheek. And then he released her, backing away, holding up both of his hands as if to show her she was free and he was…sorry? Displeased with what they'd done? Regretting the way he'd pushed her and held her and taken her as if giving her no choice? Except that wasn't how the kiss had happened at all. She'd been completely willing and involved.

Another moment and he spun away, crossing the room to return to packing his things. She shook off the daze keeping her pinned in place and scraped the loose hair from around her face, touching her fingertips to her mouth, still feeling him. Still wanting him. Not knowing how to tell him that when he'd been the one to leave. She was so tired of people leaving.

"Look. I didn't mean for that to happen—"

"Don't." She bit off the word so sharply he stopped in the act of locking his toolbox and turned. Her chest was heaving. She tried to stop it, to control her breathing, but everything around her had changed and she didn't know how. "Just don't."

"Don't what?"

"Don't apologize. Don't say you didn't want that to happen."

"That's not what I said. I said I didn't mean for it to."

"Is that different than you didn't mean it?"

"I meant every second."

"Then why did you stop?"

"I don't know."

She didn't believe him. She was certain he knew exactly why, but that he wasn't comfortable telling her. Or comfortable with admitting it to himself. And as much as she didn't want to accept the truth, he'd been right to stop. She'd been angry. He'd been reacting to that, not to her. Yes, her experience with men was limited, but she knew the heat of the moment did not lend itself to rational thought.

Still, she couldn't let it go so easily. "If you want to kiss me, then kiss me. Don't work out your frustrations with your family or use me—"

"I'm not using you, Kaylie. This…it has, had, nothing to do with my family."

"But you stopped anyway."

"I stopped because things were about to get out of hand, and this isn't the time or the place…" He rubbed at his eyes. "I'm not going to take you up against a wall in an empty house. You deserve better than that."

"You kissed me because you were angry."

His head came up at that. "I wasn't angry. I was… aroused."

"Oh, I thought…" She stopped, because she wasn't sure what she'd been thinking. Or if she'd been thinking at all. It had become habit, assuming the worst. She knew better, but old habits died hard. "I think I'm embarrassed now."

"We kissed. I got hard. It's what happens. I didn't mean to embarrass you."

"No. I mean I'm embarrassed that I didn't realize why you backed off. I thought…" And here she went again. "I thought you didn't want to kiss me."

"How could you get that out of what just happened?"

"Because you stopped. You walked away. Because you're over there packing your tools and I'm just standing here." *Like a fool,* she wanted to add, but didn't. The words she'd already spoken had said it loudly enough.

He dropped the roll of tape he'd been holding, watched it bounce from the toolbox lid to the floor. Then he walked to the sink and planted both hands on either side, leaning into them and staring out the window.

From her vantage point, Kaylie could see Magoo sprawled out asleep in the driveway, but didn't think Ten was looking at her dog. She pushed off the wall and waved a hand distractedly. "I'm just going to go make sure I didn't leave anything in the Jeep. Maybe throw a ball with Magoo for a bit."

"You're going to walk away? And leave me standing here?"

A flush climbed from her chest up her throat, heating her skin and no doubt turning her the color of a watermelon. "Ten—"

"No, Kaylie. We're going to finish this."

"I thought we did."

He bit off a sharp curse, slammed a fist against the countertop. "No, sweetheart. We were just getting started. I don't want you walking outside thinking anything else. Or thinking I don't want you. Or thinking that if you said the word, I wouldn't be dragging you upstairs by the hair."

She tried to laugh, but her heart wouldn't let her, thumping all the air from her chest. "That sounds rather caveman."

"I can be caveman. But I'm trying to be nice."

At that she swallowed, her throat working around unfamiliar emotions. Among them, a terribly unseemly longing that he show her the side of him that wasn't nice. "I'm…not very good at this. At reading signals. Usually when I've had someone walk away, it's meant they're not coming back."

Another curse and he straightened, facing the window as he shoved both hands through his hair. Frustration poured off him in waves, and in many flavors, and she wanted to go to him but held herself back, waiting, curious. Anxiously desperate to know what happened next.

"When I kiss a woman I'm interested in," he said, "or when…things get intimate, I'm there for more than what's happening physically. That means I'm not going to walk away afterward. Unless it's to slow things down. And sometimes that means"—he gestured toward his toolbox—"cleaning up at the end of the day. That's all this is. I promise."

He was interested. In her. And yet… "I was worried that I was the only one having a good time."

He held her gaze, the line of his jaw taut, his pulse a tic in his temple, the sun through the window glinting like fire in his eyes. She thought he might be trying to frighten her off, or see that she kept her distance because he couldn't be trusted to keep his. But she wasn't frightened. She was full of something big and grand, and thought if she didn't escape, she'd explode with it.

And because she was done with picking up pieces, and because he was obviously done with trying to explain, she pushed open the screen door and left him there, knowing without looking back that he watched her all the way to her Jeep, then as far as he could as she headed to the front of the house with Magoo.

From there, he wouldn't be able to see her. It was the best place for her to be until she settled the feelings he'd whipped up inside her like tornado winds.

CHAPTER TWENTY

What are you doing here?" Kaylie said when she opened the kitchen door to Ten's knock. It wasn't the welcome he'd been expecting, or the one he'd been hoping for, to be honest, but he'd shown up without calling, making it the most obvious question she could've asked. And at least she had answered. He hadn't been sure she would with the way they left things last night.

"I was hungry. Thought you might be, too."

"I am," she said, pulling the door wider and letting him in. "But I'd resigned myself to a ketchup sandwich made from the rest of the bread I picked up at Butters Bakery and any fast-food packets I can find in my Jeep. You know, since I've got to pay the exterminator. And because I don't have anything in the house but dog food."

Whew. She was sounding more like the Kaylie he'd gotten to know before he'd been stupid and kissed her. He'd been afraid he'd ruined all of that. He knew a lot of people, was close to only a few, and losing her friendship would've been a bigger blow than losing her business.

She hadn't been around today while he'd been working, and he'd gone crazy with it, wondering if she'd taken herself off so she wouldn't have to see him. The rest of this renovation would be a bear if that was the case.

"As appetizing as a ketchup sandwich sounds," he said, lifting the brown paper bag he held by the crimped top, "I stopped by Malina's. I've got meat loaf and mashed potatoes and green beans with bacon and hot cornbread. Or it was hot when I left the diner. Things might need a quick blast in the microwave."

She took the bag, set it on the island, and opened it. Closing her eyes, she leaned over the top, inhaled deeply, and smiled. That look on her face made up for all the worry of the past twenty-four hours and last night's total inability to sleep.

Looked like his fear about having messed things up had been a big waste of time. Except after yesterday's kiss, when she'd finally walked out of the kitchen, he'd had no idea where things stood between them, what she'd been thinking, how today would go down.

Though he would've been fine eating out of the Styrofoam containers, Kaylie dished out the food onto two of the stoneware plates she'd bought at Canton's Hardware Emporium, serving him more than she served herself, and grabbing them both bottled water from the fridge.

He took his drink, picked up his plate, and followed her to the dining room and the two chairs she'd brought down from Austin. There he settled into what he'd come to think of as the visitor's seat, while Kaylie curled into the big worn wingback, tucking her feet to the side, balancing her plate on her knees.

"Are you getting tired of camping out?" he asked, and when she frowned as if she wasn't sure she'd heard him, he added, "Don't you miss your things? Your TV? Your bed? A table that's not a kitchen counter?"

"We can sit on the stools in the kitchen if you'd rather."

"No," he said, smiling to himself. "I'm fine. I was just making conversation, wondering if you weren't tired of roughing it."

"A little, but not enough to complain. I've got Internet, so I can watch TV on my laptop. A bed would be nice, but my sleeping bag's well padded. I'm adaptable. I've had to be. I did a lot for myself. Even when I lived with my mother."

"You were only five when you were taken away. Seems kinda young to be doing more for yourself than playing make-believe."

"You'd think, wouldn't you?" She scooped up a bite of mashed potatoes and ate them before going on. "My dad left when I was four, and I think he did most of the parenting before then. It's the only reason I can think of that my mother failed so epically after he was gone."

"You didn't have grandparents helping out?"

"I don't even know if I *have* grandparents. Or cousins. Or aunts and uncles. I might as well have been Little Orphan Kaylie. Except for the orphan part."

He stabbed at his meat loaf, hating the way she tossed off something so wrong as a joke. Hating more that she'd been in that position at all. "You told me before that your mother was coming down off meth when the authorities showed up. That Ernest had called them."

She nodded, her focus on her food. "I'd been hungry. I went and knocked on Ernest's door, but he didn't answer.

I think that's why he took what happened so hard. If he'd been home, everything would've turned out so differently." But that was all she said, and he wasn't sure if she'd stopped because she didn't want to go back there, or because she didn't think he really wanted to know.

He did. He wanted to hear her story, to understand what she'd gone through, to learn more about her. He got that opening a vein and spilling the past wasn't easy. That's why so few people knew the details of his.

"You were hungry," he finally said, prodding.

One side of her mouth pulled up, though he wasn't sure it was a grin. "You're determined to make me talk about this, aren't you?"

"I seem to remember you saying part of coming back here was about facing your past. Can't face it if you can't talk about it." Though he had no business lecturing her, when he kept the mistakes of his own past locked away.

"I was hungry and Ernest wasn't home and my mother was passed out on the couch. She'd been there all day, ever since I'd gotten up. The TV was on, so I'd climbed up by her feet and watched some kid stuff for a while. *Sesame Street,* maybe. I don't remember for sure. I was a big fan of Oscar the Grouch. I liked that he lived in a trash can. It made me feel okay about the garbage all over our house."

"Kaylie—" he said, but it was all he got out.

"If you want the story, you can't stop me with that voice to tell me how sorry you are."

"I have a sorry voice?"

"And a sorry look in your eye."

"I promise. No being sorry. At least out loud." For her sake, he would bite back his anger at a young girl being so utterly failed by those who should've put her needs first, and hadn't.

"I was hungry," she said for the third or fourth time. "My mother only groaned when I tried to wake her up, and as I said, Ernest didn't answer when I crossed the hall and knocked."

"Five seems awfully young to cross the hall alone."

"Depends on the five-year-old, I guess. We were in an apartment building. All I had to do was open our door, take two or three steps, and ring his bell. I did it a lot, getting things for my mother, taking things to Ernest he'd called and asked for."

"Things like what?" Her mother had been a user, had gone to prison for intent to distribute. He was liking the sound of this less and less, Kaylie acting as a delivery service between a user and another man.

"I'm never going to get this story told if you keep interrupting."

He held up a hand, promising to stop, and gave a single nod for her to continue.

"Our refrigerator was pretty much empty. There was a milk carton and I drank what was left, but it wasn't enough for cereal. And we didn't have cereal anyway. No bread or cheese. No apples. Not that we ever had apples. Not even any potato chips.

"But we did have crackers and soup, and I knew which button to push on the microwave to heat it. Unfortunately, this was long before pull-top cans. I couldn't work the can opener. I knew the mechanics, but couldn't get it attached. And then I remembered having seen my father open a can of beans with his pocketknife."

"Kaylie. Crap."

She arched a brow, and her look said he was in trouble. "You've got that sorry face on again."

"Yeah, well, a sorry tale deserves a sorry face."

"Do you want to hear the rest?"

He didn't need to, but he nodded anyway.

"I got out the soup, Chicken and Stars, and pushed a chair to the counter where I knew the knife block was. And, yes, I knew I wasn't supposed to touch it, but I was hungry."

"How badly did you hurt yourself?" he asked, and braced himself for her answer.

"I didn't. Not at all. My mother came into the kitchen and screamed at me. I dropped the knife on the floor and curled into a ball in the chair, trying to hide inside my nightgown. She just looked at me, like she was imagining what could've happened. And then things got really weird."

He waited, waited, his heart in his throat, choking him. She took her time forking up the rest of the green beans from her plate, her eyes downcast and frowning, as if disapproving of this memory more than the rest. He looked down at his own food, the tomato sauce from the meat loaf seeping into what was left of his mashed potatoes. He didn't need to hear the rest of this. He knew enough.

"Kaylie—"

"She came closer and picked up the knife. Then she looked at me. She was sad. I remember that most of all. She wasn't crying, but her eyes were red and her face was…haggard. I couldn't have told you any of this at the time, but she looked exhausted and miserable and lonely."

He remained silent, the air so still he expected a clock to tick, a pin to drop. Then Magoo sat up to scratch and broke the spell.

Kaylie went on, tapping the tines of her fork to her plate as she did. "I don't know what she was thinking, my mother. I doubt she was thinking at all. She'd been out of it for days. She hadn't bathed or dressed. She barely managed to open an eye and see that I was okay. Ernest had been checking in, and I'm sure he would've stopped by that day, too."

"But you were hungry."

"Have I mentioned that?" she asked, giving him a wink before sobering. "She took the knife and ran her thumb over the blade. I remember wincing when I saw the blood, but she didn't even react. Next thing I knew, she'd cut both of her wrists, and then she looked at me and smiled, and collapsed on the floor. Her blood..."

"Kaylie—"

"It was like a faucet trickling," she said, her voice steady, though tears ran down her cheeks. "Like spilled Kool-Aid. Or the colored water from the end of a paintbrush. Except it was thicker and darker. The puddle kept getting bigger and bigger and I just sat in that chair, watching. I didn't start screaming until I saw the drops of blood on my bare toes. They were poking out from the hem of my nightgown, and it was like little red polka dots were everywhere."

"Kaylie—"

"I must've left the front door open enough for Ernest to hear me crying when he came home. He scooped me up and took me out of there. He was crying harder than I was. He called the cops, then sat with me in his lap on the steps, just rocking back and forth. And we were still huddled up together when the ambulance got there. I don't know why he didn't try to help her, wrap up her wrists or something to stop the bleeding. It was like getting me away was the only thing that mattered."

No doubt it was, if Ten's suspicions were correct. Ernest Flynn had most likely preferred her mother not be around to incriminate him as her supplier. But Ten wasn't going to share what he was thinking with Kaylie. This wasn't the time, and he had no proof, and what good would it do her twenty-three years later when she had so few positive memories of that time in her life?

"It's good they got to her in time," he said, and her head came up sharply.

"Is it?"

"Kaylie—"

"No. Don't tell me I shouldn't think that way. She was a terrible mother. Neglectful and selfish." Her eyes were angry now, red and wet, but mad like a wild dog's. "I went days without a bath. My clothes were always dirty. I didn't mind that they weren't new, because anything she picked up from rummage sales or Goodwill was new to me. But I hated the dirt. And it was everywhere. Everywhere. The floors and the coffee table, and you don't even want to know about the bathroom." She shuddered, pushed her hair from her forehead, and buried her face in her free hand.

Ten's appetite was gone. He'd made her go back there, and for what reason? To satisfy his curiosity? To fill in the blanks the gossip had left? He was no better than those who chattered behind Kaylie's back. So what if he'd asked her directly? It wasn't his business...and yet it felt like it was. Like she was his to protect.

He thought about the night he'd stopped by to look at her shutters. "That's why you've got the bowie knife, isn't it?"

She sat straight again and glanced over, her eyes doll-like and curious. "Does that seem crazy to you? That after all of that it's a knife that makes me feel safe?"

"Not crazy at all."

"I had to work up to it. The owner of the shop who helped me find one to fit my hand was amazingly patient. I must've gone in there a dozen times. But I wasn't going to order online and hope I'd get something I could handle. And I took lessons."

"So if you'd thrown at me that night in the yard, you wouldn't have missed?"

"I can split a hair if I have to," she said, and then she laughed, the tension easing. "I'm kidding about the hair, but not about knowing how to use the knife."

"Have you ever had to?"

She shook her head. "Not yet."

But knowing how wasn't the same as being able to. So he asked, "Do you think you could?"

"If someone broke into my home and was threatening me or my dog?" When he stayed silent, giving her a single nod as encouragement to go on, she gave him honesty instead of bravado. He could see it in the way she held her mouth, sense it in her hesitation.

"I want to think so. And that's not about my mother and the other knife. That's about me not believing violence is an answer."

He probably understood that better than anyone. Hadn't he watched his brother do what he'd been unable to? "Let's hope you never have to find out."

"Let's hope. And DX Security is coming next week to put in the security system, so as long as I can hold out until then, I shouldn't have to. I think the squatters have moved on, and since there's nothing here of any value to take, there's no reason for anyone to break in."

"Thieves don't always know that until after they're inside."

"Magoo won't let that happen." At the sound of his name, the dog raised his head and began to pant. "I have one blade. He's got a whole mouth full."

CHAPTER TWENTY-ONE

Luna stood in the darkened barn, a shed, really, the room still retaining the smells of the feed once stored inside. It had been fully converted to a temperature-controlled and beautifully lighted space for her weaving, but she liked to keep the twenty-by-twenty-foot room dark. At least while she was working, using only enough light to see flaws. Even then, she left some of them. Why should anything be perfect? The world wasn't perfect. Life wasn't perfect. She sure wasn't perfect.

A perfect person would never keep the sorts of secrets she was keeping from a woman she was rapidly coming to think of as a very good friend. Not only was she keeping secrets from Kaylie, she was perpetrating a huge deception, and doing so because of something *she* wanted to see happen. Could she be any more selfish? She should've kept what she'd learned to herself, never told Mitch, or at least talked to her father first, asked his advice. Now it was too late.

Mitch knew about his daughter. He'd gone to see his daughter. His daughter thought he was simply a cook come to inquire about a job. What must that meeting have been like? Had Kaylie suspected anything? How in the world had

Mitch not given himself away? Luna ached with the burden of what she'd set in motion. How was she going to make up for her hubris when everything came tumbling down around the people involved? And it would. Of that she was certain.

Mitch had been desperate to find his girl, looking for her for nearly twenty years, giving up only when the dead ends left him lost and raw. And she doubted he'd given up at all. The more likely truth was that he'd only hidden his efforts from those close to him, those who'd watched him suffer disappointment time after time.

What Luna had done had the potential to ruin so many lives. She thought back to her dinner with Will, his insistence that she owed the same truth to Kaylie that she owed to Mitch, especially since she knew that each had been looking for the other, wondering about the other, for a very long time. Maybe he'd been right, and she should've told both. Maybe he'd been right, and she shouldn't have told either.

"You standing in the dark for a reason, sweetie?"

Luna blinked away the dampness welling in her eyes and smiled as she glanced over her shoulder. "Hi, Daddy. I'm deciding on colors for a new project."

"I'd think a little light on that subject might help. Otherwise you'll end up with something that looks like a box of melted crayons."

"I already made one of those, remember? I think it was in last November's issue of *People* around Daniel Craig's neck."

"Right. I forget how much the paparazzi love you."

"Oh, Daddy. It's not me they love."

"Well, they should." Harry Meadows walked up beside his daughter, wrapped an arm around her shoulders, and faced the pegboard stocked with yarn sheared and woven from the sheep he raised. "What were you thinking about?"

"I had lunch with a friend on Tuesday. She's a baker, and she's opening a café in Hope Springs."

"The one Mitch was telling me about?"

"I imagine so, since there's only the one." But did that mean Mitch hadn't told Harry who Kaylie was, or about the rolling stone of lies Luna had set into motion? These new untruths eclipsing the others about her accident she'd kept now for over ten years?

"And you're wanting to make something for her?"

An apology, an atonement, a plea for Kaylie to understand and forgive. None of it seemed possible. Luna's shame seeped from her pores like the scent of hot rain on asphalt, pitchy and raw as it steamed. She reached for a skein as black as her heart.

And her father chuckled at her side. "Black?"

She started to put it back, then thought better. It had to be there, the remorse, the shame. Kaylie would be unaware, but Luna would know. She would always know. When the other woman was no longer a part of her life, still she would know what she'd done. She would see these threads as she wove others. She would never forget.

"An accent only. Like pepper on a salad of mixed greens." Celadon, moss, and willow. Bice blue and burgundy wine. She reached for them all, seeing them in a bowl, tossed and seasoned and dressed, and then she reached for a skein of sunflower, too.

"I don't know how you do that," her father said, looking at the collection she held and shaking his head.

Honestly, neither did she. To this day she could not explain how the colors came together in her mind. How one flowed into another as she sat at her loom. How the different strands of story became a whole. "I just see it. I don't know where it comes from. Any of it. It's just there."

Her father leaned over and dropped a kiss to the top of her head. "That's what makes you such a great artist."

Was she? Great? Was she even an artist? Or was she simply exploring the darkness that haunted her, pouring out her emotions in a way that allowed her to see them and deal with them but kept those close to her from knowing the truth?

"Have you ever wondered about the accident? If something happened then? A bump on the head, maybe, that flipped some artistic switch?"

Her father never spoke of the accident. To have him do so now, when she was overwhelmed with what the choices she'd made had wrought on others, seemed the worst kind of foreboding. She reached for a final skein the color of bitter kale.

"I don't know. I didn't have any interest in weaving before then, and may not ever have wanted to if not for being confined to bed."

"It was smart of your mother to see what you needed. I was worried we'd never get you back."

She hadn't been sure she wanted to return. Not with Sierra gone. Not with the guilt. "It wasn't easy, knowing I was still alive and Sierra wasn't."

"Your mother saw that a long time before I did."

"She's the real artist, you know. She does all of this." Luna waved her free arm in a half circle in front of the wall holding a palette of colors. "It's like a menu of every food combination possible. The ingredients to any recipe that comes to mind. I mean, look at it. Chocolate and cherries and salmon and vanilla-bean ice cream and vichyssoise and honey-fried chicken and—"

"Stop," her father said, laughing and groaning at the same time. "You just made me hungry and Mitch hasn't taken the wings off the grill yet."

"I saw the dishes you left in the sink. You ate enough food at breakfast and lunch to feed Snow White and all seven dwarfs."

"But lunch was just a sandwich, and breakfast was before dawn."

Her father loved farming, but had always hated having to get up with the sun. "Seems I remember hearing that you're the one who chose to be a farmer. That you didn't care how early your days started. Working up a sweat and feeling your muscles ache and the success of the farm made it worth it."

He got a grumpy, pouty look on his face. "I take it back."

"You can't take it back, but speaking of hungry—"

"Uh-oh."

That made Luna laugh. "I invited a couple more friends to Easter dinner. I know there'll be enough food, and that you don't care, but I wanted to tell you." To come clean.

"You don't have to tell me. Well, unless you invite a hundred of your friends."

"Daddy. I don't have a hundred friends." And she would most likely be losing the newest one she'd made.

"Well, you should. Everyone should know what an amazing woman you are."

At the sound of a throat clearing behind them, Harry dropped his arm from around Luna's neck and they both turned to see Mitch in the doorway. He raised a hand and gestured over his shoulder with his thumb. "I can go. If you two are busy."

"We're not busy. We're just having a moment." Her father gave Luna one more big hug. "But now it's March Madness time. How're the wings?"

"Ready to come in off the grill. But you're in charge of the beer, so…"

"I'm on it. You coming?"

"Right behind you," he said, turning when Luna stopped him with a quick, "Mitch? Do you have a minute?"

~

"What's up, moon girl?" Mitch asked, after Harry was out of earshot.

"I'm sorry. I shouldn't have put you on the spot in front of Daddy."

"Your dad knows we talk. You and I worked together for years. He doesn't have a lock on my friendship."

"Please promise me that I haven't ruined ours?"

Frowning, Mitch moved to stand in front of her, leaning against the workbench built into the wall beneath the pegboard of yarn. This family. The talent. It never ceased to amaze him, and yet no one he knew was more down-to-earth than the Meadows clan. "There's nothing you could do to ruin our friendship. I think of you as a daughter. You know that. And we never give up on our daughters. No matter how many years, or how many miles."

"Or how much well-intended butting-in gets in the way?"

"Luna. Don't. If not for your butting in, I might never have found Kaylie. How could I? She changed her last name, though why in the hell she chose to change it to Flynn..."

"Does the name mean something to you?"

"Yeah. And not anything good. But she wouldn't have known that. She was too little to understand who he was."

"Who he was?"

"Ernest Flynn. Our neighbor. Our dealer. Or he had been before Dawn and I cleaned up our act."

"What?" she asked, her eyes going wide.

"It's why I enlisted. I'd lost my job, had zero in the way of prospects. The service would provide for my family and keep me straight. Never occurred to me Dawn would need a reason, too. Guess with Ernest next door, she had more of one to slip back into old habits."

"I didn't know."

"No reason you should have. I can't imagine Harry talking to his girl about his best friend once being a junkie."

"But you got clean."

"Got clean. Stayed clean. I'll have one beer tonight while we go through about four dozen wings during the game, but that's it. I learned my lesson. And getting out of the service and finding Kaylie gone...I swore then and there I'd stay sober. No way was I going to risk finding my girl and then losing her again because I couldn't get through life without a crutch." He'd been watching her as he talked, as she lined up the bundles of yarn she held on the workbench where he was leaning. All the greens together with the blue and the red. The yellow and black on one end, separate.

"You're staring," she said, without looking over.

Guilty as charged. He gave a lift of his chin. "What do you think about when you're doing that?"

She shrugged. "Different things, depending on why I'm making the scarf."

"Why are you making this one?"

She twisted her mouth to one side, moved the dark red to the middle of the row of mostly greens. "It's for Kaylie."

He stopped himself from offering a lame platitude about her being sweet. Something was going on here. His moon girl didn't weave scarves for new friends. She didn't weave them for old ones, or even for family. All of her work went to the boutique in Austin. It was an agreement she and her parents had made. It kept her from being taken advantage of. He couldn't imagine her saying yes to even the most casual acquaintance wanting to place a special order.

"Why? What are you trying to make it say?"

"And here I thought you didn't get my craft."

"What? Just because I can't imagine sitting for hours at a time engaged in back-breaking repetitive motion?"

"You mean like cooking the same dish over and over again every day? And speaking of which, have you given any more thought to going to work for her?"

It was all he thought about lately. "Even if I could make it happen, I don't think it's a good idea."

"Because you'd feel compelled to tell her who you are?"

He looked down at his feet, then scrubbed both hands over his face, frustrated by the rock and the hard place hemming him in. "Lying to her is killing me. I tell myself it's the right thing to do. She's got a good thing going with her café. She seems happy. She's done something with her life. I don't want to screw that up."

"Why assume her knowing the truth will screw things up?"

"Of course it would."

"She came here to look for her parents."

"What?" he asked, looking at her over the top of his glasses.

Luna nodded. "She came back here to find out why she'd been dumped into foster care."

"She told you that?" When she gave him a look, he raised a capitulating hand. "Okay, okay. She told you. But that doesn't change anything."

She swung to face him, her hair flying behind her like a cape, her arms flung wide. "It changes everything. Are you kidding me? She wants to know why you left, where you went. You could answer all her questions. About where you were all her life. And probably a lot of the ones she has about her mother."

"Or you could answer all her questions, couldn't you? Since you've heard most of my stories over the years." And then it hit him, her need to weave for Kaylie. "That's why you're making the scarf, isn't it? Because of what you know."

When she shrugged in answer, rearranging the order of the skeins, he pushed. "Tell me about it."

"I don't know." She bit off the words, frustrated. "I see Kaylie and I think fresh, and food, and the garden she wants to put in, and the trees on her lot, and it all comes to me in green."

"Where does the guilt fit it?"

She leaned her head back, her laugh bitter. "Which part?"

He didn't like the sound of that. "How many parts are there?"

"Guilt over not telling her the truth the first time we met. Guilt over continuing to not tell her the truth now that I've gotten to know her. Guilt over not keeping my mouth shut from the very beginning."

"If you'd done that, I wouldn't have gotten to meet my girl."

"I know," she said, looking at him with big, damp eyes. "That's the only good part of all of this, except how good is it when you won't tell her who you are? I didn't get the two of you together for you not to say anything. What's the point of that?"

"Life's not a fairy tale, Luna. And happy endings can come in a lot of different colors. Just like your scarves."

But she was shaking her head. "Are you saying you'll be happy just knowing where Kaylie is? Not having a real relationship with her?"

"If I have to," he said, watching her eyes flash with disbelief.

"And what happens if *she* finds *you*? What're you going to do then? Have you thought about that? How to explain to her you were here all this time?"

Had he thought about it? Had he thought about anything else? "I guess I'll deal with that when the time comes. When it comes. If it comes."

"Mitch," she said, then stopped and breathed in, as if gathering her emotions to throw at him in a big, fiery ball.

"You know it's going to. And if you let it happen rather than making it happen, probably in a very bad way."

He had a feeling she was right, and that he was screwing up by not coming clean with his daughter. Even thinking those words, *his daughter*...

He could hardly breathe with the weight of having her near. It crushed him, a vise stealing his strength and his ability to think clearly and what passed for his soul. He'd seen her twice, and his heart had ceased to be his and belonged completely to her.

But she knew none of what he felt. She couldn't, and without his telling her the truth of who he was, nothing would change. He would carry this burden alone, and hope it wasn't as heavy as the one he'd borne the last twenty-three years. Coming home to the apartment on Harbor Lake after serving his tour of duty...

He shook his head, remembering what it had been like to find strangers living behind the door that should've opened to the rest of his life. They didn't know what had happened to Dawn and Kaylie. They didn't know who Ernest was, or where he had gone. The management office knew, at least about Dawn. Hard not to when her suicide attempt had been all over the news.

They had no forwarding address for Ernest, and not a clue about his girl. All the cops could tell him was that with her mother in prison, she'd gone into the system. But they couldn't tell him anything more, since he had no proof of who he was.

Dawn was in the wind, having vanished after her release. He hadn't even been able to rely on her to get their girl back so he could raise her, care for her, do all the things he'd never had a chance to do because he'd been young and stupid and in over his head when he wasn't out of it.

Why he'd ever thought it a good idea, having a kid with that woman…

"Mitch? Did you hear me?"

"Yeah, moon girl. You're right."

"So you'll talk to her? Tell her who you are?"

"Yeah," he said, keeping the rest to himself. When the time was right. When he could be sure he wouldn't hurt her more than he already had. When he could bring himself to face losing her again.

When he wasn't so selfishly afraid, and had the strength to let her go forever.

CHAPTER TWENTY-TWO

When the doorbell chimed through the house Thursday morning, Kaylie and her coffee were curled up in her wingback chair. May had gifted her the chair when she'd moved from Hope Springs to Dallas after Winton's death. It was worn in all the right places, the rose-and-wine print thinned to pale pink on the arms, the seat cushion shaped to fit tiny, tiny May, the lingering sheen of Aqua Net on the headrest giving up the older woman's scent when Kaylie brushed against it just right.

While the chair had been in her condo, Kaylie had slept in it as often as she'd slept in her bed, wrapped in the multicolored afghan May had given her the day she'd had the chair delivered. Kaylie had watched sad movies in this chair, read sadder books in this chair, sat and journaled and wondered why she kept reaching for the sad when she was sitting in the heart of the happiness she'd known in Hope Springs.

It was a given that she would never quit missing Winton and May, and that she'd feel their loss forever; they were her family, after all. But she'd learned to use what she felt and to live with it, to let their love push her on, not bring her to her knees with the grief of their absence. All the things she did, she did as if under their gaze. She hoped she had made them proud.

Setting her notebook and pen on the floor beside her, and burying the exterminator's invoice beneath, she headed down the hallway, reaching the front of the house as the bell rang again. She pulled open the door to a smart-looking woman she actually remembered as Rick Breeze's mother. "Mrs. Breeze?"

"Dolly. It's Dolly." Dolly Breeze brought both hands to her cheeks, her eyes going wide and inexplicably damp. "Kaylie Bridges! Look at you! Oh, it's not Bridges now, I know. It's Flynn. But look at you! Oh, come here, sugar," she said, opening her arms.

Kaylie, not usually one for hugging, allowed the other woman's embrace, smiling as she breathed in the barest hint of Chanel. "I'm so glad to see you. When Jessa mentioned you, it didn't even register that she was talking about Rick Breeze's mother."

"Breeze, Bridges. You two were always in line together, Rick in front, you behind." With a final squeeze, Dolly stepped back and this time clasped her hands to her chest as if holding them there was the only thing keeping her from reaching for Kaylie again.

"I hate to admit it, but I remember so little from living here before. Outside of this house, anyway. I think I just tried to get through the school days so I could come back here." And why in the world did she feel compelled to make such a confession to Dolly? "Come in. Would you like coffee? Or water?"

"I'm fine, Kaylie. I had coffee at home and I'll have more when I get to the office."

"That's right," Kaylie said, leading the way toward the dining room. "You work for Ten."

"I do. So I've seen some of the plans for your place. Two Owls Café. I absolutely love that you would honor May and Winton this way. May would love it so. Are you going to be serving her hot rolls?"

Kaylie laughed. "Every day. They're so easy, even I can do them, but I'd rather not have to."

Dolly took the chair next to the one where Kaylie had been sitting. The one where Ten had sat to eat the night he'd brought her mashed potatoes and meat loaf. "You'll have quite enough on your hands, I'm sure. Even with your limited hours, and your simple but absolutely genius menu, you're going to be one busy girl. And baking all those brownies. Assuming you'll do those yourself."

"I'll do some, yes, but the recipes aren't so big a secret that I won't share them with who I hire." Interesting that Dolly knew so much about Kaylie's plans. Definitely more than Kaylie had shared with Jessa, meaning the older woman must've heard the details from Luna or, more likely, Ten when he'd shown her the plans. "I'm not sure if Ten told you that this is just a part-time position. I don't want you to expect the hours you get working for him. I just don't anticipate having them. Not until I see how the café is received."

Dolly crossed her legs, smoothing out the fabric of her taupe linen slacks. "He did tell me, and said if I was interested, and you wanted me, he and I could work out a schedule for me to keep my benefits. And from the chatter already around town, I don't think you'll have to worry about your reception. You couldn't have picked a better time to open."

"Since I haven't been out much except to deal with things for the house, that's good to hear." But it wasn't the news that had Kaylie's heart tumbling. "And that's very generous of Ten."

"He's a generous man."

"You've worked for him a long time?"

Dolly nodded. "I started there about six months after my husband died."

"Jessa mentioned his passing. I'm so sorry for your loss."

Her mouth tight with her suffering, Dolly looked down at her nails. "It was hard, but that's to be expected. We'd been inseparable for most of our adult lives. Much like Winton and May."

"It nearly killed May, losing him." Kaylie shook her head, remembering.

Dolly met her gaze with a sad understanding, asking, "The two of you stayed in touch then? You and May?"

"We did," Kaylie said, "though we didn't get together as often as she would've liked. I was the one who had a hard time with it." And why was she admitting all of this to a woman she was hoping to employ? "I'm sorry. That sounds so selfish—"

"No, sugar. It sounds honest. Never apologize for being honest."

"Well, then, to be honest," she said, putting into words a truth she'd never admitted to anyone, something this house had her doing often these days, "if the state hadn't paid for my education, I probably would've stayed with them forever. It was the first true home I'd ever had. I didn't want to give it up."

"No more than May wanted to give you up, I'm sure."

Kaylie let Dolly's words settle. May had done nothing but encourage her toward the future, a new life on her own. She'd been eighteen, and it had been time. It had also been for the best, even if she'd thought differently when packing her things. May's kicking her out of the nest had allowed her to fly. *Don't look to where you've come from, Kaylie. Look to where you're going.*

She gave Dolly a wry grin. "Growing up's not for the weak, that's for sure."

"And yet we all come to that place, don't we?"

Kaylie nodded, swallowed, missing May.

"Your attending UT thrilled May to bits. You may not have known that. Or known how much. She bragged on you constantly. You always had the intelligence and the drive. You just needed the nurturing to pull it all together."

This was certainly not where Kaylie had expected this interview to go. Or where she had *wanted* it to go. This was business. Dolly's observations were personal to Kaylie, about Kaylie. And yet she couldn't deny her curiosity. "I didn't realize, when I was here before, that you and May were such good friends."

Dolly brushed at the fabric over her knee, her downcast gaze contemplative. "I had Rick late in life. May was older than me, but she was still more of a contemporary than most of the mothers of Rick's classmates. You may not remember the play your drama class did in seventh grade. *A Christmas Carol*?"

Kaylie hadn't thought of that for years. "I do remember," she said with a laugh. "I played Belle to Rick's Scrooge. May made me the cutest pink gingham dress, probably not very period authentic, but it was the most beautiful dress I'd ever seen."

"It was the first time I remember ever seeing you in a dress. You were always more the sneakers and softball glove sort. You carried that glove everywhere."

"I was afraid to let it out of my sight," she said with a laugh.

"Studies, athletics, working while going to school." Dolly smiled. "May had a lot to be proud of. And so do you."

"Well, thank you. But you didn't come here to talk about me, so..." Kaylie got to her feet and gestured behind her through the dining room. "Would you like to see the kitchen?"

"I'd love to," Dolly said as she stood. "And to hear more about your plans. Ten's told me some, but he doesn't have answers to half my questions."

Speaking of questions... "The day I put my ad in the *Courant,* Jessa bragged on your cooking. But she didn't tell me anything about your experience."

"That would be because I don't really have any," Dolly said, her laugh self-deprecating but not the least bit nervous. "Unless nearly four decades of family holidays and church socials and being in charge of monthly book club and bunco potlucks counts. I can provide plenty of references for my cooking skills, but I've never cooked in a commercial kitchen. I hope that's not a problem. I should've thought to ask about that before wasting your time, but Jessa did say this was going to be a small enterprise."

"It is going to be small, and you're not wasting my time. And I meant to have an application for you to fill out, but I've been running in circles all week."

They moved into the kitchen, Dolly walking around the island and taking it all in. "I love this kitchen so much. I was always envious of the pantry space May had. And the food stores. Lordy. The woman never met a fruit or vegetable she couldn't make into soup or jelly or just can to have on hand. Sometimes she put up enough to last to the next the growing season. And talk about a woman who could cook."

A rush of emotion caught Kaylie unawares. May had used food for so many things besides nourishment. She'd taught life lessons to the kids in her care every time they'd come into the kitchen, and done so without their realizing it. It was easy to look back now and see that, but at the time, all Kaylie knew was snack time meant sitting at the island and listening to May talk.

Clearing her throat, she said, "I have no imagination when it comes to casseroles. And I want to use as much fresh produce and local ingredients as I can."

"Oh, I can definitely help you with that. Whether you hire me or not. I belong to a farm co-op and can put you in touch with dairy farmers for your cheese and milk, all organic. The same with eggs and free-range chicken. Peggy Butters, who owns the bakery, has any herb you could possibly want. You have got to taste her rosemary-olive bread. Heaven. Absolute heaven."

Kaylie wondered... "Do you happen to know Indiana Keller?"

"Ten's sister? Well, yes, but I haven't heard her name in ages."

"I got the feeling they don't stay in touch."

"Ten's not in touch with any of his family to speak of. As far as I know, his parents are still in Round Rock. Indiana lives near Buda, I believe. I'm not sure anyone knows where Dakota is. Not even Manny."

"Manny?" Kaylie hadn't heard the name before.

"Manuel Balleza. He was Dakota's parole officer. He and Ten are still fairly close."

Parole officer. Obviously the events that had kept the two brothers from going into business together were matters of the law. She wondered why Ten hadn't told her. If it had slipped his mind or he'd thought it unimportant. Or if he'd hidden it from her. On purpose.

"Why did you ask about Indiana?" Dolly asked after Kaylie's silence had gone on too long to ignore.

"I'd like to put in a garden and be able to supply what I can of my own produce. I asked Ten if he knew of someone who I might hire to do the heavy lifting."

"And he mentioned his sister? That's really odd. She's the perfect choice. Don't get me wrong. But there are others in the area I would've expected him to think of first."

Kaylie wanted to ask the other woman why Ten's recommending his sister was such a surprise, but she realized the answer might lead to others she wanted, others that Ten might not want her to know. It was best if she asked him herself. And she would.

Not about his reasons for giving her his sister's name as a suitable prospect, but why he'd remained friends with his brother's PO. And why he hadn't told her Dakota was an ex-con. Especially when he knew her history with the law.

CHAPTER TWENTY-THREE

Leaving the parlor and heading for the back of the house and his truck, Ten found Kaylie standing in the dining room, one arm across her middle, the hand of the other in a fist tapping her chin. A row of artwork in stark white frames sat on the floor propped against the longest wall. He knew she'd decided to paint the eating areas to reflect the four seasons, and from what he could tell, the pictures she was staring at were season-based as well.

For the look of the café, she'd been consulting with an interior designer from Austin. He hadn't told her he'd heard gossip of hurt feelings from Maxine Mickels, the one and only local decorator, but the Austin designer had worked with Kaylie on the Sweet Spot, so it made sense for her to use someone she knew. Her renovations had already poured a ton of cash into the Hope Springs economy. The locals couldn't expect her to keep all her money in town.

"If you're trying to sneak up on me, you're not doing a very good job."

And here he'd thought he was doing a great one. "I was trying not to bother you. I wasn't sneaking."

"You're not bothering me. I'm bothering me." She sounded grumpy or pouty or both, and he was rethinking his decision to use the back door.

Now he was stuck. "How so?"

"I can't decide which of these pictures I like. Or if I like any of them."

He was not going to get into the middle of this. "I like all of them."

"You're no help."

"You're welcome," he said, fighting a grin as he crossed the room behind her, heading for the kitchen and escape. No good could come of his having an opinion.

"I interviewed Dolly yesterday."

"Yeah?" He stopped, shook his head, and shoved his hands to his hips. She obviously had something on her mind. He'd learned that about her. She didn't say anything without a very good reason. Even though sometimes it took her a while to get there. "How'd that go?"

"Fine. I'd forgotten that she was Rick Breeze's mother. I mean, the Rick I knew in school, not the Rick married to Jessa."

He walked closer. "That's not the first time you've mentioned forgetting something from your time here."

She shrugged. "A survival mechanism, I suppose."

"Is that your diagnosis or your therapist's?"

This time, her glare spoke for her.

"That was a joke, Kaylie."

"It wasn't a very funny one." And she obviously wasn't in a very funny mood. "I hardly need a professional to explain my issues. I'm well aware of how screwed up my life has been."

O…kay. "We're all screwed up one way or another. I think as long as we recognize it, we're doing okay."

"Dolly said something else," she said, deftly changing the subject.

Uh-oh. *Here we go.* "Should I be worried? Has Dolly been spilling all my dark and dirty secrets?"

"Is there a reason you didn't tell me your brother spent time in prison?"

She was still looking at the pictures when she asked, so he couldn't get anything from the look on her face. He came to stand beside her, stared down at what he thought was summer heatedly staring back. "Dolly told you that?"

"Inadvertently, so don't think she was gossiping about you."

"I don't see how else it could've come up."

"She mentioned Manny, and I asked who he was."

"Why would Manny come up in conversation?"

"It was innocent. I promise. We were talking about my plans for a garden. I asked if she knew your sister. The conversation progressed from there, the way conversations do." She waved a hand as if frustrated at the distraction, and turned to face him. "But that's not the point."

"Maybe not to you," he said, and moved his attention to the autumn leaves falling. "You're not the one being talked about behind your back. And this isn't the first time you've admitted doing it."

"Ten. Why didn't you tell me about Dakota?" she asked, backing away, arms crossed, defensive.

Was she throwing up a wall because he'd kissed her? Or because she didn't like him calling her on the gossip she denied? Either way, his answer remained the same, and he glanced to the picture where winter was coming. "I didn't tell you about Dakota because who he is and where he's been aren't relevant to this job."

"It's relevant to me."

"I don't see how," he said, glancing off spring as he turned to her.

Her expression was a mixture of things, but betrayal most of all. "After what I told you about my mother? Don't you think I might want to know?"

"Why? Your mother went to prison for drugs, and for putting you in danger. My brother went to prison for…" He paused, realizing that for the first time in his life he was going to admit to a much larger truth than the facts he'd stuck with all this time. Facts were easy. Facts got the job done. Facts came without emotions attached. "Dakota did something I should've done."

"I don't understand."

He did not want to talk about this. Not to anyone. Not to Kaylie at all. And yet the way she'd been so open about her own past, which far out-tragedied his, made sharing this particular event less a wrenching of his gut than he'd been bracing for.

He moved to the kitchen door, leaned the back of his head against the frame, and looked up at the dining room's ceiling, where the new tracks for the lighting ran east to west. "Dakota's two years older than me. I was a sophomore when he was a senior, and that year, over spring break, a friend of mine came and stayed with us."

"The friend you mentioned before. Who turned out to be not much of one."

"Yeah. Him. His parents had planned a family vacation, but he didn't want to go. My folks said he could spend the week at our house, and he took full advantage of every minute he was there."

"Advantage of your parents? Of you?" She paused. "Of your sister?"

He ground his jaw, thinking of Indiana, how he'd failed her, and how much better things had been since he'd decided to pay for that crime by removing himself from the family circle and making sure he never failed them again. "He tried. One night when my parents had gone out to some…saving the planet benefit rescue dinner thing. Indy fought him off, and used my dad's shotgun to force him out of the house."

He sensed Kaylie's eyes widening, heard her sharp intake of breath before she asked, "And you didn't know? Or hear?"

"Indy's room was downstairs. Mine was up. So was Dakota's. We were playing video games in his, and had the sound system maxed out. We couldn't hear anything but what was coming through the speakers."

"Did your sister tell you? After he was gone?"

He shook his head. "I finally realized Robby hadn't come back with the pizzas he'd gone to get out of the oven. I went downstairs, found Indiana sitting at the table with the gun. I ran back for Dakota, and she told us what had happened. Made us swear not to tell our folks."

"Why wouldn't she want them to know?"

"Our parents were…" Flakes? Crunchy hippies? Parents in name only? "Our mother would've flipped out, tried to calm everyone with lavender oil and magnets. Our father would've wanted to start a campaign to bring Robby to justice, rather than let a lawyer and the cops handle things quietly."

"So you and your brother agreed not to say anything. To anyone."

"We didn't really discuss it. Things just went down that way. I looked at Dakota, basically telling him it was up to him. He nodded, didn't say a word. Just dug his keys from his pocket and left the house."

"To hunt Robby down."

Ten nodded. "He found him at a local arcade. Went after him with the baseball bat he kept in his car. Then because he was eighteen and a legal adult and refused to tell the cops why he'd beaten Robby to a pulp, Dakota went to prison for aggravated assault."

Kaylie's throat worked as she swallowed. "I can see why Robby wouldn't admit what he'd done and risk charges, but why didn't Dakota say something?"

He pushed off the doorframe then, crossed his arms, and looked back at the paintings. "He was protecting Indy. He'd promised her. She didn't want anyone to know. He took the fall so she wouldn't have to finish school being *that* girl. The one Robby Hunt tried to rape."

"Oh, Ten." Her voice was soft, her hand at her mouth hiding most of it.

"He did his time. We stayed in touch. When he was paroled, I tried to get him to come work for me. I wanted to pick up where we'd left off. Keller Brothers Construction. He wasn't having it. Once he was free of Manny and had his life back, or most of it anyway, he left. I don't have a clue where he is. Haven't heard from him in years. Wouldn't know where to look for him."

"But you're still in contact with Manny, right? Would he know?"

"Dolly tell you that, too? About Manny?"

"She said the two of you had become friends."

"We did. We still are." No reason to hedge. "When Dakota wouldn't come work with me, I felt like I needed to do something. I don't know. It sounds dumb, but I thought if I couldn't help him, maybe I could help others. So Manny would send me parolees who had construction backgrounds, or had done similar manual labor. I'd take them on, give them a leg up with the jump back into the real world."

He saw the gears in her head grinding, wasn't surprised when she asked, "Do you have any ex-cons working for you now?"

He nodded.

"Will? Is that why he's been out of pocket for a while? Because he's been in prison?"

He nodded again.

"What did he do?"

This time he shook his head. "That's his story to share. Or not."

"I can't believe you didn't tell me any of this." She came for him then, pushed at his shoulder to turn him toward her. "Don't you think that you should have? Before you brought him into my house?"

Fear was in her face, and anger, disbelief. And the knife and the blood and her mother. "I don't hire violent criminals, Kaylie. And I don't hire junkies or dealers. I hire guys who found themselves on the wrong side of the law for doing the right thing."

"You think Dakota taking a baseball bat to another kid was the right thing? Because that sounds pretty violent to me."

"Indy was a minor. Robby was not. Dakota did what he thought he had to do. What I should've done."

"What if he'd killed him?" she asked, her voice rising.

"Then he'd still be in prison." *Where I should've been.*

"What if *you'd* killed him?"

"I wouldn't be standing here talking to you."

She buried her face in her hands, shook it off, her whole body shuddering. "I'm having trouble getting my head around any of this. I don't understand why you didn't call the cops."

"Calling the cops would've turned Indy's life upside down."

"And losing her brothers didn't? One going to prison, one just…going away?"

This time he spun on her, advancing, the actions of his past rising like a tsunami behind him. "You don't think I haven't thought about that a million times since? Wondering what we were thinking, taking matters into our own hands? We were kids who'd pretty much raised ourselves. We didn't have much of a bar to use to measure our behavior."

"But your parents—"

"Our parents weren't exactly candidates for any parenting awards." Funny how he and Kaylie had that in common, and yet nothing about their situations growing up was similar at all. "We loved them, they loved us, but they had trouble keeping even one foot in reality.

"They put a roof over our head, then spent most of their time out of the country, or at least out of town. They fed us and clothed us, then did the same for kids living in poverty all over the world. We had the material things we needed to thrive, but we didn't have the emotional guidance that probably would've kept Dakota out of prison, and helped Indy deal with what had happened…"

"And kept you at home," she finished for him because she knew him that well. "Do your parents still not know what happened?"

He shook his head. "Why tell them now? They're happy. Their oldest is out of prison. All three of their kids are now responsible adults. They can continue to pretend everything in their life is fine."

"Do they know where Dakota is?"

"I don't know."

"Because you don't talk to them. Or to your sister."

"I called Indy about your garden. Left her a message."

"Like I said." She gave him a knowing look. "I realize my aversion to anything that smacks of wrongdoing comes from a very personal place. I'm probably way too sensitive—"

"With good reason."

"Maybe. And I probably need to work on that. But in the meantime, please don't keep things from me. Not things like…this."

"Kaylie, listen to me. I'm never on a job long, and the parolees I hire aren't at any one location more than a few days. Will may be the exception, but that's the usual rule. I do what I can to help them fit in. I don't take them on jobs with kids, no matter what their crime, but that's my decision. And I clear everything through Manny first. They're good men who made bad choices. Hard for me to write them off for that when I would've done worse if my brother hadn't."

"Would you have? Really?"

Had he learned to hide that side of himself so well that she didn't think he had it in him? Or was she asking something else, wanting to know if he was someone she needed to fear, someone dangerous, someone unbalanced, like the woman who'd slit her wrists in front of her five-year-old daughter?

"Yeah. I would have. Dakota just got there first."

CHAPTER TWENTY-FOUR

By the time lunch rolled around on Friday, Kaylie had already interviewed four applicants for the cook's position. Each had potential, but none clicked with the same compatibility Dolly had. And none came close to measuring up to Mitch and his ideas. Talking to Dolly was as comfortable as talking to May. Talking to Mitch, well, he was a lot like Ten, though she would never tell either man that because of those very similar natures.

She was still digesting what Ten had told her about his brother, and she had yet to figure out why she was letting Dakota's history bother her. She didn't know him, and from what she'd learned, his incarceration had been a punishment he'd chosen to accept even before he'd delivered a retaliation he and Ten agreed was deserved.

Ten was right. His brother standing up for his sister's honor had nothing to do with his work as her contractor. And yet prison and an ex-con's time served always brought her back to her mother and her inability to settle her feelings about the past. She'd been in Hope Springs two weeks now, and she had yet to do anything that wasn't related to the conversion of the house into a café. Next week, she swore. No matter if the chasing down records meant a whole day spent away.

Hearing a car door slam, Kaylie looked out the kitchen window to see the fifth woman of the morning walking up her driveway. Except she didn't have the day's fifth appointment scheduled until later this afternoon. The woman, big sunglasses hiding much of her face, appeared to be close to Kaylie's age, and similarly sized, sharing the same taste in boots, T-shirts, and jeans, though where Kaylie drove a Jeep, this woman drove a low-slung sports car splattered with mud, and that careless contradiction had Kaylie smiling.

She put aside her paperwork, told Magoo to stay where he was stretched out on the kitchen floor, and met her visitor at the back door before she could knock. "Hi. Can I help you?"

"I'm looking for Kaylie Flynn," she said, and when she pushed her sunglasses to the top of her head, Kaylie knew who she was. "I'm Indiana Keller."

She had Ten's eyes, and the same caramel-brown hair, though hers was twisted into an unruly rooster tail against the back of her head. Kaylie wondered if Indiana knew her brother was here, if she would care. Wondered, too, what she'd thought about him getting in touch on behalf of someone else, not because they were family and close.

Though little about the reasons why made sense, he'd made it clear they weren't. Close, anyway. He couldn't do much about their being family. "I'm Kaylie. I'm so glad to meet you. But full disclosure in case you'd like to go somewhere else to talk, Tennessee's here, working upstairs on some wiring issues."

"Then I guess it's a good thing I need you to show me around outside, isn't it?" she asked, before a joyless smirk caught at her mouth. "I'm kidding. Ten's a man alone by choice. A ridiculous choice, if you ask me, but what do I know? I'm just the sister who managed to screw up both of her brothers' lives."

Wow. Kaylie wasn't sure what to say to that. She certainly hadn't expected such a forthright confession from a woman she didn't even know. But then she'd been doing a lot of confessing herself lately, hadn't she, sharing pieces of her life with strangers she now called friends. This house. Something about it was magic…

She took in Indy's expression, saw a flicker of anxiousness beneath the bravado. "Ten's told me a lot of what happened with the three of you. I hate that such a sorry person had this impact on all of your lives."

Indy's head bobbed, and this time her smile was true. "I like that he told you. I like it a lot. Almost as much as his finally, *finally*, calling me. When I heard his voice on my machine…" She let the sentence trail, reached up with a shaking hand to rub at her eyes. "I can't wait to grab him for an appropriately embarrassing public hug. Stupid, hardheaded man." She stopped and blew out a long breath. "But now I should shut up and pretend I'm a professional instead of dying to see my brother. Show me what I've come here to see."

Indy's honesty, her frankness…Kaylie liked the other woman already. Stepping outside, she led the way through the breezeway to the back side of the garage. "I need to get a landscaper out here to do something with the flower beds. Right now the whole place looks abandoned. Which I guess makes sense. It's been a while since anyone has lived here."

"Are you living here now?"

"I'm camping out. I didn't want to move all my things until the renovations were done. Easier to clean up the postconstruction mess when it's on the floor and not in the creases of my clothes."

"Good call. I had my living room painted recently, and even with drop cloths covering everything, I keep finding bits of the old stuff that was sanded off the door and window facings."

Kaylie feared even with her precautions, she'd be finding the same. "I appreciate you making the drive. Dolly Breeze told me you live in Buda?"

"I rent a small place in town," Indy said, pushing her sunglasses back in place. "But I spend most of my time at the greenhouse several miles away. I'm thinking now I need something like what you have here. A home and a business all in the same spot."

Kaylie laughed. "It may turn out to be a disaster, but since I always take my work home with me anyway..."

"This way you don't have to panic in the middle of the night if you've forgotten something in the office."

"Oh, I'll still panic, but I'll be able to run downstairs and hopefully find it," Kaylie said, stepping over a fallen limb. Yeah, she really needed to get in touch with a landscaper. She wondered if Ten knew someone... "Do you provide landscaping services, too? Or do you just supply produce? Ten didn't explain all of what you do, just that he'd talk to you about the garden."

"Nope. I'm strictly fruit and veggies. Even if I wanted to, I wouldn't have time to take on something new. But I can give you a half dozen names of businesses who'll do right by you."

"Thanks. Ten's been great to recommend local services, but I hate to go to him for everything."

A wry smile crept over Indiana's mouth. "Oh, I doubt he minds. He likes to help and, well, not to be jumping to conclusions, but you're exactly his type. Or what I last knew to be his type, anyway."

Warmth spread over Kaylie's chest, up her neck, along her hairline, prickling uncomfortably. Talking about Ten to Luna hadn't caused this sort of awkwardness, but then Ten wasn't Luna's brother. "He's made it a lot easier for me to navigate the local waters. Things have changed a lot since I lived here before. I'm still getting my sea legs, as it were."

"I didn't know you'd lived here before."

Meaning Ten hadn't talked about her to his sister. And that realization brought with it a frown. "What exactly did Ten say in the message he left you? I'm really hoping he didn't beg a favor because you're family. If you don't normally provide this sort of consultation—"

"Don't worry about it," Indy said, waving her off. "I have to meet a vendor in San Antonio this afternoon, so I'd already cleared my calendar today. As long as I'm not imposing on you by showing up unannounced, we're good."

That didn't exactly answer her question. "I don't even remember what imposing means. I've had people coming and going for two weeks now. Which is another reason I'm waiting to move in my things. I'm just using the bedroom and I'm rarely out of sight of my laptop…"

"Oops," Indy said, and Kaylie laughed.

"It's okay. No one's inside at the moment except for Ten. And probably Will. I haven't seen him, but they usually show up about the same time."

"Will, huh? Is he one of Ten's pet projects?"

Did that mean that even though she wasn't in contact with her brother, Indiana knew about the parolees? "He just came to work for him recently," she said but left it at that. She was still working through what she felt about Ten's outreach.

"Ignore me," Indy said a few moments later, blowing out a breath heavy with exasperation. "I shouldn't be digging for news on what's going on with him."

At the sound of Magoo's bark, Kaylie turned, needing a moment to get her bearings. He was racing toward her, obviously freed by someone going into or out of the house. She walked backward as he ran up to her, bending to snuggle his face before he bounded off again.

"I'm sorry Ten doesn't stay in touch," she finally said to Indiana.

"Love the dog," the other woman replied, then, after watching Magoo nose at the ground, added, "Ten seems to think keeping his distance is the best way to hold the family drama to a minimum, or so I'm assuming, since I honestly don't know what he thinks. But his telling you about what happened…I really want to take that as a sign that he's coming around and getting over this whole guilt-trip thing."

Kaylie didn't want to give the other woman false hope. Everything she'd learned about Ten said he was mired in self-blame. "He did tell me about Dakota, but he only volunteered the information after one of the women I interviewed for the cook's position let it slip."

"Or wanted you to know what you were getting into?"

"I suppose that could be the case, but it seemed very innocent."

"Oh, I'm sure it was. I'm the cynical Keller. You'll have to forgive me. Change of subject." She waved both arms in an arc. "How big is your lot, and how do you feel about taking out trees?"

Not any better than Ten had felt about taking out walls. "It's just over an acre, and I'd like to keep all the trees if I can."

"You need direct sunlight for a garden to do you any good."

That much she knew. "There's a big spot that was cleared years ago. It's where we played softball when I was a kid. It's a mess of brush right now, with some smaller saplings I don't mind getting rid of. But it's close to the wooded acreage next door, so the wildlife might be too much of a problem."

"We can take care of that with eco-friendly fencing and repellent, but you might want to consider a greenhouse. Show me the place and let's see what you have to work with."

The women spent the next thirty minutes walking the edge of Kaylie's lot, and oh, the memories. The trees she'd climbed. The cozy little hideaways where she'd sat with a book, or slept, or daydreamed, or made notes about the brownies she'd taken to school, what the kids liked, what they thought gross and disgusting.

The trees were older, some brittle and broken with weather and time, some stronger than ever, and taller. If she scaled to the top, what would the view be like now? Would she see more than downtown Hope Springs? The spire on the top of the Main Street Bank? The bell that rang from the top of Second Baptist's steeple?

Thinking about it now, she realized she hadn't heard the bell since she'd been back. Next time she was in town, she'd drive by and see if the building was still standing. And she'd ask Jessa or Dolly about Pastor Ross. If he'd been charged in the sex scandal that had driven him from town. Funny that she'd remember the gossip surrounding his downfall and so little else.

As they returned to the house, the conversation slowed, both women lost in thought, and then Indiana's steps slowed, too. Kaylie glanced over, wondering what Ten's sister was thinking. And then followed the direction of her gaze to where her brother stood, hands at his hips, watching the two of them make their way back to the house.

Ten was the first to speak. "You two have been gone long enough to get the garden planted and the first harvest in."

Indiana looked over at Kaylie. "In case you haven't run into this yet, Tennessee likes to keep an eye on things. Like clocks. And if you're not careful, every move you make."

"I've noticed," Kaylie said, cutting her gaze back to Ten. The smile he had for his sister had her melting.

"Good to see you, Indy," he said, stepping toward her.

She met him, an audible sob breaking in her throat, before he'd made it halfway. "You could've seen me anytime you wanted to, and you know that."

And then her arms were around his waist, his around her shoulders, his cheek resting on top of her head and his eyes closed. Kaylie held one arm tight to her midsection, pressed the fingers of her other hand to her mouth. Why in the world would he deny himself this...veritable joy as he held Indy and rocked her and finally picked her up and twirled her around?

Indy beat her fists on his back, laughing and then stumbling backward when he finally let her down. "Don't do that again," she said, trying to catch her breath. "And I don't mean the hug. I mean the silence and the absence. Enough is enough."

"We'll see," he said with a wink; then sobered, he added, "I'm sorry. I didn't know how to make up for what I let happen. The distance, not seeing you…it made it easier not to think about all of it. Except I've thought about it every day since."

"You didn't *let* anything happen, Ten. Stop beating yourself up. You have nothing to make up for, not to me or to Dakota. Well, nothing besides the distance thing." She reached up and rubbed at his shoulder. "I couldn't believe it when you called," she was saying as Kaylie finally pulled herself together and walked closer. "I heard your voice on the machine and screamed so loud Anne, the girl in the office who keeps me sane, came running. She caught her shoe on the edge of her floor mat and sprained her foot, and now she's on crutches, and I'm no longer sane. So you owe me."

"Remind me not to leave you a message again."

"You'd better leave me a message," she said, slapping playfully at his biceps. Then slapping again, this time harder, with a little bit less play. "You'd better leave me tons of them."

Ten gave her a lopsided grin, rubbing at his arm. "I guess this means I'll be seeing a lot of you from now on?"

"More than you were ready for."

"Did you decide on a spot for the garden?" he asked of Indy as he looked sheepishly at Kaylie.

"We did. I'm going to send out a crew to get started. Most likely it'll be next week. And since we're right on the edge of when I like to plant, we'll use starter plants rather than new seedlings."

"Girding your loins against summer?"

"Something like that," she said, her gaze drawn past Ten's shoulder as Will Bowman came around the edge of the house, his arms hooked over the bundle of two-by-fours he held at his neck. Kaylie decided it made him look like he was in stocks, a visual she found inexplicably troublesome knowing where he'd been the last few years.

Ten followed the direction of her gaze and motioned the other man over. "Indy, this is Will Bowman. Will, my sister, Indiana Keller."

"Mr. Bowman," Indy said, offering him her hand.

"Ms. Keller," he said, dropping the bundle to take it, giving off the same hungry vibes Kaylie had sensed the morning he'd met Luna.

She looked at Ten. Ten looked at her. She wasn't sure which of them was the first to roll their eyes.

CHAPTER TWENTY-FIVE

Meadows Land sprawled over eighty-five rolling acres on the outskirts of Hope Springs. Kaylie made the trip alone, having left Magoo at home, pouting. She knew her dog, his friendly temperament, his loyal, protective nature, but was well aware his size and his teeth often gave strangers pause.

And then there was the fact that he put his own ninety-pound spin on rambunctious, which she just couldn't see being compatible with kids in their Easter best. She promised him and herself she wouldn't be gone long. And with a reluctant, hangdog sigh, he'd curled into a ball and watched her go.

Spending Easter Sunday relaxing, instead of working, with people she didn't know wasn't exactly how she'd thought she'd wind up the month. In fact, spending it in Magoo's company would've been fine. And even though Indy Keller would have a crew out to put in the garden next week, Kaylie couldn't imagine a better use of the quiet day than clearing the easily managed detritus from the area, leaving the larger downed limbs and buried stumps to the pros.

Winton Wise had been the one to plant in her the seeds of self-sufficiency and independence. While May had nurtured her emotions, Winton had fed her practical nature, and the lessons had stuck. To this day she had no trouble changing the oil in her Jeep, or replacing a toilet's ball cock, or installing a garbage disposal in the kitchen sink. She paid others who were more efficient to do those things, but in a pinch, she was there.

She also knew football and baseball, though Winton had never understood how to follow a rugby scrum. They'd laughed about it one day when rewiring May's washing machine after a rat made its way into the mudroom and chewed through the cord. Dealing with the dead rodent had grossed out both of them, and they'd laughed about that, too, but only until May had tossed it into the yard and buried it, then ordered them to bleach every inch of the room.

Turning in at the sign to Meadows Land, Kaylie found herself swept gladly back in time. It had been forever since she'd thought of that day, the hilarity as May grumbled about having to be the one to change diapers and gut fish and now deal with a fried rat because Winton had no stomach for the squickier things in life.

Winton had apologized with a bouquet of sad wildflowers picked from the patch of yard set to be Kaylie's garden. She'd remembered the picnics and softball games when walking the patch with Indy, but she'd forgotten about the sweet pastels, the blues, pinks, and yellows that had brought a very naughty smile to May's face.

As she navigated the farm's long, narrow road, Kaylie lowered her window. She breathed in air musky with grazing sheep and tiny lambs bouncing on springy little legs, and thought about true love. Not the love of exotic hothouse blooms, but the day-to-day emotion binding two people. Love that saw past bouquets of thin wildflowers to the intent and the eyes behind. Strange thoughts to be having, she knew, but the last week of revelations shared with Luna and Ten, Dolly and Indiana, had left a strangeness in its wake.

Parking to one side of the paved circle in front of the house, she turned off the Jeep, pocketed her keys, and headed in the direction of the noise. It spilled from the yard behind the Meadowses' sprawling stucco ranch. Smoke rose from a barbecue pit built out of a fifty-five-gallon drum, and monstrous bowls of potato and macaroni salads, baked beans, and buttered corn on the cob weighed down picnic tables covered in red-and-white gingham cloths.

At least two dozen kids scampered around in a flurry of spit-shined shoes and yellow-dotted Swiss and seersucker shorts and bow ties and cowboy boots. Kaylie smiled at their contagious exuberance, wondering if she'd ever been that young…and, of course, she had. Just never free to run like the wind when the Easter bunny had still been real.

She was late in arriving, the festivities already under way. Men stood huddled in groups of three and four near the beer kegs and ice chests, no doubt solving the problems of business and politics and sports. Women clustered in similarly sized groups near the tables of food, no doubt solving the problems of children and men and home, after which, she mused, they would tackle business and politics, and some of them sports.

Her smile widening, she glanced toward the far side of the yard, where the pit was set up at a distance from the big patio, and caught Mitch Pepper's gaze. She lifted a hand in greeting. He returned her wave, hesitated, and then left his tongs on a table next to several foil-covered platters and walked across the grass to meet her.

"I wasn't sure you were going to make it," he said when he drew close, almost as if he'd been waiting for her.

"I was slow to get moving this morning," she admitted, shoving her hands in her pockets and breathing in the smell of smoke he brought with him. "It was so quiet around the house I didn't want to leave. And I promised Magoo I'd be back by the time he finished his morning nap, so I probably won't stay long."

"Guess it's been pretty noisy lately. The construction and all."

"The construction. The deliveries. The installations, both Internet *and* an alarm system," she said, getting an acknowledging nod in return. "I'm putting in a garden, too, so there's been that planning. Plus all the interviews I've been doing for the cook's position."

Mitch gave a snort at that. "Found anyone to fill the bill?"

"A couple of applicants look promising," she said without mentioning his name or Dolly's. "We'll see what happens."

Nodding absently, he looked off toward the children scrambling to get close to Luna for the start of the egg hunt, his expression drawn tight and grim. She thought of what Luna had told her, of Mitch returning from his military service to find his own family gone. She wondered if it was hard for him to be here, if he thought about the Easters he'd lost with his child. Wondered, too, if Luna had somehow filled that void in his life.

"She really enjoys this, doesn't she?" she asked, canting her head toward the other woman. Luna waved her arms, and the kids swarmed around as if she were the Pied Piper, or the Easter bunny itself.

"She does," Mitch said, his hands in his pockets as he mirrored Kaylie's pose. "So do her folks. For some reason, this is the holiday they make a big deal of."

"I think it's great. They've got something special. Not all families get a chance to share this kind of fun."

"Did you? I mean, with any of the people you stayed with?"

"In Hope Springs, I did. The Wises loved all holidays equally. But they did birthdays better than anything."

"You were with them a while, I think you said."

She nodded. "I celebrated eight years there. Balloons and hats and streamers and candles and the most amazing cakes. All of us kids were allowed to spend five dollars on each other, and then May and Winton gave us one gift. None of us expected much, but that one gift, knowing it was just for us…it was the most magical day."

When she looked up, Mitch was frowning. "You didn't get things at Christmas?"

"Sure, but usually things we could share. Games, puzzles, big boxes of crayons. Footballs and soccer balls. Stuff like that. This necklace," she said, reaching for the small gold heart she wore. "I got this when I was sixteen. I was a jock, so I never had a lot of time for girly things, and when I opened this teeny little box and found this inside, I started bawling. May thought I was disappointed, but it was the best gift anyone had ever given me."

"Sounds like you landed in a good place," Mitch said, clearing his throat. "Though it's too bad about Christmas. That things had to be shared."

Oh, but he had it wrong. "I didn't mind. Especially since I had a few years in other places where I didn't get anything at all. But then I also had the years with my parents and those gifts."

"Yeah?" He crossed his arms, gave her a curious look. "You remember back that far?"

"Some of it," she said, pushing aside the worst memories and digging for the best, the one she'd thought of the night she'd found Ten in her yard shining a flashlight over her shutters. "I got a big stuffed puppy once. All pink and sparkly. I was little, but I remember using it for a pillow, in bed, on the couch, the floor." She laughed then, thinking about trying to clean it with soap and a rag and rubbing it bald in one spot. "It got pretty dirty after a while."

Mitch looked away again, rubbing a hand over his neck. He'd been courteous. He hadn't really wanted to hear about her Christmases past. And she'd gone and made him uncomfortable by opening a vein and pouring herself out there the way she'd been doing so often these days. "I'm sorry. I don't know why I told you that."

He waved her off with a "Don't worry about it." But he didn't look at her as he said it. Instead, he pointed toward the barbecue pit and took a step in that direction. "I hate to cut out, but I've got to get back to the meat before Harry decides he knows how to cook. I'll, uh, see you soon, I guess."

She gave him a wave, then for no reason that made sense, mentally added, *You will if you're lucky.*

Weird, she mused, watching Mitch go, deciding he must think her a loon. Who in their right mind told a virtual stranger about a toy they'd slept with at four? Honestly, after the few short weeks she'd been in Hope Springs, she doubted her employees in Austin would recognize her. There she'd been all business, keeping her private life private. Here she was pouring out her life story to everyone she met.

Shaking off the strangeness of the moment, she turned back to Luna and saw Ten walking toward her, a sugar cookie frosted with thick yellow icing in his hand. Flutters of unexpected delight tickled her as she breathed in, then worked their way lower to coil in her belly and burn. They made the next breaths she took a struggle, yet she held on to them anyway, digging her nails into her palms, letting the flutters fill her.

Ten said nothing as he stopped beside her, watching with her as the kids lined up at Luna's command. She raised one hand overhead until all eyes were on her. Then, with a flourishing sweep of a scarf, she brought her arm down to signal the race was on, jumping and clapping as the kids nearly mowed her down.

Kaylie was pretty sure the other woman was having more fun than the children. She bumped her elbow against Ten's. Accidentally, she told herself, though she wasn't sure that was the case. "Did you ever hunt Easter eggs when you were a boy? You and your brother and sister?"

He grunted. "Is this your way of getting me to talk about them? Or to find out why I don't talk about them? Except, it seems, to you."

"Either. Both." It had actually been neither. She'd only been asking about eggs. But to know that he felt free to talk of them to her…her heart tumbled at that, the honor, the privilege. She felt flushed with a satisfaction almost too intimate to bear.

Ten popped the rest of the cookie into his mouth, talked around it. "How 'bout I just say yes? My brother and sister and I hunted Easter eggs as kids."

"That's it?" she asked, looking up.

Brows furrowed, he looked down. "What more do you need?"

She was hungry for everything about him. His hair in the sun. His eyes on hers. His tongue flicking out to catch cookie crumbs. His Adam's apple bobbing as he swallowed. "Did you hunt them at home? After Sunday school? With the other children in the neighborhood?"

"Again. All of the above," he said, and turned back to watch the kids, as if having changed his mind about sharing things about his family with her.

Fine, but he was the one who'd opened the door. "If you don't talk to your sister, why did you ask her to come by?"

"Because you wanted to put in a garden," he said, shrugging as if it was obvious. "And no one knows gardens like Indy."

He'd done it for her. Put what she needed for her café above his desire for the separation from his family that even Indy wasn't clear on—a thought that had her returning to Winton and May and the way each looked to the other's needs first.

"Thank you," she said, asking, "What?" when he responded with a weighty sigh.

"Nothing," he said, pinching the bridge of his nose. "You're welcome."

She reached for his arm, tugged him to face her. "No, it's not nothing. What's wrong?"

"Nothing's wrong." He puffed out his cheeks, then puffed out a gust of air. "I just don't want you to think it was a tit-for-tat thing. I'm not expecting anything in return."

"Anything?" Oh. "Like another kiss?"

"I'm not expecting another kiss, no."

But the way he said it… "Do you want to kiss me again?"

"Kaylie—"

She raised her chin and looked up at him, shading her eyes from the sun when it got in the way of her drinking him in…the way he ground his jaw, the stubble of beard he hadn't bothered to shave, the curl of hair that cupped his ear because it wasn't as long as the rest hanging over his collar.

She remembered the feel of it in her hands, the strands coarser than corn silk, and textured, like raffia, or hemp. She remembered his scent and caught hints of it now, spicy and fresh and of the woods. His mouth had been fresh, too, wet and warm and sure. And the discoveries she'd made of his body…

She used the hand at her eyes to push her hair from her face, catching back strands stuck on her lips where she'd slicked them with her tongue. "I want you to kiss me again," she said into the moment bubbled around them, close and fragile. "I want to kiss you."

He said nothing as he lifted one hand, hooking a flyaway lock of her hair behind her ear. She leaned into his touch, the bubble tightening, the holiday crowd and noise and watercolor eggs fading into the watercolor distance.

She nuzzled her cheek to his hand, and he swallowed hard, his throat working around the words caught there. "You're making it hard to say no."

"Then don't say it," she said, wondering what he had done to her, because she was not herself at all.

"Time and place, sweetheart," he finally said, as if it had taken him longer than he'd expected to find a response. "Do you think either is right?"

"No." But that didn't change any of what she was feeling.

"Later," he said softly, leaning closer to whisper, "Promise," against the shell of her ear. "You and me. No distractions."

Nodding, she moved away, because her hands were numb and her heart tumbling and her skin prickling with fever. "I'm going to go find Luna. She promised to show me how to work a loom."

"You're going to take up weaving now? On top of baking brownies and running a café?"

"No, but I have a toolbox needing to be packed and it's calling my name," she said, and his laughter echoed behind her all the way to the weaving shed.

CHAPTER TWENTY-SIX

As Luna Meadows was rushed by a three-foot-tall screaming mob, Mitch sought out his daughter where she stood beside Tennessee Keller, still wondering how he'd made it back to the barbecue pit without breaking down after hearing her talk about Christmas. He'd woken this morning, too little sleep under his belt and sweating bullets. It was Easter. The one day each year he couldn't get out of going to Meadows Land. And yet today, of all days, Meadows Land was the last place he wanted to be.

It had been bad enough seeing Kaylie at the Gristmill. What had Luna been thinking, bringing her to Gruene for lunch, knowing he liked to spend his breaks on the patio or the deck, visiting with diners, making sure the food was well received? Turning the corner and seeing them there…no way could he have retreated unnoticed. But he'd wanted nothing more than to drop his gear, wave a white flag, and run.

Stopping at their table when he'd told himself to stay away had killed him. He'd wanted to sit in the chair beside Kaylie, listen to her and Luna talk, learn what she liked, what she thought, what she wanted. Listen to her laugh. Soak up the things she shared with her friend that he would never know because he *could not see her.* He could…not…see her. The pain of that truth was worse than what he'd felt when he'd first found her gone.

But no matter all the reasons it was a particularly bad idea for him to be at Meadows Land today, he couldn't get out of it. Calling in sick to the barbecue would have Harry dropping his basting brush and coming after him, propping him up in front of the pit if he had to. So he'd made the trip over not long after dawn, put the meat in the marinade, and started the fire. Then he'd stood there, smoke making his eyes water, and watched for Kaylie, his palms clammy, his ulcers developing ulcers and burning hot pokers all the way to his spine.

He didn't feel a whole lot better now, having talked to her. Those few minutes…he'd wanted to pull her aside and ignore everyone around them and memorize every single word that came out of her mouth. And then she'd remembered the puppy. The cheap, stuffed arcade dog he'd won shooting at a target of a moving reindeer.

Of all things for her to remember, though, at least it was a good one and not the day he'd told her good-bye. He shook off his musings, focused on his daughter again. She wore boots and jeans, as always, though today with a pullover sweater. It was cashmere, he was certain, and pink, a color that sent him back in time…

…to patent shoes with bows on the toes and buckles too tiny for his tweaking fingers to fasten. Her socks had been the littlest things, the tops folded around her ankles, the lace on the back of one torn and dragging beneath her heel. He'd pulled out his pocketknife while she wasn't looking and sliced the loose strip away.

Her dress had been pink, too, like a tutu, the skirt made of some sort of mesh he thought looked like crap, but not Kaylie. She said it was what princesses wore. And ballerinas. And as much as she'd wanted a tiara, she'd had to settle for the ribbons Dawn had made out of a trashy lace teddy, tying up her hair like Madonna's in strips of pink and white.

He'd looked at her that day, her little fingers wrapped around the handle of a cheap plastic basket nearly as big as she was, everything she wore used or torn or an unwanted hand-me-down, the smile on her face brighter than all the bulbs in the apartment lamps shining at once, and he'd dropped to the floor full of shame.

What the hell kind of father let his daughter wear a torn-up teddy in her hair? So what if he couldn't afford to buy her a new dress. So what if the next year he'd cleaned up his act and bought her one with a big velvet bow in the back. He'd let her mother pull a piece of crap lingerie out from under the bed and tie pieces of it into his daughter's hair.

He turned away and walked from the pit to the fence edging the nearest pasture, a sob caught in the back of his throat and choking him. He didn't deserve to have her in his life. He didn't deserve anything good after the four years he'd wasted. He'd been given the greatest gift a man could wish for, and he'd been too stoned most of the time to even register the worship in the big green eyes looking up at him.

And yet, whether a higher being had answered his prayers, or if it was simply Luna being in the right place at the right time, Kaylie was here. His girl was here. And he couldn't turn his back on her again. Facing the direction he'd come, he watched from a distance as Kaylie leaned into Ten Keller, as the other man reached up to tuck her hair behind her ear.

Mitch may not have done right by her in the past, but he'd damn sure do it now—whether she knew he was looking out for her or not. And if that meant going to work for her, seeing her every day without her knowing who he was, so be it. He could cook for her café. He could wash her dishes, mop her floors, whatever he had to do. He was not letting her out of his sight again.

Ever.

He wasn't going to think about her discovering his deception until he had to. Being near her after all the years and all the damage and all she'd gone through because he'd left her behind was the only thing that mattered. And he was willing to take whatever risks that required.

~

"When you said farm," Will said, minutes after Luna had extricated herself from the egg hunt and led him to her weaving shed. He circled her loom on his way to the pegboard holding her rainbow of yarn. Red on one end. Violet on the other. A spectrum in between. "I was expecting corn and wheat fields. Not sheep."

Luna found that remarkably funny. "Did you think I used flax fibers or stalks of grain in my weaving?"

"Farming. Weaving. I wasn't associating the two." Will chose a skein of sapphire blue and flipped it in his hand like a juggling club. "And I didn't connect either with you being famous for your scarves."

That took her aback, but in a good way. "Thank you. I needed that."

"How so?"

She pulled the scarf she wore from around her neck, looped it around his. Circles woven in the colors of marshmallow Peeps peered back at her like wide, frightened eyes against his wolf black. "I'd obviously started believing in my own press."

Will laughed, lifted the scarf to his nose, and breathed in. "I didn't mean that as an insult. And I sure didn't mean to hurt your feelings. And this smells like you, only closer."

The wolf smelling her marshmallows did something sharp to her tummy. "You didn't hurt my feelings. Not at all. I forget Hope Springs is barely a pinpoint on the map."

"And everyone in this pinpoint knows you?"

"Obviously not," she said with a laugh. "But those who do are good to keep my secret."

"Which secret would that be? Your true identity?" He sniffed at her scarf again, his lashes like a sweep of feathers as he blinked. "The one you're keeping from a new friend? Or the one you hide with your hair?"

She was not going to get into this with him today. She was not going to let him draw a dark cloud over her fun. And yet she found herself asking, "What did you mean that my scarf smells like me, only closer? Wouldn't I smell the most like me?"

"Your work holds your blood, sweat, and tears."

"And that's what you smell."

"Call me…"

"Crazy?" she finished for him when he let the sentence trail. Except *crazy* wasn't the right word. He was intuitive, intelligent, the strangest being she'd ever met, and he frightened her more than a little bit, the way he saw her. Knew her.

She didn't want anyone being that close…which was exactly what Will was saying. He had looked at her work and learned the things weaving drew out of her. The stories she told in her work because she couldn't share them elsewhere. She swallowed, wondering about his magic.

He held her gaze, lifted a hand, and moved his thumb a scant quarter inch from his index finger. Then he smiled. Then he winked. And her heart flipped as if from a high wire. *Crazy* wasn't the right word. He was dangerous—to her, certainly, but she couldn't help but wonder if he was a danger to himself.

Returning the skein to the pegboard, he said, "Your father raises the sheep, shears them. Your mother spins their wool and dyes the yarn. And then you get to play. This is some kind of gig you've got going on."

"It's not play." But it was, wasn't it? She played and had fun and got paid ridiculous money for a job she sometimes went days without doing. "Okay, yes, I play. I work the hours I want. I work when the mood strikes. I answer to no one but myself. When I try to help around the house, I get shooed out. It's a wonderfully amazing life."

"And you keep waiting for it to fall down around you." He walked back to her loom, dragging a finger along the frame, bending to peer through the shed of yarn, raising only his gaze and snagging hers as he said, "No, wait. It already has, hasn't it?"

"What has what?" she asked, because she was caught by the look in his eyes, piercing, seeking, as if he'd found a crack and peered into places she no longer looked.

He straightened, picked up an empty boat shuttle, and turned it over and over in his hands without looking at it at all. "Your life. It's not the amazing wonder you say it is. Something happened and you're living a lie because of it."

"That's nonsense," she said, grabbing the shuttle and returning it to the shelf. He had no idea. She was not that transparent. Surely she was not that transparent. "You have secrets. I have secrets. That doesn't mean either of us is living a lie."

"What if I am?"

"Then you probably don't need to be working for Ten Keller. He's not big on dishonesty." She narrowed her gaze. "Besides, I don't think you could get away with living much of one. Not while you're on parole."

He gave her that with a nod that had his hair falling forward to his brow. "That leaves your secret, and I'm thinking it's more than keeping a father from his child."

Avoiding his gaze, she glanced toward the door, wondering how Mitch was faring, knowing who Kaylie was, unable to say anything. Had he stayed after seeing her? Or had he let Luna's father take over the cooking chores and driven away?

"It's Mitch, isn't it? The friend who came home from the service to find his daughter gone."

She pressed her lips tight, holding in the truth and then looking over to ask, "What makes you say that?"

"Seeing the two of you together. I'd say you're as close to him as you are to Harry, who's a great guy, by the way. I dig him."

Dig him? Really? "I'm not talking about this with you. It's done. We put the subject to bed a week ago."

"Any regrets?"

"About what? Inviting you here today?" She nodded, being honest. "A few."

He laughed, that wicked-sounding thing he did deep at the base of his throat. "Then I appreciate the tour. Since I won't be seeing you for a while."

"Are you finished working for Ten?" she asked, confused.

He shook his head. "I'm not ready to get mixed up in anything."

"Anything?" Arrogant, arrogant man. "You mean me."

"It's complicated. I'm complicated. I'm pretty sure you're more complicated than anyone I know."

It was probably for the best, Luna mused, as they walked toward the door, Will continuing to lift the scarf to his nose, rubbing against it. She wasn't sure how to react, or what to think about this man who, in the end, hadn't made a pass at her but still brought to mind hungry, devouring wolves.

"It's Kaylie. She's Mitch's daughter."

How in the world… "I didn't say that."

"You didn't have to."

She shook her head, not admitting, not denying. Not giving him the satisfaction, or herself a reason to keep him close. She turned away and opened the door to make her escape before it was too late.

"Hi," said Kaylie, stepping forward, her gaze going from Luna to Will and back. "Am I interrupting anything?"

Two Owls' Nutty Chocolate Brownie Buddy

a peanut walked into a chocolate bar

The Chocolate Part

½ cup unsalted butter
4 ounces semisweet chocolate
2 ounces unsweetened chocolate
⅔ cup flour
½ teaspoon baking powder
¼ teaspoon salt
¾ cup sugar
3 large eggs
2 teaspoons vanilla

The Peanut Butter Part

¼ cup melted butter
½ cup powdered sugar
¾ cup smooth peanut butter
½ teaspoon vanilla

Preheat oven to 325°F. Grease or spray with cooking oil and flour (or line with aluminum foil) an 8 x 8–inch baking dish.

The Chocolate Part

Melt the butter, the semisweet chocolate, and the unsweetened chocolate in a double boiler (or in a microwave), stirring often so as not to burn the chocolate. Cool. Whisk the sugar into the cooled chocolate mixture. Add the eggs one at a time, mixing until smooth, then stir in the vanilla. Sift the flour, the baking powder, and the salt into a bowl. Fold the flour mixture into the chocolate mixture.

The Peanut Butter Part

Stir all the ingredients together in a bowl until smooth.

Pour half the batter into the prepared pan. Drop the peanut butter mixture by tablespoons on top. Cover with the remaining batter. Swirl the peanut butter mixture into the batter with a dull knife.

Bake 40–45 minutes, or until an inserted tester comes out with a bit of batter attached. Cool completely before cutting.

CHAPTER TWENTY-SEVEN

Ten made his reluctant way from the third floor of Kaylie's house to the first, slowing his steps the closer he got and grimacing. While tearing into a kitchen wall this morning, he'd found one of the studs slightly damp. Knowing the only water she'd been using besides that on the ground floor was in her bathroom, he'd headed upstairs. And sure enough, he could hear dripping beneath her pedestal sink.

He didn't like being the bearer of bad news. Especially on top of Will discovering the termites not even two weeks ago. Thing was, until the pipes in the rest of the house were checked, he wouldn't know the full extent of the damage. It would be hard to give her an estimate of the delay or the repair cost. And figuring the best way to let her know that was stalling him further. But he was mostly stalling because of the way she'd looked at him yesterday when she'd asked him to kiss her. Her mouth, her eyes...it had taken willpower he didn't know he had not to tumble to the grass on his back and pull her on top of him—

"I can hear you not walking out there," she called, her voice carrying through the empty house as clearly as his footsteps. Or the lack thereof.

He found her in the front parlor, sheets of butcher paper on the floor cut and taped into squares. He liked this about Kaylie. No computer programs for this one. No mock-ups of how the tables she'd ordered would fit. She got down and dirty and figured things out for herself. "You decided on the four-tops for this room?"

"I think so. The space is smaller. Makes sense for seating smaller parties. Or not. But I think so," she said, nodding as if she'd won the argument with herself. Then shaking her head before nodding again. "What do you think?"

"I think it's fun to watch the two of you argue."

She glared at him, but did so while still looking at the floor. "What was with the not walking?"

He shoved his hands to his waist, weighing the words, not weighing them fast enough, obviously, because his delay earned him a "Spit it out."

"I've got some bad news."

"Then never mind. Don't spit it out."

"Okay," he said and turned for the kitchen.

She groaned. "Can it at least wait until I finish getting over and paying for the last bad news you brought me?"

"It could, but since it's more of the same, I thought you might want to take care of it all at once."

She pushed a hand from her forehead into her hair. "More termites?"

"Not bugs this time. Water."

"Water?" she asked, cocking her head as if she didn't understand. "You mean from the damage to the shutters and window casings? A leak where rain got in?"

He shook his head. "An inside wall. The third-floor bathroom. I doubt it would've showed up had you not been using it there the last couple of weeks."

She blew out a breath bursting with frustration. "So you're saying it's a good thing."

"No, I'm saying it'll be a whole lot easier to fix now than later."

"Then it's a bad thing."

"I don't think the one leak is that bad, but I won't be able to say until I get a plumber out here to go through the whole house."

"The whole house?"

He nodded. "The whole house. Unless you want to risk another leak from the second floor dripping onto your customers' heads while they're eating."

She groaned louder this time, pulled at more of her hair. "Fine. Get a plumber out here. The sooner the better."

"I know a guy—"

"Of course you do."

When he laughed, she gave him a look that had him thinking of backing away. Then had him thinking of pushing forward and slamming his mouth down on hers. She was beautiful. Angry beautiful. Aggravated beautiful. Just beautiful. "Would you rather I ran my finger down the yellow-page listings and had you yell stop?"

"No," she said, her gaze withering, her tone skating straight into sarcasm. "I'm very glad you know all the guys you do. Now call one of them so I'll know the money part of the damage. If I'm going to have to sell my soul, I'll need to start lining up buyers."

He thought she was probably exaggerating; she'd paid cash for the house, after all. But just in case… "We can slow things down, you know. If you need to. But I don't think it's all bad."

"How can it not be all bad? Do you know how soon Memorial Day weekend will be here? What if all the plumbing has to be replaced? How many walls will have to be torn apart, and floors and ceilings, and…I can't deal with this right now. I just can't."

"Yeah. You can. You'll figure out a way because that's what you do."

She looked up when he said it and asked, "What's that supposed to mean?"

That was more like it. "It was a compliment, sweetheart. You're better than anyone I know at that making-lemonade thing. I just hate having to be the bad guy."

"Ten, you're my contractor. You're not a bad guy—" She stopped herself, then swallowed, then added as if she'd been thinking about it for a while, "Yesterday at the farm proves that, don't you think?"

He liked that she had yesterday on her mind. It had certainly been on his. And now she'd brought it into the open, into the right time, the right place, and it was growing, heating, taking up space he needed to breathe. The tension in the room rose with the beat of her pulse in her throat, and beneath his skin, his blood raced.

"Say it." He nearly strangled getting it out.

She shook her head. A brief shudder. "I said it yesterday."

"Yesterday doesn't count. Say it now."

Her breathing as ragged as his, she smoothed a hand over her head to the band holding her ponytail, tugging it free and shaking out her hair. It wasn't the practiced sort of move he'd seen from celebrity starlets. It was just Kaylie being Kaylie, finding her balance, taking her time.

Or so he thought until she bit at her lip, and he realized the truth in her intent. She stepped on the paper on her way to him, but her gaze held his, unwavering. He left his hands at his hips; he wasn't sure he could've moved them with a crowbar. He was mesmerized, hypnotized, growing hard.

When she reached him, she wasn't fast to move, placing her palms against his chest. His heart pounded, and she smiled, and she liked it, and he liked that she did, liked her, too. Slowly, she flexed her fingers, as if testing the play in his muscles, then slid her hands to his shoulders, then behind his neck, then to the base of his skull, then her fingers found their way into his hair.

She lifted her gaze, met his, held it as she pulled him down for her kiss. At the first touch of her lips to his, he wrapped his arms around her waist and brought her into his body, sliding a boot between hers and pressing his thigh to the vee of hers. She wiggled closer, whimpered into his mouth, and he let go of his reserve, slanting his mouth over hers and going in search of her tongue.

She rubbed against him, a cat arching, purring, and played her tongue along his. He thrust, he stroked, he tempted her into his mouth, returned to love her in hers. He wanted her closer, he wanted more, and placed one hand between her shoulder blades, sliding the other lower, to the small of her back, then lower still, past her waistband to her bottom, cupping her, pulling her higher against him.

She squirmed in response, her hands slipping to his shoulders, kneading there, gouging there, digging in to hold him, and then she raised up onto her tiptoes as if she wanted him closer, wanted more, too. Wanted the same things he did, without clothing, without stopping, never coming apart until they both were racked and spent.

It was Magoo's bark signaling the arrival of visitors that came between them, echoing as it did through the near-empty house, bouncing off the walls and into their kiss like an explosive charge. Kaylie took a step back, stumbled, her eyes wide as she brought both of her hands to her mouth, pressing her fingers there, smiling behind them.

"Wow," she finally said. "That was nice."

Nice? *Nice?* Did that mean they were done here? That she'd gotten her kiss and that was it? Except when Magoo barked again he knew they were, at least for now. He also knew what they'd started was headed for a big finish. And with the house a veritable beehive these days, he'd been stupid to think anything about kissing her in the middle of it was right.

"It *was* nice," he said. "Next time it will be even nicer."

"If there is a next time," she replied, her tone and her smile both teasing as she reached for his biceps. Holding him, she pressed her lips quickly to his, then brushed by him and scampered off to answer her dog's insistent call. All Ten could do was shake his head, and hope they could get to a time and place that worked before the wait killed him.

CHAPTER TWENTY-EIGHT

At the sound of yet another truck door slamming, Kaylie decided to buy noise-canceling headphones. Or else sell the house and buy a Caribbean island. Not really, of course. She loved her house. And a Caribbean island would've been out of her price range even before she'd had the funds transferred to the Colemans.

A vacation in the Caribbean sounded really good right about now, though. Things would calm down once the construction was finished and Two Owls was open for business. Or at least the slamming doors would mean customers instead of delivery trucks and installers and locals stopping by to introduce themselves. Which she did not mind at all. Most of the time.

But today she was tired. She shouldn't be. She wasn't the one wielding power tools, the one hoisting sheets of drywall and buckets of paint up the driveway and through the house. She was making a lot of decisions, a lot of trips up and down the stairs. She was visiting the clearing at the back of her lot where her garden would go. She was the one throwing the ball for Magoo, at least until he lost interest and left it for her to retrieve, but that was about it.

Still, the last few weeks of very little sleep were catching up with her, and today was the first day since moving to Hope Springs she felt she could take time for a nap. She wanted to close her eyes and dream about yesterday's kiss with Ten. But the knock on the back door followed by the squeaky opening of the screen meant she'd have to put both on hold. She needed to see who'd come a-callin'.

Uh, yeah. Full-on sleep deprivation here.

"Hello?"

Hmm, she mused, rubbing at one eye. That sounded like Mitch Pepper. "In here," she said, raising a hand and waving over the top of the wingback chair.

"Kaylie? Am I interrupting?"

"Nothing but a nap." When Mitch came into her field of vision, she gestured toward the other chair. Ten's chair. "Sit, please."

"I didn't mean to wake you," he said, perching on the edge of the seat.

"I wasn't really asleep. Just…daydreaming."

"Ah, fake napping. I do it a lot. Usually to Doyle Bramhall's *Jellycream* album. Then it's back to business."

"I might have to try that. Though I can't imagine anything called jelly cream being good for me."

He thought a minute, his mouth twisted. "Give Neko Case a try. *Middle Cyclone.* I think it would be a good fit. Or Amos Lee's *Mission Bell.*"

"Thanks. I will." She curled her legs to the side in the chair. "It was good to see you this weekend. I'm sorry we didn't have more time to talk."

"And I'm sorry I don't have more time today. I've got to get to work. But I was wondering..." He stopped, looked down at his laced hands.

"Yes?"

"If you haven't hired anyone yet, and are still taking applications, I'd like to throw my name in the hat for the cook's position. I haven't talked to the Gristmill yet about reducing my hours there, but if you want me, I imagine I can work something out."

For several days now she'd been turning over an idea in her mind, and now that he was here... "How would you feel about sharing the kitchen duties?"

"Sharing?" He blinked, scratching the back of his head. "The cooking or the cleaning? All of it?"

"All of it," she said, hoping Dolly would agree, because she really thought this could work. "Whatever the two of you think best."

"I'm always up for a division of labor. Tell me more."

Kaylie sat straighter, leaned toward him. "The woman I've been most interested in doesn't have professional experience, but comes with amazing personal references. Everyone I talked to said they'd been begging her for years to open a restaurant or start a catering business."

Mitch squared one leg over the opposite knee. "What's she doing now?"

"She actually works for Ten Keller. My contractor. In his front office. And it turns out I went to school with her son. Their last name is Breeze, and at the time mine was Bridges, so we were always lined up together."

Mitch looked back at his hands. "She's a friend of yours, then."

"I didn't remember her until I saw her again, but then that's not a surprise."

"Why not?"

She didn't want to get into the reasons why, but… "I've forgotten a lot of things about my time here. Not in the house, or with my foster family. But other things. Kids I went to school with."

"You remembered getting a stuffed animal for Christmas when you were a kid," he said, his voice so soft she almost couldn't hear.

"I know. And that surprised me." Probably as much as she'd surprised him sharing the memory. "Dolly, that's the woman's name, Dolly Breeze, she had to remind me about a school play I was in with her son."

"Oh yeah?"

Something in the way he asked, as if he wasn't making conversation but truly wanted to know, had her saying more. Again. "It was seventh grade. Our drama class put on a production of *A Christmas Carol.* Now that I *have* remembered it, I can say it was pretty bad."

"Hey, it was seventh grade. I don't think much about the seventh-grade experience is good for anyone."

"That's probably true. But I really think you'd like Dolly."

"If she keeps your contractor on his toes, then you're probably right," he said, his mouth pulling into a smirk.

What was it with these two men? "Will you think about it?"

"I don't need to think about it." He slapped both palms to his thighs. "I'm in."

"Great," she said, more excited than ever to get the menu settled. "I'll give her a call and see what she thinks. If she's on board, I'll see about setting up a time for all three of us to get together."

"Sounds like a plan," he said, getting to his feet.

"I'll be in touch, then," she said from her chair, offering him her hand.

He gave it a quick shake, held it for a second longer, and then let go and offered her a single slicing wave in parting. Kaylie listened as his steps carried him through the kitchen, listened to the bang of the screen door as it slammed. She closed her eyes, waiting for the next interruption, and was still waiting when she fell fast asleep.

CHAPTER TWENTY-NINE

"Where would I find your newspaper archives? I'm looking specifically for the *Austin American-Statesman* from twenty-three years ago?" There, Kaylie mused. She'd said it. Put into words the reality of what she'd returned to Hope Springs to do. The only thing left to figure out was why irritation rather than anticipation had hopped onboard for the ride.

For some inexplicable reason, she'd made up her mind after yesterday's nap that today was the day to visit the small town's even smaller library. Whether due to the remains of a fleeting dream, or having Dolly remind her of seventh grade, or the conversation with Mitch where she'd remembered a childhood Christmas, she'd decided it was time—even if she'd lost what had once been a keen interest in her life's missing parts.

As bits and pieces of those years had continued to return, she'd found the pull to look into the past diminished. Her present was wonderful. Her future promising. Turning around and walking in the other direction seemed such a wrong path to take. For so long she'd thought learning about her parents would give her strength to close the door on her old life and open the one into the new. But she was finding that wasn't the case at all.

She rarely thought of them these days. Rarely wondered where her mother had ended up, where her father had gone, if either of them had been curious about her, had ever tried to find her. Had even cared what had happened to her after the state had taken her away. If everything was as perfect as it felt, what good would it do her to dredge up these things? She was happy. *She was happy.* She didn't need to know; why had she ever thought otherwise?

The librarian was saying something, leading her to a quiet corner near the rear of the small room, but all Kaylie could hear was May Wise's voice. *Don't look to where you've come from. Look to where you're going.* Clinging desperately to those words, she swiped at the hair sticking damply to her forehead, and focused on the woman in front of her, giving Kaylie directions as they walked.

"…on microfilm. The spools are in the cabinet next to the table, and the instructions for loading them into the viewer are on the poster above it. It's fairly self-explanatory, but if you need any help at all, I'll be at the desk. Just give a wave. I'm not exactly overwhelmed, as you can see."

"Thanks very much. I think I can manage, but I'll let you know if it turns out otherwise."

"Not a problem," said the other woman, leaving Kaylie alone with her past. She did not want to be here. She wanted to be at Two Owls, seeing how the repairs to the plumbing were going. She wanted to be talking casseroles with Dolly and Mitch. She wanted to be walking through her yard with Ten, throwing the ball for Magoo. But more than anything in this moment she wanted May Wise at her side.

Since that was the one thing she couldn't have, however, and since she was already here, she pulled out the chair and sat. Finding the spool with the right range of dates, she loaded it and rolled it forward, advancing from page to page, scanning the headlines, smiling at the ads for sunglasses, cringing at the models' hair, rolling her eyes at the poster for *Young Guns II.* Boy, had those guys changed.

She spent at least an hour getting nowhere, or reading too much about the year she'd turned five. And then she stopped reading and stared at the image in front of her taking up a quarter page of the local news. The crime-scene photo...Why did it look so familiar? Frowning, she leaned closer, reading the print beneath the headline, knowing she'd seen it before...or someone had shown it to her before. This wasn't new. It was...

Dear God. The story! It was *her* story! *Her* life. The headline, the copy, the image showing the yellow tape—grainy in old black and white—across the door to the apartment where she'd lived. This was her past, her mother being wheeled out on a gurney, one bandaged wrist handcuffed to the metal frame. She'd seen this all from another view. From above, on the apartment staircase...*There!* That was her wrapped up in a blanket and sitting in Ernest Flynn's lap!

Her heart like a balloon swelling at the base of her throat, she read the reporter's words and knew this wasn't the first time she had. When had she seen this before? Where? Why hadn't she remembered any of this article? Why had she blocked out the very things she'd come to Hope Springs to find?

She printed the page and dug in her wallet for change to pay for the copy. As she made her way to the front desk, she wondered if this was how it was always going to be, bits and pieces she'd have to sift through for details that might lead her to the truth. Was it worth knowing if the discovery was dragged out over weeks or months, even years? When all of it, the whole shebang, might already be locked in the back of her mind?

She hated this...this...defense mechanism, or whatever it was. This ridiculous memory lapse her subconscious thought it was protecting her with. She didn't need protection. Ten had told her she was better than anyone he knew at making lemonade when life served up lemons, and he was right. She'd dealt with everything her twenty-eight years had thrown her way. Foster homes, course finals, three a.m. doughnuts, termites.

All of those things she'd had no choice in, and she'd survived with only a few hard knocks. Looking back instead of moving forward...this she could choose. As she made her way to the farthest of the six parking spots and her Jeep, she folded the sheet of paper and stuffed it into her purse. Her head pounding, her stomach in knots, she chose, in this moment, the only thing she could.

To go home.

~

The next night, Kaylie lined up her ingredients on the kitchen island, found her measuring cups and spoons, a saucepan and glass bowl large enough to use as a double boiler, and her favorite aluminum baking pan. The utensils and cookware she'd brought with her from Austin last week. The food items she'd bought this morning at Tandy's Grocery.

She hadn't planned to bake brownies until her new kitchen was done, but she was itchy with the wait. Her baking muscles felt flabby, like those of a runner kept too long from the trails, or a cyclist grounded, a swimmer landlocked. A bit of an exaggeration, she knew, but it had been weeks and she was going, well, stir-crazy.

She turned on the oven, then secured her favorite recipe to her magnetic stand, doubting she'd look at it again but wanting it there anyway. She knew this recipe by heart. She didn't need the lined steno sheet May had written it on, the ink from her blue ballpoint faded into the paper along with drops of vanilla and butter smears and dribbles of melted chocolate wiped clean. This one was embedded in Kaylie's heart as well as her head.

Peeling away the paper from the unsalted butter, she thought back to the first time she'd watched May turn what had seemed like unrelated food items into the most glorious dessert she'd ever put in her mouth. The chocolate had been rich and sweet but not too much of either, the texture more cakelike than a gooey fudge, though she'd grown to appreciate both.

May had asked her if she wanted frosting, and she couldn't imagine adding anything more to what her young palate, which had known only Hostess and Little Debbie snacks, thought was perfection. Over time, she'd learned a little something extra was often a very good thing. But only a little. Too much meant ruin. And she feared her feelings for Tennessee Keller had become too much.

She added the chocolate to the butter in the double boiler, and while those melted, she measured sugar into a bowl. The salt and vanilla and flour she put into miniramekins, and the eggs she set in a saucer that had enough of a lip to keep them from rolling into the sink. Rather than use an electric mixer, she chose her favorite wooden spoon. It had been May's favorite wooden spoon first, and it had somehow survived the years and the change in ownership with no more than a chip in the handle.

When she'd sought out a general contractor, she'd never thought she'd get more in the bargain, but she was pretty sure Tennessee Keller was fast becoming her very best friend. She'd never had a best friend, though most of her closest ones had been male. She wasn't sure why, except she didn't think that she had ever made a very good girl. Her hair was usually in a net, or beneath a white chef's hat, any attempt at style lost to her trade. She bought clothes that would last, and often paid more because of that, so she rarely needed—or had time—to shop, no matter how much she enjoyed it.

Makeup was nothing but mascara, powder blush, and lip gloss, if that. Baking was a sweaty business, sometimes a messy business, and her sensitive skin fared better when bare. And yet she found herself spending more time in front of the mirror these days, wondering if Ten liked what he saw. She supposed he did; he'd kissed her and made sure she knew he meant it. But what she was more interested in was why, when she was honestly quite plain.

Ten, on the other hand, was anything but. He was...a surprise. His body beautifully built, his hips lean, his stomach flat, his legs thick but not bulky with muscle. He wore his jeans with purpose, the denim modestly covering his most intimate parts, while conversely showing them off. She liked that, the hint of sexuality she could choose to ignore if she wanted. She didn't. She indulged. The way she was indulging now, breathing in the rich scent of chocolate as she stirred the batter until glossy.

As much as she'd had the urge to flex her baking muscles, she'd also needed the emotional release baking never failed to provide. Yesterday's library visit had left her unable to sleep last night. She'd tossed and turned, disturbing Magoo as she'd pictured her life laid out in print for anyone to see.

They'd always been there, those newspaper archives, the rest of the public records. The years she'd lived with Winton and May…How many people had been curious enough to hunt for the truth? The Wises wouldn't have talked. She knew that. But had any of their friends heard gossip and felt compelled to share what they'd learned?

The worst part was, forcing herself to dig for information—in the library as well as previously on the Internet—had been next to fruitless. In all her searches, she'd turned up nothing on Dawn Bridges other than the date of her release. Where had she gone after prison? Where had she been since? Kaylie didn't want the expense of a private investigator, though hiring one might be her only option in the end. If she decided to go forward with her search. And that was a decision she was seriously rethinking.

Since losing May Wise, Kaylie had been obsessed with her parents—which made no sense at all. They were nothing to her. They never had been. Why in the world had she thought finding them mattered? She'd upended her life over a ridiculous fixation…yet had absolutely no regrets. Her return to Hope Springs had been the best move she could ever have made. She was happier than she'd been in years. She was blossoming. She was finding herself. She was falling in love.

Were all these things possible because she was finally, without even realizing it, listening to May? Maybe what she was looking for all along was more of what the Wises had given her. A home and a family. One filled with people she cared for, not people with whom she shared blood. Wasn't that what she was finding with Luna and Ten? With Dolly and Mitch and Will? With Indiana? It was sobering, truly, to realize that a search she should never have made in the first place had given her exactly what she'd been looking for all along.

Two Owls' Chocolate Brownie on the Brain

the brownie to cure all ills

4 ounces unsweetened chocolate
4 ounces unsalted butter
1 teaspoon vanilla
1¼ cups sugar
⅛ teaspoon salt
2 large eggs
½ cup flour
½ cup cacao nibs
½ cup semisweet chocolate chips
½ cup chopped pecans

Preheat oven to 400°F. Grease or spray with cooking oil and flour (or line with aluminum foil) an 8 x 8–inch baking dish.

Melt the chocolate with the butter in a double boiler (or in a microwave), stirring often so as not to burn the chocolate. Add in the vanilla, the sugar, and the salt. Whisk in the eggs, one at a time. Mix in the flour, blending until the batter is smooth. Stir in the chocolate chips, the cacao nibs, and the nuts.

Pour the batter into the prepared baking pan. Bake for 18–20 minutes, or until an inserted tester comes out with a bit of batter attached. Cool completely before cutting.

CHAPTER THIRTY

Kaylie! You've got visitors!"

As if that was anything new? She closed her laptop, setting it and her legal pad in the dining room's wingback chair. It was where she did all of her business these days, and strangely enough she'd grown used to the inconvenience. Eventually she'd set up an office on the second floor, but for now she liked being in the thick of things.

With the major construction due for completion this weekend, the truck with the café's furniture would arrive on Monday. The curtains and blinds were scheduled to be installed the following day. The middle of next week, the deliveries of the remaining supplies for Two Owls would begin. Meaning this had to be about the garden. *Finally!* Not that it had been long since she and Indiana Keller had talked, but she was as anxious to get her starter plants in as she was to open the café in just over six weeks.

"Thanks, Will," she said as she reached the kitchen. She wouldn't be able to use her own produce until later in the year, but the garden going in where she'd once played softball and eaten thick slices of ham on even thicker slices of May's bread, and where spindly watercolor wildflowers had grown, made her so happy she wanted to spit or skip rope or something.

But she didn't do any of that since Will was still there, biting into the brownie he'd snitched from the plate on the kitchen island. It must've been the fifth he'd eaten after arriving this morning to discover she'd baked late last night. "No, *thank you.*"

She loved that her brownies were a hit with her contractor and his ex-con crew of one. And why she'd thought that about Will now when she hadn't for days had her wondering when his being on parole had ceased to matter. Because it had. And she was glad.

She was very, very glad. "You're welcome, but if you get sick while three stories up on the ladder, give a warning to those of us below."

"Yes, ma'am," he said, his laugh a wicked howl that might've sent shivers down her spine if she wasn't getting her shivers elsewhere these days.

And that had her wondering about seeing Will with Luna at Easter. Something had been going on when she'd interrupted the two of them in the weaving shed. Something dark and intense, something private.

She'd wanted to ask Luna about it after Will had left, but intuition told her to stay quiet. And though she'd thoroughly enjoyed hearing Luna talk about weaving and watching her demonstrate the workings of her loom, the other woman's distraction had been obvious, her smile an afterthought, her gaze drifting to the door.

Kaylie, shaking off her own distraction, had just grabbed a bottle of water to head out when Ten stuck his head inside. "Your gardening bunch is here."

"I know. Will just told me."

"Oh," he said, coming in even though it was obvious she was going out. But now that he was here and she had Will on her mind…

"You haven't said much about how Will's working out."

"Fine. Not a problem." He glanced out the window as if checking to see that the other man was back at work. "I could see hiring him on full-time."

Well, that had to be good. "I didn't think you had full-time employees?"

"I don't, but even if I did, Will wouldn't stay."

"How do you know if you haven't asked him?"

"Because I know him," he said, and looked down at her. "I've known a lot of men like him. He's the loner he wants you to think. He's only here because he has to be."

There was more to it than that. Not why Will wouldn't stay, but why Ten was so sure. The connection wasn't that hard to make. "He reminds you of your brother, doesn't he?"

Ten shrugged, reached for his fifth brownie, too, and said nothing as he bit it in half.

"C'mon," she said, rolling her eyes as she turned and shoved him toward the door. "Walk with me to the garden plot. Make sure I don't forget anything."

"These are Indy's employees. *She* won't have forgotten anything."

"Walk with me anyway. Tell me what's bugging you about Will."

He chewed as they walked, stopping to dust off his hands once he'd finished the treat. "By the way? I'm pretty sure you said the first batch of brownies in the new house was for me, not for public consumption."

Oops. "Did you not just eat five?"

"Maybe, but that's not the point."

She reached up and brushed crumbs from the side of his mouth. "I'd had a bad day. I needed to bake. And I said new kitchen, not new house. I baked these in the old oven, so not the same thing."

"Why was yesterday bad?" he asked, frowning down at her, his tongue darting out to catch a crumb she'd missed.

Of course that was the part he would pick up on. "I don't want to talk about it," she said and started walking again. And it wasn't yesterday that had been bad.

Yesterday had been wonderful, measuring, stirring, dipping her finger into the batter the way she'd done as a girl and licking away her fill of chocolate. The sugar had made her that much more sleepy, but it was a good sleepy. Especially compared to the insomnia she blamed on the microfilmed images she wanted to wipe from her mind.

Except they'd been there all along, those images. Seen from the other side of the camera, and with five-year-old eyes. What she couldn't figure out, wasn't sure she wanted to figure out, was why they'd seemed so familiar, printed on the page.

Stopping on the far side of the garden plot, Kaylie watched the IJK Gardens forklift lower a pallet of starter plants to the ground. The three other members of Indy's crew consulted a clipboard of instructions before setting up surveying equipment to mark the plot.

Ten's sister obviously ran a tight ship. No haphazardly hoed rows for Indiana. Like brother, like sister? The attention to detail, the controlling, hands-on nature. Was this how the tragedy in the past had taught them to cope with life? Had it done the same to Dakota?

Or had his time behind bars made him a different man? Kaylie cut her gaze up to Ten's. "I promise to make you your own batch of brownies. But I want to know why Will reminds you of Dakota. And, no, those two things are not related. They just both happen to be on my mind."

He rocked back on his heels, arms crossed. "So you get to skate on answering my question, but I have to answer yours?"

"I asked mine first."

He blew out a huffing breath. "It's probably not what you're thinking anyway. About Will."

She didn't know what she was thinking, just that there'd been something new in Ten's eyes when the other man was around, and she was pretty sure she could time the change to Indiana's reappearance in her brother's life. "You miss him. Dakota."

"Yeah, but that's not really it either. I mean, I don't look at Will and want him to be my brother or anything."

"You wonder what he did to screw up his life?"

"Something like that. Manny doesn't tell me and I don't ask. Some of the guys he sends over will end up talking about it over a beer or something, but that's up to them. If they need to unload, I'll listen. I don't expect it, and I don't go digging. It just happens sometimes."

"But not with Will."

"Nope."

"And not with Dakota," she said, because she knew his brother hadn't confided in him after his release.

He turned then and walked away, leaving the garden behind for the edge of the newly cleared brush marking the back of her lot. She followed, wondering if he was distancing himself from someone or something…the job and Will, the garden and his sister, the house. Her.

"Manny asked me a couple of weeks ago if it was getting to be too much, me giving these guys a job when they get out. He accused me of doing it out of guilt rather than some greater good or charitable whatever." He dropped his gaze to the ground and kicked at a big rock buried there. "I think he might be right."

That he was driven by guilt didn't surprise her. That he'd been able to admit it…that wasn't something she'd expected. "Because of Dakota."

"It's always been because of Dakota. I mean, it's my fault he went to prison—"

"It's not your fault, Ten—"

"Yeah, Kaylie. It is. You weren't there that night. I saw the look Indy gave him, her eyes all big and scared and mad at the same time. Pleading. And then he looked at me, and I knew what he was going to do, and when I nodded…" He brought his boot down on top of the rock, shoved at it with his heel. "Dakota was a power hitter. He was going to play ball at UT. In his hands, that bat was a deadly weapon."

She wrapped her arms around herself and fought off a shiver before asking the one thing she never had. "How bad was Robby hurt?"

"A guy he was with warned him Dakota was coming at him. He ducked, I guess. Kinda swerved. The bat glanced off his jaw, broke it. Broke his shoulder on the second swing. It was bad enough, but it wasn't life-threatening. Dakota was only charged with assault, not attempted murder."

Even though he'd gone after the other boy with murder on his mind. "That had to have been a relief."

His head came up, his eyes angry. "My brother was going to prison because I hadn't stopped him from trying to kill the prick who went after our sister with rape on his mind. I failed both of them. Dakota *and* Indy. I'm not sure what part of that is supposed to have been a relief."

Her first inclination was to argue. He was being hard-headed, shouldering blame that wasn't his. But then the bigger picture came into focus. And his words were like a truckload of bricks falling on top of her head. "Then tell me something. How is cutting yourself out of their lives supposed to protect them from you failing them again?"

"That's not what I'm doing. I'm just…" He let the sentence trail, finally dislodging the rock he'd been using to vent his frustration. "I shouldn't have let Robby go downstairs when I knew Indy was there by herself. And I shouldn't have let Dakota go after him alone. My brother went to prison, and my sister had to live with the memory of that asshole's hands grabbing at her. I got hit with…nothing. I didn't have to serve time. I never had to look over my shoulder to see if Robby was coming. I just went back to life as usual."

He thought he deserved to be punished. He didn't think he deserved to have his siblings' forgiveness. Why hadn't she seen it before? Sadness swept through her, powerfully deep. Did he not understand there was nothing for them to forgive? That he was the one who was going to have to forgive himself? Doing that after all this time living under a cloud of guilt…

There was nothing more she could say, and yet she had to ask. "Don't you think staying in touch, being there for them now, would be a better plan? Or at least for Indy? I saw the two of you together. She's desperate to make up for lost time. She's missed you terribly."

"She tell you that?" When Kaylie nodded, he bit off a sharp curse, stepped back, and kicked violently at the rock, sending it what seemed like halfway across the yard. "I let her down in a massively huge way. Why would she think she could count on me now?" And with that, he turned and walked away, never giving her a chance to respond.

She wanted to beg him to think about what his misplaced guilt had cost him, but she knew instinctively he'd been aware of it for years. And so she watched him go, his shoulders tight, his gaze cast down, his steps having no purpose, as if only carrying him back to the house because they knew of no place else to go.

~

The next ten days brought a flurry of activity—Kaylie's prep work for arranging her belongings in her living quarters, Dolly and Mitch brainstorming menus and recipes and the balance of place settings, Will and Ten finishing up the detail work of outlets and fixtures, and best of all, deliveries for the café.

Tables and linens and chairs. The Nottingham lace panels and natural wood blinds. Chandeliers and baker's racks. Hutches and sideboards and buffets. The commercial appliances for the new kitchen. The braziers and serving dishes and flatware. And then there was the ongoing traffic to the garden.

A moving crew had brought her biggest pieces from Austin, storing everything but her bed on the second floor for her to deal with later. She would need to make one last trip to her condo, pick up the boxes of the most personal items she wanted to see safely to the new house herself. She would drop her keys at the complex's office, and make a final drive by the Sweet Spot, and that would be it.

Austin in her rearview mirror.

Hope Springs and the rest of her life ahead.

CHAPTER THIRTY-ONE

How's the search for your parents going?" Ten asked from where he stood half-wedged behind the new commercial fridge.

Kaylie blinked, surprised by the question. Today was Tuesday. Since Friday a week ago, when Ten had insisted he'd failed his siblings, their conversations had been shallow—about the house, the new flower beds, the space for customer parking, her garden, her brownies, her dog. They'd both been busy, surrounded by other people, crossing paths with hurried smiles and quick hellos. More than one night he'd gone home while she was tied up fine-tuning her first quarter's food and service details with Dolly and Mitch. The longing remained, pulling at them both, but she was pretty sure Ten was still waging a war with the things he'd told her, as well as battling the things she'd said to him.

"Okay," she said, hedging. "For the little bit of time I've had to spend searching."

He scooted out, checking the readings on whatever meter he'd been using to check whatever settings needed checking. "You haven't said anything about it. I thought you might've changed your mind."

She wasn't yet sure if she had. She certainly hadn't been in the mood to go through any more archives or battle another bout of the emotional aftermath. But neither was she ready to admit defeat and disappoint Ten or herself. "I'll get back to it. When I can."

He squatted in front of his toolbox, slid the meter into its case, and then stood, jotting a note in the spiral pad he kept in his back pocket. "The bad day you had. The brownies. Was it the article in the *Statesman* that got to you?"

What? She crossed her arms, frowned. "You know about the article in the *Statesman*?"

"I did mention my Google-fu," he said, looking down as he flipped to a new page.

Obviously he was a better Googler than she was. She'd only found it when she'd viewed the library's archives. "But you didn't mention you'd been putting it to use."

He closed the notebook, held her gaze as he tucked it away. "I've been waiting for you to tell me if you'd found anything."

So her business was his business now? She was supposed to come to him with what she'd learned? Or—wait. Was he badgering her because he didn't think she'd done anything toward finding them? As if he had any say, any right? She didn't know whether to be angry…or angrier. "That sounds strangely like an accusation."

"It was a question, Kaylie. That's all."

Whether he *was* making an accusation, or just asking a question, she had to admit—anger aside—he had grounds. She'd put off the digging she *had* done way too long. That didn't mean she liked him snooping into her past. She hadn't snooped into his…much. She circled the island, climbed onto a bar stool, and rubbed her thumb along the edge of the stainless-steel sink. "I actually went to the library a couple of weeks ago."

He waited a minute, as if giving her time to say more. When she didn't, he asked, "What did you find out?"

Her thumb stilled. She cut her gaze up to his. "Why don't you tell me what *you* found out?"

"Not a lot, really." He joined her at the island, but stayed on his side. "Nothing about your father, but I guess that's not a surprise, since he was already out of the picture by then."

Then meaning the date of her mother's attempted suicide. "I don't know why she didn't list him on my birth certificate. Who cares if they weren't married, which I'm assuming is the case. But not even to list him? Like *I* might not someday need that information?"

"Maybe she regretted the relationship, or wasn't sure he was father material, and left him out of the picture to save you the grief."

"I don't know. Maybe she was just the self-centered person everything I remember leads me to believe."

"Yeah, there wasn't a lot in any of the articles I read to make me think she might win mother of the year."

That would've made her laugh if it hadn't been so sadly accurate. Then she latched onto what he'd said. If he could tell her what she wanted to know, it would be *so* much easier to deal with coming from him, filtered through his knowing her. "I only read the article in the *Statesman.* Did the others...did you find out anything else?"

He shook his head. "Not really. Details of her arrest and trial, and later her release. I didn't dig any deeper, and only went looking on a whim, wondering if there was anything about where she went after that."

Wondering, *wondering*...Kaylie frowned, rubbed at her temple and the weirdest, dizzying sense of déjà vu. She'd been here before, listening to someone tell her about her mother and the information he'd found. Except the *he* wasn't Ten. It was someone else. A boy. Older than her but not a man.

She could see the straps of his book bag hooked on his shoulders, his wire-rimmed glasses half hidden behind his fall of sandy-blond hair. She'd been a lot shorter, and looking up she had seen the same color hair on his chin, wondering if he didn't know he needed to shave, or couldn't be bothered with personal hygiene because he had equations to solve and code to write and dragons waiting in his dungeon.

He held several sheets of paper, copies he'd made of newspaper articles. And another from public court records...

"Is this about you? Is this your mom?"

Kaylie tore the papers from his hand, read the headlines, scanned the accompanying photos. Then she shoved the sheaf in her binder and pushed by him down the hall.

He followed, leaning a shoulder into the bank of lockers beside hers, pushing his glasses up his nose with one finger. "Is it?"

She grabbed her texts for English and algebra, hiding the pieces of paper detailing her past behind the stack of books on cooking due back to the library. "I don't know. I don't have time to look. I've gotta get to class before Mr. Alexander starts timing our test."

"I'm pretty sure it is."

Slamming the locker door, she whirled on him. "Why are you doing this? It's not any of your business. It's my business. Mine."

"I just thought you'd want to know. I mean, everyone is wondering why you got taken away from your parents."

"Then everyone needs to stop wondering. And don't you dare show that stuff to anyone else. I swear, if you do—"

The bell rang, cutting her off.

"I hate you, Morris Dexter. I hate you."

"Wow," she heard herself say, coming back to the present from the past. That day in the library. She'd been right. She had seen those images, that article, before. "Morris Dexter. I haven't thought about him in ages."

"What about him?" Ten asked.

Kaylie's gaze snapped to his. "You know Morris Dexter?"

"Sure. He owns DX Security. They installed your system." A look of amusement played across his face. "You didn't know that?"

Was he kidding? Morris Dexter had been the ultimate tech-geek high school cliché. Bullied by the jocks. Made fun of by the jocks' girlfriends. Hung out to dry by his so-called friends, who ran at the sight of the jocks. And then there was his need to stick his nose in everyone's business. Including hers. Especially hers.

"I had no idea. I never talked to him when I called. Just scheduled the consultation and dealt with the tech who came out."

"What's your history with him?"

She left the stool, needing coffee. "For some reason during our sophomore year, he decided he wanted to know why I was in foster care. And he went looking."

"Why would he do that?"

"The same reason you did, maybe?" she asked, and glanced back.

She watched a vein tic in his jaw before he said, "I doubt that."

She waited for him to elaborate, but he didn't. And so she asked, "What's that supposed to mean?"

He brushed off the question, nodded toward the pot, and changed the subject. "I'll take a cup. Did you know Suzi Gish?"

She recognized the name… "She was on the dance squad. One of the officers, I think."

He nodded. "They got married right after both graduated from A&M. And then they got divorced."

"You didn't go to school in Hope Springs. How do you know about Morris and Suzi?" she asked, filling both of their mugs.

"Same way you knew things about me before we met."

The news media had nothing on small towns. "This isn't making any sense. Suzi hated Morris. I mean, no one really liked him. He was such a know-it-all…" She paused. "And obviously with good reason, since he pretty much *did* know it all."

"He still does."

She handed him his mug. "I wonder if he's still a jerk about it."

"If he is, I don't think it matters," Ten said, smiling. "If you think the gossips talk about me, you should hear what they say about him. Especially since he's single again."

"Huh." She reached into the old refrigerator for cream, had a thought, and glanced back at him with the straightest face she could manage. "I'm going to have to have a talk with Luna. She's supposed to be keeping me up-to-date on the local bachelors."

"I don't think so," he said, sliding from the stool, so large when he stood, and coming closer, his gaze both hooded and sharp.

She backed away, her stomach tightening around the nerves he continued to stir there, until she hit the edge of the counter and was all out of room. She lifted her chin, breathing hard, then held up her hand like a stop sign. She shouldn't have started this. Right place, but wrong time. This conversation had taken a strange turn the minute she'd remembered Morris Dexter.

And that got her back on track. "I don't like you thinking I'm not capable of finding out what I need to know about my parents."

He stopped, his puckish expression quickly becoming a frown. "I don't think that."

"Then why are *you* spending time looking for information?"

"What? I told you—"

"I don't need a head start, Ten. I don't need things made easier for me." Did he still not understand the life she'd lived? How nothing about it had been easy? That even the time she'd lived in Hope Springs, as wonderful as those eight years had been, had not been a walk in the park? "I'm not weak or helpless or—"

He moved again, so fast she didn't have time to dodge him. She'd been waiting for this part of him, his hand holding her wrist, the fire in his eyes. His lust. That most of all, because her own had been building since the last time he'd kissed her. She liked it when he was bold. She hated that they hadn't further explored that connection…except the moment the wait was over, this moment, when it was finally, *finally* over, was exquisite.

And the feelings—the physical longing as well as the wild rush of emotional hunger—left her breathless and aching, and aware of the rough skin of his fingers, and the pulse beating for her at the base of his throat. Left her aware, too, that this bond between them, so potent, so rare, would take years of moments to explore. Years with him she wanted. Years she could see in his eyes.

"I don't think you're helpless," he said, reaching for her other wrist with his free hand. "I don't think you're weak," he said, tugging her arms around to the small of his back and pinning her there. "I think you're one of the strongest women I've ever met. And if I'm making things easier on you, it's because I'm selfish."

"Selfish?" The word came out on a breath of air, and when she pulled in her next she smelled him. His skin, his sweat, paint and wood and oil from his tools. She breathed again. Then asked her question again. "Selfish?"

"I want you to make things easier on me." And then his mouth was on hers, his body flush to hers, both hard, both demanding. She twisted her wrists to break his hold, then slid her palms up the plane of his back.

He groaned, brought his hands to her waist, and lifted her to sit on the counter's edge. Without thinking, she wrapped her legs around him, hooked her heels around him, moved her arms from his back to his neck and locked her hands around him. His tongue was in her mouth, his lips hard on hers, and she pushed against him, her pressure, her heat, her need for him. And she did need him, for this, but for more.

To let her try, and fail, then to catch her. But also to let her fall if the lesson could only be found on her knees. She needed his shoulder, and his hands, and his heart. Because if she couldn't make her own way in the world, how would she ever be able to share his?

CHAPTER THIRTY-TWO

Coming around the side of the garage, Ten heard voices and slowed his steps so as not to interrupt. He'd been checking the flow of the buffet room's new exhaust vent and hadn't seen Luna arrive. But the female voice was definitely hers, and the other sounded like it belonged to Mitch Pepper.

One half of Kaylie's new cooking duo had been a constant around Two Owls the last few weeks. Understandable since he was working with her and Dolly Breeze on menus and stuff. But Ten didn't have to like it. It was bad enough that their conversations had been casual, and often made in passing, but Kaylie's having to spend more time with Mitch than with him grated. There was something sketchy about the other man. Something Ten seldom felt from the ex-cons he put on his payroll. He'd tried to keep his suspicions from Kaylie, but he was pretty sure she knew he wasn't a fan of her cook.

"Are you going to tell her?" This from Luna, and Ten stopped, waiting and curious, instead of politely turning away as originally planned.

"I haven't decided. I mean, how do you just come out with something like that?" And that from Mitch. Ten moved closer to the corner.

"You just do. Choose a time when it's quiet, get her alone—"

"It's never quiet here, moon girl. It's a madhouse all day long."

"Mitch—"

"Luna, crap. What am I supposed to say? 'By the way, Kaylie, when you hired me on, I forgot to mention that I'm your father'?"

And...that was it. Ten shot around the corner, steam coming out of his ears, his heart thwapping like an air gun against his ribs. He slammed to a stop, sending dirt over the toes of his boots and theirs. Luna frowned and reached down to brush hers clean. Mitch looked down, too, but with guilt.

Ten's gaze traveled from one to the other. "Tell me I didn't just hear what I think I heard."

Luna turned away, gnawing at her thumbnail as she pressed her fist to her mouth. Mitch set his hands at his hips and followed the direction of her gaze. And in that moment, not any that had gone before, Ten saw Kaylie in the other man's face.

Mitch wore his gray hair short, and time had etched itself into his skin, but he held his mouth the same way Kaylie did when she needed to think about what to say, and the length of his nose, the slant...Ten blew out a breath, one fiery with the anger boiling in his veins.

"What is wrong with the two of you? Luna? You brought him here," he said, waving toward the man he wanted to deck. "What were you thinking? How could you do this to her?"

Luna spun back, gestured wildly with one hand. "I haven't done anything to her. And I knew Mitch long before I met Kaylie."

"That's not an answer. That's not even an excuse. That's…nothing," he said, his fury shooting at his words like clay targets. "Nothing."

"Well, I don't know what you want me to say," she shouted, angry, petulant.

She didn't have cause to be either. She was the one in the wrong. How could she not see she was in the wrong? "I want you to talk to me. Give me something here that makes sense."

"Don't take this out on Luna," Mitch stepped in front of him to say.

"You…" Ten pointed a finger into Mitch's chest, still struggling for coherence. "You shut up. You…shut…up. You don't have any rights here. You don't have a say. Not in what I do. Not in anything."

Mitch puffed up, sputtered, grew hot. "I have every right in the world. Kaylie's my daughter. *My* girl. She's been mine for all of her life. Long before she was ever yours, if that's what's happening here, what's pissing you off."

"What's happening here? *What's happening here?* Are you kidding me? What do you *think* is happening here? That I'm pissed off because you're going ruin something for me?" He jerked away, spitting curses and putting distance between himself and the other man. Then slamming a fist into the bark of a tree so he didn't slam it into Mitch's face.

Luna stepped in front of Mitch as Ten turned back. "Stop it, Ten. Don't make this about your relationship with Kaylie."

"You're blaming the wrong man for that, Luna."

"Maybe so, but Mitch is right. Kaylie is his family."

"You think that's how she feels? Have you even asked her how she feels?" He looked from one to the other, so angry with both he couldn't think beyond the moment to how he could possibly make things right for the woman he loved.

He loved her. He did. The feeling swept through him on a buoyant wave, lifting him above the madness, his chest tight, his eyes damp. He had to set this right for her. He had to do it without her getting hurt. But these two people…What they'd done was unconscionable. It was sick and twisted and selfish. Could they not see that? Were they that self-involved?

He shook it off, jamming his hands to his hips and snorting through his nose like a mad bull as he looked at Mitch. "You know she came here to look for you."

Mitch said nothing, just took a guilty step back.

"It's the reason she came back to Hope Springs," Ten said, digging at the sore spot to make Mitch hurt worse. "To find out what happened to her parents. What *she* did to make her mother try to take her own life. What *she* did to make her father leave and never come back."

Mitch was shaking his head. He couldn't stop shaking his head. "That's just wrong. She didn't do anything. I left to make a better life for her and Dawn."

"Does she know that? Does she have a single *effin'* clue? Of course she doesn't. Because you've been too busy getting what you want out of this to think about her—"

At that, Mitch swung, connecting with the corner of Ten's jaw. Ten stumbled back, righted, fisted his own hand but held his rage in check, watching as the older man scrubbed his hand back and forth over his head.

"I have done *nothing* but think about her," Mitch said, pacing in circles, his voice breaking. "Every day of my life. Every moment I was overseas serving my country. She was the only thing on my mind. Getting back to her. Taking care of her."

Ten hadn't known any of this, Mitch's service, his making a better life. Down the road the truth of where the other man had been, and why, might lessen the hate eating him up, but not now. "You've got a messed-up way of showing it, then."

"What would you have me do? Just come out and tell her? Upset everything she's made for herself?"

"Because waiting makes it better?"

"No," Mitch said, wilting in front of Ten, his fight gone, sadness taking over, guilt hard on its heels. "Waiting's never what I meant to do. I just needed time. I had to get to know her. In case once she did find out, she kicked me out of her life for good. I had to have this time."

Ten pulled in a deep breath, blew it out, popped his neck, and worked his jaw as if that would ease the pain of Mitch's fist slamming into his face. "If she does kick you out of her life? It won't be about where you were for most of hers. It'll be about this. About the lie. About coming here and passing yourself off as a cook."

"I am a cook. It's what I know. Her mother made sure I wouldn't have a chance to be a father."

That was a crock of crap. "You've had an entire month to be a father. Now it's time to be a man."

"Ten—" Luna said, but he cut her off because he didn't care if he was out of line. All he cared about was what these two had done to Kaylie. He couldn't go back in time and stop it from happening or fix it now that it had. He couldn't make up for failing to protect her, for letting this hurt come her way. But he could see things set right. And he would.

"Here's what's going to happen. I was supposed to drive Kaylie to Austin on Sunday to pick up the last of her things. But something's going to come up. I'll have to pick up supplies in San Antonio or something, and I won't be able to. Instead of leaving her stranded, I'll have arranged for you to go."

Mitch's face blanched. "I have to work at the Gristmill on Sunday."

"You *did* have to work. But you're going to call in sick, or have a family emergency, or just bring in a temp to cover your shift. I don't care what you do."

"And what are you going to do, Ten?" Luna asked. "When this all hits the fan. What are you going to do?"

He couldn't think about that now. Not about what he might lose if Kaylie found out the part he'd played here. It was hard enough imagining how hurt she was going to be. Those thoughts seized at him, tightening his gut until he thought he might puke. "This isn't about me."

But Luna pressed on. "You know this ultimatum of yours that Mitch tell her the truth could very well ruin your relationship. And the café's set to open in a month. She's doing a trial run on Friday night. She's got a lot on her plate. Why force this on her now? Why not let things settle—"

"And how will letting things settle help? Once the café opens, she'll have no choice but to stay here when she might want nothing more than to leave and never see this place again."

"She loves this place," Luna said. "She came back here because she loves it so much. This is her home now. You can't take that away from her."

"Me? Uh-uh. I didn't do this. You want to place blame, you look in the mirror."

Luna turned away, swiping her fingers beneath her eyes.

"Ten's right," Mitch said. "I've gotta come clean."

"Yeah. You do. You're going to be here bright and early that morning with your truck. You're going to drive her to Austin. You're going to load up the rest of her things. And on the drive back, you're going to ruin her day and tell her every bit of the truth."

"No. Not like that."

"Yes. Just like that. You'll have the time—"

"Not enough. Not for everything that needs to be said."

"Then you pull over to the side of the road and say it. I don't care as long as you don't let her out of your truck until she knows. When she gets back here, I don't want there to be any question in her mind that you are who you say you are."

CHAPTER THIRTY-THREE

"We're going to need a better way to serve the salad dressing. The cruets will tip too easily if the table is jostled."

"A squatter style of cruet, then. You know, shaped like a genie's lamp or something. Ladles make too much of a mess. Pouring makes more sense."

"What makes more sense is to be able to see if the dressing is about to run out."

"Crystal cruets. Short, squat. Solves both problems."

"Crystal's too fancy. I saw some in Williams-Sonoma made of laboratory glass. Simple, clean designs. No muss or fuss."

"Laboratory glass. Sure. Why not?"

"Well, I'm glad you agree. I'll pick them up this weekend."

Standing in the doorway between the kitchen and the room designed especially for her buffet, Kaylie smiled as she listened to Mitch and Dolly bicker over the table's accessories. She'd been so right to hire both of them. And as much as they squabbled in the kitchen, the two had become fast friends.

The produce for tonight's trial run had come from Indy's greenhouse, but Dolly had made the dressings from scratch. She and Kaylie had worked in the Breeze family kitchen last week to perfect them; the kitchen at Two Owls had been in complete disarray, but everything had come together since then.

Mitch had turned out three gorgeous test casseroles: chicken spaghetti, shredded pork enchiladas with a lime-cilantro cream sauce, and a grilled sirloin and egg noodle stroganoff. The scents of onions and cheeses and spices had her stomach rumbling. Dolly had baked May's hot rolls, and Kaylie had gone all out with a trio of brownie varieties for dessert.

She walked into the room, her hands full with the tiered stand that held them stacked two deep on all three levels. Mitch caught sight of her, turned, and stepped forward, his arms outstretched. "Here. Let me take that. Smooth out the cloth at the end of the table there, would ya, Doll?"

Kaylie grinned as she handed off the brownies. She loved how Mitch had come to shorten Dolly's name. "Thanks. I probably went a little overboard for a trial run, but I couldn't resist."

"The entire buffet says overboard for the number of people who'll be eating, but I absolutely love that it does," Dolly said, rotating the dessert stand a quarter of a turn, as if where Mitch had set it didn't quite measure up. He rolled his eyes and Kaylie's grin widened. Then Dolly clapped her hands and said, "I think that's it. I'm going to run freshen up before everyone arrives."

Watching her go, Mitch shook his head. "That woman. Has to have everything just so."

"The very reason she's here," Kaylie reminded him. "I don't have time or patience for the *just so*, and you don't have a knack for it."

"Yeah, well, you got me there," he said, rubbing at the back of his neck.

"But you make up for the *just so* with the beef and pork and chicken, and those sauces. They smell so good I want to dive in and swim laps." She stepped closer to the table and held her shirt to her body so as not to drag it through the food when she leaned down to breathe it all in. "This right here," she said as she straightened, her encompassing gesture taking in the whole spread, "this is why *you* are here. And I am so, *so* glad you are." Then before she thought about what she was doing, she wrapped her arms around Mitch's neck and gave him a hug.

He grew stiff, and she knew she'd caught him unawares, but then his arms came around her gently and he returned the show of affection—just with a little less show. And that was fine, she mused, stepping back as she released him. The exuberance making her feel like she was floating through the house in a bubble was enough show for the whole town of Hope Springs.

"Listen, Kaylie," he said, moving to the end of the buffet. "I want to thank you for this. I really wasn't interested in taking on another job when I had a good one—"

"But Luna made you come."

"She did. And I was curious. But this thing you've done..." He swept his arm in an encompassing gesture to indicate the whole of the room...the furnishings and the food and the tongue-and-groove walls whitewashed to look like a general store, the decorative license plates and old milk bottles and gas station signs Dolly had hunted down. "I couldn't be prouder of y—of how this turned out had I done it all myself."

What had he stopped himself from saying? *I couldn't be prouder of you?* Did he think she wouldn't welcome his pride?

She circled the table to where he stood. "We've done this together, Mitch. I would never have pulled it off this beautifully without your input and Dolly's *just so.* You've been vital to the planning every step of the way. I'd thought from the very beginning that it would be a good idea to have my cook on board early, but having you here has been absolutely crucial."

"I don't know about that—"

"I know about that," she said, reaching for his wrist and squeezing. "Please don't ever doubt how much it means to me having you here."

"If you're sure," he said, his hands going into his pockets when she released him. "Doll can do most of what I can, so if it turns out you don't need the both of us, keep her. Let me go."

That sounded like he *was* making plans to leave. She scrambled for something to say to convince him otherwise, but Dolly returned then. Humming beneath her breath, she took in the table once more, adjusting the fold of the napkin covering the hot rolls, lining up the slotted spoon in front of the casserole, doing the same for the salad tongs, and earning another roll of Mitch's eyes and Kaylie's laugh.

When the front door chime rang moments later, Kaylie circled her two cooks to answer, giving both a smile and a pat on the back. Dolly returned her smile reassuringly. Mitch seemed agitated, which Kaylie, her own anxiety rising, could totally understand.

The next two hours were a madhouse of food and laughter. Kaylie walked between the tables, talking to everyone, watching to see who returned for seconds, who for thirds, what dish went the fastest, how many hot rolls everyone ate. She kept an eye on the floor space, the elbow room, checked the lighting, the room's temperature. Refilled iced tea and coffee like a proper hostess, and had the time of her life.

"Kaylie, aren't you going to eat?"

The question came toward the end of the meal from Jessa, and had all heads turning toward Kaylie, where, taking a break, she leaned against the door to the dining room. Rick's gaze searched her out, as did his mother's and Carolyn Parker's and her husband Wade's. Will was the only one who didn't stop eating, but when he looked up it was straight at Indiana.

She was looking at Kaylie, too, as were Peggy Butters and Maxine Mickels and their spouses. And Manny Balleza, who sat next to Ten. And Max and Josephine Malina. And Mitch, who watched her with his hand around his tumbler of iced tea, waiting.

All of these people...her café...after so many years... "I'm actually not very hungry. And besides, y'all are my focus group, so I've got to see if you're focused."

Her sixteen guests sitting at four tables of four laughed as one, Carolyn saying, "Well, it seems hardly fair that we're having all the fun."

Kaylie met Ten's gaze across the room. He had done this for her. Yes, it had been her idea, her dream, but Ten had made it happen. And yet...there was something in his expression that led her to believe he was less than happy. It made her think of Mitch's earlier agitation as the guests had arrived, and the tension in the room had her suddenly feeling the need to escape.

"I'm going to check on the food, see how everything is faring on the buffet." She turned, an overwhelming pull of emotion leaving her struggling for balance, and for the life of her she didn't know why. This was what she'd wanted, what she'd planned for and worked for. But she'd never expected to feel so...empty.

It didn't make sense, she mused, frowning as she tested the heat of the hot rolls and tucked their linen covering closer. None of what she was feeling made sense. She should be pleased, content, full of the joy she'd seen on the faces of her friends. And she did feel all of that. She did. But something was wrong. Something was missing.

She had her dog, her café, her three-story Victorian on the corner of Second and Chances. But she didn't have Winton or May, and that loss, one she'd thought she'd come to terms with, one that had been a part of her past now for years, suddenly crushed her, and she stumbled into the corner, dropped to crouch there, and stayed.

Ten was the one to find her no more than a minute later, as if whatever he'd seen in her face had led him to her. He swore beneath his breath, came down on one knee, and wrapped his arms around her, pulling her against him, holding her until the worst of her shaking subsided. When she nodded, he helped her to her feet and guided her through the buffet-room door into the kitchen.

Once there, she eased from his embrace, uncomfortable to have been found so weak, equally uncomfortable at the possibility of one of her guests seeing her so. Most of all hating that he was the one who had found her. He'd said that he thought her the strongest woman he'd known. She didn't want to give him a reason to think otherwise.

"I really am okay," she said, crossing the room to stare out the window above the kitchen sink. Her guests were parked in the small lot accessed from Second Street. All but Ten. His truck sat in her driveway, behind her Jeep, as if he belonged there with her. As if this was his place as much as it was hers.

She closed her eyes at the thought, let it infuse her like amaretto into a fresh strawberry cake. He did belong here, with her, to her, and she to him. Her limbs tingled with the realization and with wanting him, her belly, too, and then he was there behind her, his hands on her shoulders, squeezing as he leaned forward and nuzzled his nose to her ear.

"You stay here," he said, his voice deep, a vibration that lifted the hair at her nape. "I'll play host, make sure everyone gets their fill, then clean up. I'll say you're not feeling well—"

"Dolly will never believe you." Though being alone with him was the only thing she wanted, and it sounded like heaven, and she couldn't wait. "She'll insist on helping."

"And I'll insist on her doing what I say if she wants to keep both her jobs."

"You wouldn't dare," Kaylie said, staring into the window at his reflection.

"Watch me," he said, and then he was gone.

~

"I'm sorry," Kaylie said a half hour later, once they had the house to themselves. "I'm fine, really. I promise."

"I know you're fine," he said, his voice soft, his words for her ears alone. "You're exhausted, excited, I doubt you're sleeping. You're running on empty. But I know you're fine."

She looked up at him, the circles beneath her eyes like bruises marring her tender skin. "If I could just get a full night's sleep, it would help."

He wanted to hurt everyone responsible for the nightmare that kept her awake. "What if I stay? I can camp out down here. You won't have to worry about…whatever it is that has you sleeping with a knife."

"That's not how it works," she said, stepping into him and cuddling against his chest. "I'd still wake up."

His arms went around her, tightened, absorbed her trembling until they both stood still. "You don't know that. You haven't tried."

"But I know me." And then she leaned back to look him in the eye. "It might work if you were in the same room…"

The tension that had been floating around them like ground fog rose along his limbs. Ten felt it in the tightening of his muscles and skin, in the way he forgot how to breathe, in his clothes that felt heavy and damp, in his urge to shed them, to rid her of hers, too. "I can stay. In any room. Wherever you want me."

"I think I want you to stay in mine."

Desire gripped him, and he battled a rising groan. "Uh-uh. Not if you think. You've gotta know."

"I want you to stay in mine," she said, no question, no doubt, no fear. "Will you please stay in mine? Will you please stay there with me?"

His jaw tight, he took her by the hand and tugged her behind him up three flights of stairs to the bedroom where she slept.

And where tonight she wouldn't.

CHAPTER THIRTY-FOUR

"Are you sure?" Ten asked, still fully clothed and stretched out beside her on top of her quilt-covered queen-sized bed.

She was nervous. He could have no idea how nervous she was. But he could know how happy his being here made her. How ready she was for him. That she'd been waiting for him longer than even she could believe. And no matter how the night went, it would be perfect.

"Very. Are you?" She rolled toward him, slipping one leg between his, hooking her ankle behind his and winding their feet close.

He rubbed his knee along the inside of her thigh, the friction of the denim on denim warming her skin. She wanted to take off her jeans, but she didn't want to move. His weight on the mattress, his heat, the scent of sunshine and sawdust and spice...She shivered and nuzzled close.

"Very very," he said, though it took him a minute to respond, and his breathing shifted with the wait, growing ragged as if his racing heart was slamming into his lungs.

She reached up and brushed his hair from his forehead. She'd known him now for two months, and she didn't think he'd cut his hair in all that time. She liked it long. She loved how it curled over his collar, how she could tuck it behind his ear. She loved his ear, and got a shiver out of him when she tugged on the lobe. She loved his jaw, how defiant the line, sharp and strong, and the stubble he always wore, she loved that, too.

"Your eyes are closed," he said.

"I know," she replied.

"Are you falling asleep on me?"

"Not a chance."

He laughed at that, a deep, full-bodied growl that she felt with her leg between his. "Good, because I don't plan for either of us to think about sleeping for a while."

She liked that, his confidence, that he would make such a threat, and that he meant it, because she knew he did. "I never mind missing sleep for a good reason."

He moved his hand to her throat, trailed his fingers to the hollow, then lower, to the top button of her rose Henley tee. "This will be a good one. I promise."

She opened her eyes because she wanted to watch, to follow the shifts in his expression as he touched her, to see his fingers, his hands, his skin against her skin, which was lighter than his, pale where his showed his time in the sun. He freed a second button, then the third, and pushed aside the fabric to slide beneath, sweeping his fingertips over the swell of one breast, then the other. Her nipples tightened and she shuddered, shuddered again when he slipped into her bra to feel for himself.

"I like that," he said, his voice gravelly.

"I like it, too," she whispered. "I like it a lot." She thought she would really like it if he used his mouth, but she wasn't ready to say that. She spoke with her hands instead, mimicking him, releasing the snaps of the work shirt he wore, two, then two more, then another two until she'd bared most of his chest. He was fit, his muscles solid when she pressed her palm there, his hair soft, silkier than that on his head, a pleasure to her fingers.

She learned what he liked, playing beneath his shirt, listening to the sounds he made, feeling his temperature rise. Beneath his hair, his skin was smooth, and she lifted up onto one elbow to taste him, lowering her mouth to kiss him, flicking her tongue over the hard center of his nipple the way she wanted him to flick hers, circling, drawing on him with her lips, biting softly until he growled and pushed her to her back. He hovered over her, delivering on his earlier threat and thrilling her.

His eyes were bright and flashing when he said, "My turn," and lifted her shirt by the hem to bare her, slipping a hand around her back to release the clasp of her bra. He pushed it out of the way and leaned down, wetting her, sucking her, lapping at her with the flat of his tongue before moving his mouth to hers and slipping inside. It seemed she'd been waiting hours to kiss him again.

She brought both of her arms around his neck to hold him close, slanting her head to meet his, bumping his nose with hers, laughing and then finding him again, his lips, his teeth. His breathing grew harsh and hot on her cheek, and she wondered if he felt the same warmth from her exhaled breath.

And then he was gone, sliding down her body, finding her nipple again. The contact had her arching her back, pressing into him. She wanted more. Oh, so much more. And she used her hands on his back to tell him, her nails scraping him lightly through the fabric of his shirt.

She wiggled her hips, working her way underneath him, feeling the hard bulk of his erection first at her hip and then at the juncture of her thighs. It was a glorious sensation, having him there, knowing she was responsible for that thickness and weight. She lifted into him, and he ground down, rubbing her just right so that she thought she might die.

She shivered, felt the hairs on her arms flutter, and her belly grew heavy and tight, and it fluttered, too. "Do that again."

He growled out a laugh, kissing his way down her torso, stopping when he reached her waistband to deal with the button there, to unzip her fly. On his knees now and bracketing her thighs, he told her, "Raise up," and when she did, he worked her jeans down her hips and off. He tossed them to the floor, his gaze on the damp fabric of her panties striped in lilac and white.

"You're so beautiful," he said, still staring below her waist, a focus that brought a smile to her mouth, then brought a laugh. "What?" he asked, looking at her then, and she swore she saw a flush stain his cheeks.

"Nothing."

"You laughed. It's not nothing."

"My laughing bothers you?"

"I'm about to get naked. And I am nowhere near as gorgeous as you are. Yes, your laugh bothers me."

"Don't let it. It's a happy laugh. I'm glad you like what you see."

"I'm not sure *like* is a strong enough word. You're just… amazing."

"So…get naked."

"Yes, ma'am," he said, and this time he laughed, though she wasn't sure he was amused as much as trying to stave off the shift from playful to intense. He straightened and shrugged out of his shirt, baring his shoulders and chest and the flat, flat plane of his abdomen where a strip of dark hair left her mouth dry.

Another part of her, a part that was already damp, grew wetter, and ached. She clenched her muscles there, slid a hand down her belly to her panties that were in the way. But before she could push them down, Ten shook his head and said, "Wait."

Leaving her hand where it was, she gave in, her gaze following as he stepped off the bed and out of his jeans. He wore boxer briefs, black or navy, she couldn't tell, and the fabric clung to his thickly muscled thighs. Clung, too, to the head of his penis where it bulged atop his erection. She swallowed, nervous, hungry, anxious, but hungry most of all.

She didn't know this side of him, but she was certain he'd be as focused and exact as he was with everything he did. The idea of having all of that for herself…she was about to burst with the want, she was consumed with anticipation, and she was so, *so* ready.

As if reading her mind, he removed her panties, used his knee to spread her legs, and cupped her sex with his palm. His fingers were deft and clever as he parted her where she was slick, dipping lower to ready her, to stretch her…

She dug her fingers into his biceps. "Ten?"

He didn't answer except to stop, going stiff above her.

"I think I should tell you something."

"I think you just did."

CHAPTER THIRTY-FIVE

"You're a virgin." It was such an oversimplification that it sounded ridiculous, but it was the only thing Ten could think of to say.

"I know." Her grip on his arms lessened. "I'm the one who hasn't had sex."

He wasn't going any further until he understood what they were doing here. This was major. A big, big deal. But when he tried to pull his hand from her sex, she tightened her muscles and held him. That, of course, sent a new surge of blood to where he was already thick with it.

So all he could ask was, "Why?"

She looked up at him, her gaze smoky, her smile sure. "Is that really what you want to ask me?"

No. What he wanted to ask was, why him? "Why didn't you tell me?"

"I just did." She moved her gaze to the side of his face, his hair, brushing her fingers through it to tuck it behind his ear.

He couldn't think for the way she was touching him, with purpose, with design, distracting him, luring him in, lingering. "I mean before."

"Before I took my clothes off?" she asked, and her hand stilled, her gaze returning to his.

"Something like that," he said, wishing they weren't having this discussion with their clothes off. He was having the worst time staying on track, what with her thighs so smooth where they rubbed against his, and her breasts plumped like cushions for him to rest on.

"Because I didn't think it mattered."

That brought his mind back to business. "How could it not matter?"

"I want to be here. I want to make love with you. As far as I'm concerned, that's the only thing that does."

He wanted to believe her, to agree with her, but…a virgin. He didn't want her to regret her decision, or to hate him afterward because he wasn't the right man. He wanted to be the right man. He wanted tonight to be unforgettable. He wanted—

"Ten?"

"Yeah?"

"Did you forget about me?"

"Never, baby," he said, then added, "Not a chance."

"Do you believe me?"

He nodded, swallowed, and nodded again, staring into her eyes as he did, and falling. How could he not believe her when her skin was flushed and her pulse visible beneath the translucent skin of her neck? Her eyes bright, the color lost to arousal, like he was lost to his.

"I believe you," he finally said, the words scratching their way up his throat.

"Then can we stop talking now?"

She had no idea what she was in for. "I guess this is when I should tell you that I'm a big believer in talking during sex."

Her lips parted, and she caught at the lower with her teeth, teasing him, and it worked because nothing about the move was practiced. It was pure Kaylie, genuine and unaffected and true. "Then *don't* stop talking or…anything else."

He took a deep breath, shed his hesitation along with his briefs, and settled between her legs. "I don't want to hurt you."

"You're going to. I know that. But it's okay."

He couldn't say anything to that. All he could do was bring his mouth down on hers in a kiss so soft she sighed beneath him, melting and spineless as she lifted her legs, dragging her heels down the backs of his thighs. He wasn't quite as soft after that, his tongue hungry in her mouth, his body shuddering from her touch.

"You like?" she whispered, her lips at the edge of his.

"More than you know."

"Tell me."

"Kaylie—"

"I don't want you to hold back. I want everything. I want all of you."

And so he told her, moving down her body with his mouth, whispering against her skin, licking certain spots and making her squirm, smelling her and squirming, too. She was soft and sweet, her scent of sun-soaked flowers so familiar he felt a tug in the center of his chest. But he didn't talk about that. He couldn't talk about that. Not when she'd brought her thighs up his sides in invitation.

He knelt on the bed between her legs, holding her as he kissed her the way he'd been wanting to for days, tasting her, drawing her hips off the bed as she pushed against his mouth, whimpering as if asking for more.

"You like?" he asked, his voice like sandpaper to his ears.

"More than you know."

"Tell me."

"Unbelievable. Please. Oh, please. I want..." She stopped, shivered, gooseflesh pebbling the skin of her thighs where he held her.

"Are you cold?" he asked, pretty sure her trembling wasn't about the room's temperature.

"No." She shook her head on the pillow. "I want more of your mouth. And I want to come. And I want to feel you inside me. That's what I want most of all."

Magic words. All of them. Words that had his body tightening, growing harder than he already was. But since he knew this wouldn't be easy on her, he held himself in check and lowered his head.

He used his tongue to lick and pierce her, his lips to suck and kiss her. He pulled on the hard bud of her nerve endings, applying the pressure her movements told him she liked, listening to the noises she made each time he shifted, or adjusted, or slid deep, or withdrew.

He tasted the metallic salt of her release before she gave in, flinging her arms to her sides and fisting her hands in the sheets. She cried out, stiffening, shaking, shoving herself against him where she most needed his touch to finish. He let her use him, giving her all that her body asked for, then reaching for the condom he'd tossed to the foot of the bed.

At the sound of the packet tearing, Kaylie opened her eyes and rose up onto her elbows. She watched while he rolled the protective sheath into place, then parted her legs and lifted her gaze to his. He crawled over her and lowered himself into the cradle of her hips, one hand holding his shaft as he probed at her entrance, pushed at her barrier. And then he was inside, sliding into her, a slow, easy penetration that had her eyes going wide, her teeth grabbing for her bottom lip, her hands pulling the sheet to her sides.

When it looked like she was about to punch holes through the fabric, he stopped, said, "I'm sorry."

"Don't stop," she said. "And don't be sorry."

"I'm hurting you."

"Yes, but I think it's going to get a whole lot better from here."

It was, for both of them, but he needed to be sure. "Tell me how you want me to move, to make it easier. Tell me what to do."

"Tennessee Keller. I don't want it easier. I just want it. And I want it from you. And I really, really want it now."

"You're killing me, Kaylie. You know that, right?"

"That's good, because I wouldn't want to be the only one here dying."

And with that, his elbows braced on either side of her head, he began to move his hips, easing in and out with long, gentle strokes, holding himself to that rhythm as long as he could, in and out, in and out, his gaze holding hers as he did. Her breathing increased to match his, a rough digesting of the air between them. And her pulse in her neck beat like a drum, pounding and labored like his.

He increased his speed, and she raised her knees along his sides, lowered them, raised them again, urging him on with her heels to his backside, smoothing her soles down his thighs to his calves. She squeezed her legs around him, squeezed her sex around him, too. He couldn't have found the words, even if he'd had any brain left for speech, so he grunted to tell her she was doing everything right.

She responded in kind, moans and whimpers and panted breaths, but soft ones, where his noises were crass and heathen. *He* was crass and heathen, and she was beautiful and thoughtful and so hungry. He fed her the only way he knew how, pumping ever harder in response to the insistent, greedy push-pull of her hands and feet on his body, urging him to hurry.

He didn't want to hurry, but he couldn't take his time. Not when she was so demanding, and when he was enjoying finding out that she was. He wasn't sure what he'd expected to discover about her in bed, but this wasn't it, this total lack of inhibition, and Kaylie a virgin. The thought had him burying his head in her pillow, his face against her neck, and increasing the speed of his hips.

He knew she was climbing with him, her whimpers now desperate cries. He bit her neck, sucked on the skin, soothed the wound with his tongue, and she let go, arching upward, drawing her fingers down his back, then turning her head to bite him. At that, he surged into her, the hot physical rush followed by a burst of complex emotions, and then he collapsed, finishing in a quaking shudder that left him spent.

Long minutes later, Kaylie shifted beneath him. He started to roll away, stopping when she reached for his shoulders and held him still. "No. Stay."

He'd be content on top of her for the rest of the night, but she had to be sore, and they both needed to shower. He wanted her again, but he wanted her to recover. And sleep was sounding better and better. But first there was the condom to deal with.

Leaving her with a kiss, he rolled off the bed and headed into the bathroom. He'd just turned on the bathwater when he heard her behind him. He looked back without thinking, then sucked in a breath and stepped into the claw-foot tub, closing the curtain around him and flipping the lever for the showerhead.

He'd had her naked beneath him. He'd been buried inside her. But seeing her without her clothes, head-to-toe bare walking toward him…he forgot how to breathe, how to think, how to do anything but grow thick and hard.

"Do you want company?" she asked, her voice nearly lost in the steam filling the room. "Someone to wash your back?"

At the moment he couldn't think of anything he wanted more. Thing was… "There should be another condom on the floor by my jeans," he said, then stuck his head under the spray. He'd leave it up to her and not press, but just in case, he had to be ready.

Moments later he felt the curtain against his shoulder move, felt the brush of Kaylie's hair as she reached around him for her sponge and flowery body wash. He didn't ask about the condom. They'd get to that.

He faced her and asked something else instead. "Do you want to tell me why you're still a virgin?"

"I'm not still a virgin," she said, her smile coy and honest as she sponged his chest, her gaze following the trail of suds down his torso.

He closed his eyes, thought about the basketball game he'd missed tonight. Thought about the mess still to clean up in the kitchen. Then he thought about Mitch and Luna's deception, and that effectively took his mind off Kaylie's hands. "You were until a few minutes ago."

"And it's so nice the way you took care of that for me."

"That's not an answer."

"I don't know that I have one," she said as she moved to wash his arms. "Except that the time was never right. And the man was never right. Until now."

He turned so she'd wash his back and not…anything else. "You're gorgeous, and you're willing, and you're a whole lot of fun. I've gotta think you've had more offers than you can count."

She continued to soap him. "I knew what I wanted. I don't know how else to explain it. I had a lot of opportunities, and it wasn't always easy to say no. But it wasn't right. And I'm afraid if I say anything else, I'll scare you off."

"Then scare me," he said, his hands laced on top of his head as he looked over his shoulder. "I really need to know."

She stilled, the sponge in one hand, the soap in the other. "I couldn't give myself to someone who I might never see again. I'm not the one-night-stand type. Or the casual-sex type. And that's why I didn't want to tell you. I didn't want you to stay with me because I guilted you into—"

"Kaylie, stop," he said, spinning to grab her by the wrists. "I'm here, and I'm staying, and there are many, many reasons why, but the most important one is this." He used the long edge of his index finger to lift her chin, forcing her gaze up to meet his. "I want to be here with you. I don't want to be anywhere else. Guilt has nothing to do with it."

The sunshine of her smile lit him up, a warmth more comforting than the water soothing his tired back. And then she leaned into him and wrapped her arms around him, her skin on his skin, her heart beating with his. "I didn't think that you did, but I still had to say it. Don't be mad."

"I'm not mad. I just want to understand," he said, holding her.

"I've lost everyone who's ever mattered to me, Ten. Or everyone who should've been there for me. It's not hard to figure out why I go into relationships looking to make exits easier, for me, for the other person. It's a coping mechanism, I guess. Or a defensive one. And it's probably why I don't have many friends. Any friends, really."

She was breaking his heart, always alone, having no one. "Oh, baby. You have me. And you have Luna and Dolly and Indy. And Carolyn and Jessa. And Will." He forced himself to add, "And Mitch."

She let him go, looking up with a sharp eye. "That hurt, didn't it? Putting Mitch in there."

"Are we done here?" he asked instead of answering. "Because I'm pretty sure my prunes are pruned."

She swatted him on the bottom, pulled the curtain aside, and handed him the first towel, stepping out and wrapping herself in the second. They were barely dry before he met her in the center of the bed, spooning his knees into hers, wrapping his arm around her waist, nuzzling his cheek against her hair spread out on her pillow. "Do you want me to come with you to Austin on Sunday? To get the last of your things?"

"I thought you had to go to San Antonio for supplies. I thought that was why Mitch said he'd go."

"I do, but if you want me there, I can change my plans." He could hear the hesitation in his offer, and he had no doubt she sensed his reluctance that was bigger than changing some plans. He loved this woman. He did not want her hurt. And he'd set her up to be devastated. It was hard to think about his killing her Sunday after she'd loved him so thoroughly tonight.

She tucked her shoulder into his armpit and wrapped herself tighter into his arm. "I'll be fine with Mitch. It's just a walk-through of my condo, and telling Austin good-bye."

His responding laugh was low and gruff and rife with his gut-roiling guilt. "I hope it's as easy as that."

She wiggled against him. "You saw through that, did you?"

"I know a little bit about leaving behind something you love."

But she didn't answer, already fast asleep.

CHAPTER THIRTY-SIX

When Luna walked into the parlor of the house at Second and Chances Saturday morning, Kaylie looked up from the floor where she was sorting linens and grinned. "We missed you the other night."

"I'm sorry I couldn't make it," Luna said, dropping down to sit, and to help. She'd spent the night in her weaving shed, lost in the penance of the repetitive motion. "I wanted to, but...something came up."

"I would ask if that something was Will Bowman." Reaching for a stack of forest-green cloths, Kaylie arched a fine brow. "But since he was at my place..."

Luna smiled. Maybe one day she'd tell Kaylie about her adventures with the wolf. Just not today. "Will and I are just friends."

"You say that like it's a good thing."

"It is. Will's a little too intense for me." And yet she was here because of him. Because he'd made her realize she owed Kaylie the same truth she'd given Mitch. And he'd done that before Ten Keller had issued his ultimatum.

As right as Ten was, she'd come to this decision before he'd discovered the secret she'd been keeping. This was her own heart, her own heartbreak. And because of Will, she had to tell Kaylie good-bye. "I don't think I'm in the right place for a relationship anyway. I've got some personal things to sort out first."

"Can I help?" Kaylie asked, reaching over to brush Luna's hair from her shoulder to her back. "Can I do anything?"

"No. I screwed up. I've got something I need to fix." More than one something. And after Luna made things right with Sierra's family, she'd come back here and try to do the same.

"Do you want to talk about it?"

Strangely enough, she did. "I had an accident," she began, smoothing the russet-colored napkin she held. "In high school. I lost my best friend. I was confined to my bed for weeks. It's when I took up weaving. But I never told Sierra's family the truth of what happened. I never told my parents, either. I've been carrying it around all this time. And it's refusing to stay in the corner where I tucked it away."

"Oh, Luna," Kaylie said, her face pale, her eyes like moss and sorrowful. "I'm so, so sorry. I know what it's like to have something eating you up. It doesn't matter what it is."

"I owe it to you, actually." And to a wolf. "You being brave enough to face your past."

Kaylie gave a snort and went back to her linens. "Brave is about the last thing I am. If I were brave, I would've actively been looking for my parents. I've done next to nothing."

"Do you not want to know?" she asked, because tomorrow was coming all too soon, and if Luna needed to put a stop to Mitch's revelation…

Smoothing the napkin she held against her thigh with one palm, Kaylie shrugged. "I think I'm scared to know."

Luna pressed. "Scared of what?"

"That everything is going to change. I'm happy," Kaylie said, her hands stilling in her lap. "Or I think I'm happy. But then I wonder if I even know what being happy means."

"And you're afraid learning what happened to your parents will mess that up somehow."

She nodded, solemn like stone. "What if finding them, or finding out what happened to them, ruins what I have?"

"I guess it could," she said, but being Mitch's friend, too, she couldn't help but look on the bright side. "But what if it makes things so much better you're left laughing at all your doubts?"

"It's all the unknown, isn't it?"

"The unknown's a monster. It really, truly is." Dark and haunting and waiting in the wings. "With jaws that bite and claws that catch."

"I love 'Jabberwocky,'" Kaylie said, swatting at Luna's arm with a towel.

Luna swatted back, smiling. "I read it over and over when weaving during a really bad time. I think that resulting scarf went for more money than anything I've ever done. If it didn't hurt so much to be in that emotional place, I'd stay there. It was some nice cash."

Kaylie got back to folding. "It's wonderful that you have that outlet. I just...bake. Usually brownies. And then I have to get rid of them before I take the whole pan to bed with a gallon of milk."

"I think I've done that before," Luna said, and Kaylie laughed with her, though the laughter quickly faded, and Kaylie sighed.

"I think the worst part for me is wondering if I really did do something to make them want to leave me. I mean, I was only four when my father left, five when my mother tried to check out. It's not like I could've done anything too terrible. And I tell myself anyone who could blame a young child for anything isn't much of a parent. But then I wonder, what if they never even wanted me at all?"

"Kaylie—"

But Kaylie pushed on. "My mother could've found me if she'd wanted to after her release. She would've had access to my foster-care records. She could've asked questions of my caseworker, followed whatever trail was there, found me in Hope Springs, or even later in Austin. But she didn't."

Except there was another option. "Maybe she did. Maybe she realized you were settled and happy, and left again."

"Isn't that the same thing?" Kaylie asked, the green of her eyes so sad.

"It depends on what she was thinking, I guess." And that was something Kaylie might never know. "That she'd done enough damage and didn't want to make things worse. Or maybe she talked to Winton and May, and they thought it best that you not see her."

Kaylie shook her head. "I just don't get it. She got out of prison, and she was in the wind. As if she never existed. As if she wanted to erase everything of her previous life. Part of me thinks I should respect that and let things go." She paused, lined up the napkins at her side, then pushed them and the conversation away. "But you didn't come here for all this."

"It's okay. But yes. The reason I came here is this." She handed Kaylie the shopping bag she'd set beside her, watching the other woman's face light up as she reached in and unwrapped the scarf.

"Oh, this is gorgeous," she said, her eyes going wide. "But...this isn't the scarf you talked about in Gruene at the Gristmill. When we came up with the coconut and caramel brownies."

"I haven't done that one yet. I thought about it before Easter, and wanted to get started, but I was standing in the shed with my dad, looking at all the yarn I had to work with, and these colors made me think of you."

Kaylie brought the scarf to her face, breathed it in, rubbed it against her cheek, then, laughing, she hurriedly looped it around her neck. "Is this right?"

"Here." Luna adjusted the drape and the cowl, straightened the fringe, and pulled free strands of hair Kaylie had caught in the wrap. "There. It's perfect. You should see your eyes. Such a beautiful green."

"Like salad? This makes me think of salad. And of my trees. And the garden. I love it." She pushed onto her knees, grabbing Luna in a hug. "Thank you so much."

"You're welcome," Luna said, hugging her back as tears fell. "I hope you think only good things when you wear it."

CHAPTER THIRTY-SEVEN

"I don't know why I didn't have the movers bring this stuff to Hope Springs when they delivered the big pieces to the house last week." Kaylie shoved what she thought should be the final box of her things into the bed of Mitch's truck. "I guess I just needed to be the last one here, to say good-bye."

"Makes sense." Mitch pushed his own box farther toward the cab. "You've lived here a long time."

"Ten years. In Austin, anyway. Five in this place." She looked back at the sidewalk winding to her door through tiny squares of mulched flower beds and monkey grass. Poor Magoo, cooped up for two years with only a daily leashed walk and the occasional weekend trip to the dog park. "You'd think it would feel more like home than it does."

"What's the saying? Home is where the heart is?" Mitch used a foot on the bumper to vault himself onto the tailgate, moving into the bed to snug the boxes close. "I guess the house in Hope Springs was more home to you."

"It was. It is." She shrugged, moving out of the way as he jumped down. "It's hard to explain why."

He slammed the tailgate shut. "You don't have to explain."

"I know, but I think about it a lot. Wondering why it's meant so much to me. And it's more than the house. It's all the years with Winton and May." She pushed her sunglasses to the top of her head and turned for the condo. "It's where I found out what it means to have a family."

Mitch was quiet as they walked back to her place, his hands shoved in his pockets, his gaze cast down. And then Kaylie realized what she'd said.

She reached for his arm, stopping him, giving a squeeze before letting him go. "I'm so sorry. I wasn't thinking. I know from some things Luna has mentioned that you haven't seen your family for a very long time."

"Don't apologize. It is what it is," he said, and started walking. "And I was lucky enough to find a family with Harry and Julietta. It's not exactly the same, but I can't complain. They're good people, the Meadowses. Luna's a peach."

"I'm so glad I met her. And her parents. They throw a mean egg hunt and barbecue."

A smile appeared and softened Mitch's features. "Did she tell you it's always been her favorite holiday? More so than her birthday or Christmas?"

"Really? Do you know why?"

He laughed as they went inside to walk through her condo one last time. "I don't. I just know how excited she gets when it's time to have the children hunt the eggs."

"She told me this morning she spends a good hour hiding them."

"It's a wonder they all get found. I think she draws a map."

"Good for her."

"I keep telling her she'll be the Easter envy of all the mothers," he said, heading into the kitchen. "She keeps telling me she's not having kids."

Kaylie mulled that over as she checked inside cabinets and the top corners of closets and behind doors. She'd honestly never thought about having kids, which made sense since she'd honestly never thought about getting married. She knew a lot of women raised children on their own, but doing so wasn't an option for her. Living alone with her mother wasn't what had taught her that. She'd learned her lesson from her time living with Winton and May.

"Is it hard saying good-bye to this place?" Mitch asked on their way to his truck.

"Not the condo, no," she said, climbing into her seat as he double-checked the tailgate before taking his place behind the wheel. "Drive three blocks west and make a right. I'll show you the hard part." He did, and less than a half mile later she gave him directions again, pointing to the curb in front of the Sweet Spot. "Pull over right here."

Mitch eased the truck into place, shifted into park, and shut off the engine, staring along with her at the frosting-pink awning with the chocolate-colored polka dots shading the bakery's front door. "This was yours?"

"For almost five years. I baked the best brownies in town, bar none, and that's not a pun, or an exaggeration," she said, making the long-running joke one last time. "But then I know what you think about my brownies."

"I've got a feeling they're the best in more places than Hope Springs and Austin. I saw them in a shop in Gruene once."

"And?"

"Oh, I didn't buy any," he said, laughing. "I thought about it, but mostly I wondered who this upstart was peddling desserts in my town."

And now he was cooking for the upstart. A nice bit of poetic justice. "So Gruene's *your* town, is it? From what I've heard, it's not even its *own* town anymore."

He smiled at that. "I've worked there longer than I was in the service. Hard to believe that much of my life has been spent in a place like this."

"Where did you think you'd spend it?"

He stared straight ahead, one wrist draped over the steering wheel, his fingers tapping the dash. "With my family. Anywhere we wanted to go. But nowhere in any plans was I forty-seven and on my own."

He did such a good job of hiding his pain, but it was there, this time, in his voice, the set of his shoulders, the tension weighing him down. "I'm sorry. Truly. No one should have to go through that."

"You're right. No one should." After a moment of silence, he reached for the keys. "Ready to go?"

"I am," she said as he started the engine. She'd been ready to go for years.

~

"I need to tell you something," Mitch finally spit out as his truck hit speed outside of Austin. All day long the words had been clawing up his throat, screaming to get out, burning.

He'd swallowed them down repeatedly, waiting for the right time to say them, and now he was running out. He had less than an hour to tell her his story. Less than an hour before losing her again.

"Okay."

He heard the frown in her voice and could only imagine what she was anticipating. A change to the menu. A problem with the equipment in the kitchen. His resignation before they'd even opened the doors. "It's not about Two Owls."

"Okay," she said again.

This time he heard curiosity, but something more. Suspicion. Trepidation. As if she were expecting bad news. Was this what it had always been like for her? Waiting for the roadrunner to drop an anvil on her head? To be swept out of one home and tossed like trash into another? How many times had she had to fall before she stopped looking for anything good?

His throat was swollen nearly shut, his heart racing. He took a deep breath and wiped first one palm and then the other on his thighs. "I'm not sure what all Luna's told you about me. Not about our working together, but my life before that. Before I joined the service and met Harry."

"Nothing, actually. And I know very little of what came after."

One thing about Luna. She knew how to keep a confidence. Another deep breath, and he backhanded the sweat beaded above his lip. "I got into some trouble early in my life. With drugs. I thought I was holding things together. Most junkies do. But then I lost my job. I tried for months to find another. But there wasn't anything to be found."

She let that settle for several seconds, then asked, "What about your wife? Did she work?"

"We were never legally married. And she stayed home with our daughter. Said that was her job, though I told her I could be the at-home parent for a while." He paused, took a breath, and wiped his palms again. "Her habit was worse than mine. Looking back, it's pretty easy to see she didn't want to work because she preferred stoned to sober."

In the seat beside him, Kaylie tensed, her fingers flexing against her thigh. "I once knew someone who held the same view. Or so I've come with time to believe."

Mitch turned his head, his gaze moving between his side mirror and the road. He swallowed hard, cursing Dawn for not being there when their little girl needed her. Cursing Ten Keller for making Kaylie revisit this part of her life. Cursing himself for listening to Luna. He should've stayed away from Hope Springs, let Kaylie find him.

The miles clicked by and the silence deepened and time continued to run out. He felt their lost years like a bottomless moat between them, too wide to cross safely, to deep to survive.

"Anyhow, one day I was standing in front of the pantry, my daughter in my arms, looking for something to feed her for lunch, and there was literally nothing but a can of Crisco in the house. It was the wake-up call I'd been needing. I had to find some way to provide for my family. So I enlisted. I was twenty-three. And I believed all the recruiter's promises. Four years and an education on Uncle Sam's dime."

Again, she took her time digesting his words before asking, "But it didn't work out?"

"I didn't mind the service. I met Harry Meadows in boot camp, and we shipped out together, were given most of the same assignments. But, yeah, it was tough being away from my kid. I called home, though it was rare if anyone answered. And I wrote letters, but no one wrote back. I figured I'd been dumped, and it wasn't the worst thing in the world. I'd already planned to file for custody of my girl, even though my odds weren't good."

Kaylie gave a sharp, knowing snort. "I've heard courts like mothers."

He nodded, wondering if she'd started putting two and two together, wondering if he could finish before she got to the bottom line. "Problem was, my girl's mother and I weren't married. And I wasn't listed on the birth certificate as the father. It hadn't seemed like a big deal at the time. We were together, and I knew what my responsibilities were. It's just when I got my discharge and came home, I didn't have any grounds to claim her from the state."

"From the state?" she asked after at least a mile had passed, her tone level but the words shaking their way out of her mouth.

He pressed on, his hands shaking, too, his whole body stiff with dread. She had to be close to figuring it out, and he wanted to be facing her. He needed her to see his sorrow and his sincerity because he didn't think any of it was coming out with his words. "After finding someone I didn't know living in what I thought was my apartment, I learned from the manager some of what had happened. Then I went to the cops for the rest."

"The cops?" she asked, half shriek, half whimper.

He nodded again, glanced in his rearview mirror, slowed to let an approaching car more easily pass. "My ex had tried to kill herself. No doubt she was wasted, or crashing after a really bad high. A neighbor heard my daughter crying. He came in and got her out of there and called the cops. They took my ex to the hospital. She ended up in prison. And my daughter went into the system. I never saw her again. I had no rights, according to the state, so I hired a PI. But no dice."

"Why are you telling me this?" she asked, her voice tiny like a little girl's, hollow and frightened and so afraid she'd done wrong.

"Because I've kept it from you too long, Kaylie," he said, his chest ripping open, his heart bleeding all over him as if he'd been shivved. "I should've told you the first day I came to ask about the job. I wasn't really there about the job. I just wanted to see you. To see if it really was you. I'd stopped looking for you several years ago. I couldn't take it anymore, coming up with nothing. But I'd been looking for Kaylie Bridges all that time."

"I changed my name when I was eighteen. I didn't want to have the same name as that woman," she said, and her sob rent through him, and tears welled in his eyes, blinding him.

He swiped them away, but he still couldn't see as he made the turn onto Chances Avenue. "I'm sorry. About everything. Today. The last month. That I left you with your mother in the first place. That I couldn't find you the nearly twenty years I looked."

He pulled into her driveway, turned off the truck, then turned to her to ask for forgiveness. But it was too late. She sat stiffly, staring straight ahead. "I'm sorry, too, *Mitch*, but I don't think I can have you working at Two Owls."

She pushed open her door, jumped from the cab, and ran to meet Magoo, who exited the house in front of Ten Keller. She knelt in front of her dog, buried her face in his ruff, and threw her arms around him. Then, shoulders still shaking, she stood and headed for the house.

Mitch watched beside his open door. Ten watched from the driveway, waiting until the screen slammed behind her before moving. Mitch wasn't in the mood, so he headed to the bed of his truck, untying the knots of the ropes holding Kaylie's things in place.

Keller spoke first. "I guess that didn't go so well."

"It doesn't matter how it went. It's done."

"Yeah." Ten slapped his palm against the truck bed and turned back to the house.

Mitch reached out, bringing his hand down on the other man's shoulder. "Leave her alone. Let her work through it. Help me get her things inside, and do not ask me anything. Not about what I said. Not about what she said. I'm done talking about this."

Twenty minutes later, his truck was unloaded and Ten was gone and Mitch was sitting behind the wheel. He started the engine and shifted into reverse, then back into park before moving. Reaching across the cab, he opened the glove box, pulling out the stack of letters bound by the chain of his dog tags.

He held them, his hand tight, the words pouring over him as if he'd written them this morning and not twenty-three years ago, twenty years ago, fifteen years ago, when he was all out of ideas on how to hunt her down.

Before he could change his mind, he walked to the house, into the kitchen, left the bundle there in the center of the island, and then he walked out on his daughter, leaving her to fend for herself for the second time in his life.

~

Kaylie was buried beneath her afghan in the wingback chair when Ten found her there in the second floor's living room, where she'd moved it. "How long have you known?" she asked before he could say anything.

He stood in front of her, shoved his hands in his pockets, and shrugged. "Since Wednesday."

At least he didn't deny knowing, though she'd only guessed that he had. "And you kept it to yourself."

"They promised to tell you."

"They?" Her mind raced. "You mean Luna."

"Yeah."

Kaylie closed her eyes and let her head fall back. She was tired. So unbelievably tired. "That's why she gave me the scarf."

"What?" Ten asked, but her answer was more for herself.

"I thought it was a gesture of friendship. But it was an apology. Knowing about Mitch and bringing him into my life without telling me who he was. I can't believe she would do that. What kind of friend does that? And you," she said, her eyes flying open. "You're no better. You knew and said nothing."

"Wait a minute." He held up a hand and backed away. "I hadn't said anything *yet.* And only because I was giving Mitch a chance to come clean. That's why I had him drive you to Austin. To give him the time to say what needed to be said."

"And that makes things okay? The fact that you arranged this...kidnapping? This forced confession?" She was being ridiculous, a harping fishwife, but she couldn't bring herself to care. "I want you to leave."

"Not like this. I'll sleep in my truck, but I'm staying."

She pulled her afghan up to her chin, tucked it beneath her toes. "I don't need you here."

"I need to be here."

Why did he have to have such a hard head? "Ten, please. Don't do this."

He made a sound that was half laugh and half snort. "Don't care about you? Don't worry about you? Don't want to make things up to you?"

"Don't...smother me."

"Oh," he huffed out. "So now I'm smothering you?"

"I didn't mean that. I just..." She was so lost, her thoughts everywhere, racing. "It's not fair, you know. Life. Keeping us apart. Making me think...oh, the things I've thought about him, the reasons I made up for why he left us."

"You didn't drive him away," he said, his voice firm but soft.

"I know that now. And I probably always knew it at some level. But that doesn't help when I remember the horrible things—"

"Kaylie, stop," he said, hunkering down in front of her, his hand on her socked foot where she hid it beneath the afghan. "You couldn't have known. You only had a small piece of the picture. And for a lot of that time, you were a child."

"I haven't been a child for a while, Ten. And I've still had those thoughts."

"So, put 'em away," he said, as if it were nothing, easy. Nothing.

She would. But she couldn't do it with him here. "I need you to go. I need to think. And to sleep. And I need to be alone."

"If you're sure."

She could hear the hurt in his voice, but she couldn't look up. "Just for tonight. I just…need time. To process all of this. I just…" She stopped, as what felt like a knife blade pierced from her stomach all the way to her spine, nearly doubling her over.

"Kaylie," Ten said, surging forward to catch her.

"I'm fine." Oh, what a lie that was. "I think I may have an ulcer, but I'm fine."

"Do you need a doctor? Something to drink?"

She needed him to let her take care of herself. "No. I just need you to go."

"I don't like leaving you like this."

"I promise I'll call you if it gets worse. But I need to be alone now. Please. Don't make me ask you again."

CHAPTER THIRTY-EIGHT

Kaylie hadn't been asleep for more than an hour when Magoo woke her with intent. He wasn't growling at the window as he had when Ten stopped by, or whimpering to be let out for a trip to the yard. This was purposeful, his nudging at her shoulder, at her collarbone, her face. Exhausted, she pushed him away, pushed a second time when he insisted.

It was when he nipped at her cheek that she jumped, angry. And then she smelled smoke. Not the smoke of something burning in the kitchen. Neither she nor Dolly had cooked in the house today. And Mitch hadn't been by since their trip two days ago to Austin. But this wasn't the smell of food anyway. It had a harsh metallic tang. The smell of a cord burned through.

She jumped out of bed, scrambled into her pants, and grabbed her boots, her laptop, her phone and her knife, her keys and her tiny wallet. Barefoot, she ran down the stairs, one flight and then another with Magoo practically nipping at her heels. Her heart pounded in her chest even louder than her feet did on the new flooring as she crossed the kitchen, Magoo's nails scrabbling behind her.

Ten never left any of his tools plugged in. Neither did Will. The appliances in the kitchen were all new and shouldn't be shorting out or sparking. The renovations hadn't required much in the way of new wiring, and every single connection and outlet had been tested within an inch of its life.

Dear God, what was burning? Where was the smoke coming from? She punched 9-1-1 on her phone as she ran out the kitchen door to her Jeep. Magoo jumped in first, and she tossed everything but her keys into the backseat, starting the engine and backing down the drive.

"Nine-one-one," said a gruff male voice. "What is your emergency?"

"My house. I smell smoke. I think it's on fire. At the corner of Second and Chances. My name is Kaylie Flynn. Hurry."

Once the dispatcher assured her help was on the way, Kaylie dialed Ten. And it was just as he answered that she saw the first flame licking at the glass in the third-story window.

"Kaylie? Baby? Is it the nightmare?"

It was, but oh, this was so much worse. "My house is on fire!"

"What?" He yelled the word into the phone, and she heard him knock something over, cursing in the distance, coming back to her seconds later. "Where are you? Do you have Magoo?"

"We're both in my Jeep. I pulled out onto Chances."

"You need to get out of there."

"Okay," she said, but she wasn't going anywhere. "Magoo woke me up. He smelled the smoke. If not for him—" A sob grabbed the rest of her words.

"Kaylie, I'm coming, baby. It'll be fifteen minutes, but I'll be there."

As he said the last, the wail of sirens reached her. "I'll let you go. I hear the fire truck."

"Okay. Hang on." He paused, then added, "I love you."

"I love you, too," she said, and that was it. The emotion tearing through her spilled in buckets.

Hot tears streaked down her cheeks, blurring her vision, wetting her neck, her pajama top. Magoo stepped across the console onto the edge of her seat, and she wrapped her arms around him, buried her face in his ruff. He smelled smoky and doggy and was so solid, his breath warm as he panted against her neck.

"Oh, Goo," she said, straightening, swiping her sleeve over her snotty nose. "What're we going to do if we lose our house?"

He gave a single bark, then began to growl as the fire engine and police cruiser both pulled to the curb on Second. "It's okay, Goo. They're the good guys." She found her boots in the back and slipped them on, then gave Magoo his visual command, followed by a verbal "Stay."

She climbed down from the Jeep, circling it to lean against the hood, waiting as the team of volunteer firemen got busy hooking up their gear. It wasn't long before the man in charge approached, crossing the yard at a rapid clip.

"Miss Flynn? Kaylie? Are you all right? Is there anyone inside?"

Wade Parker. Carolyn's husband. She'd met him during Two Owls' trial run. "I'm okay. I was the only one inside besides my dog. He woke me or I don't think either one of us would've gotten out."

He gave her a nod. "Do you have any idea what we're looking at? I know the place has been under construction."

"It has, and I think I smelled something like wiring, but not from the first floor."

"What I'm hearing is that it's on the third. We'll see if we can keep it from spreading. But I'd like you to move your Jeep a little farther down the street to be safe."

"Okay," she said, climbing behind the wheel and backing down the road, stopping when a set of headlights appeared in her rearview mirror, and a truck she could tell was Ten's slid to a stop behind.

He was out and running toward her before she could do more than shift into park. As she turned off the engine, he jerked open her door, and she fell into his arms, holding him, her tears already shed.

"God, Kaylie. Did I do this?"

She stayed glued to him, shook her head against his chest. "No. I saw flames on the third floor. I think it was electrical. Something in the way the smoke tasted."

He brought up a hand to cup the back of her head. "I'm so sorry. Is Wade here? Have you talked to him?"

"I just told him what I knew. I guess now all we do is wait," she said, and hearing Magoo whining behind her, she reached back. Ten kept his hand on hers as she held the dog's head to her shoulder. Beneath her cheek, Ten's heart raced as fast as hers, and she wondered if tomorrow she'd find bruises there.

"I cannot believe this is happening. I should've checked all the connections upstairs. You're living there, for chrissakes. I should've checked everything."

This wasn't his fault. It wasn't anyone's fault. The house had fallen into disrepair, and she'd rushed the renovations. Nothing had turned up in the original inspection to lead her to believe she was living in a tinderbox, but she should've been more diligent, more thorough. She shouldn't have been so desperate to get the renovations started.

She shouldn't have used the house as an excuse to avoid the search for her parents.

A man moved into her peripheral vision, smeared as it was by her tears. He wore a T-shirt and jeans and, she thought, sandals. Mitch. Her father. The man she'd so cruelly assumed had never wanted her and walked out. The man who'd spent his life looking for her, giving up only when he'd run out of places to look.

She'd hated him for so long, hated him without knowing him at all. She'd imagined the worst possible reasons for his abandoning her, and every imagining had been so far from the truth it hurt. She'd thought more than once since she'd met him how cruel Mitch's family had been to leave him. And here she was, that very family who'd left.

Just as she started to go to him, a loud crash from the house had her whipping her head around. Sparks shot from the roof like fireflies to disappear into the dark. Flames licked toward the branches of the nearest trees. *Dear Lord, please not her trees!* She hugged Ten tighter and watched the spray of water soak the leaves, turning the ground below into muck. Her azaleas would be ruined!

And then she started crying again. How many things had she lost? She was safe. Magoo was safe. She had her laptop with ten years of her life's records. But she didn't have May's wingback chair, or the bed where she'd made love with Ten. It was a sentimental loss; her memories were safe, her heart full of them, but losing her bed so soon after giving herself to him seemed so huge in the moment, she almost couldn't breathe.

When she looked back for Mitch, he was gone, and she shook off the strange need that had her wanting to follow. How had he known about the fire? Where had he been that he'd arrived so quickly after she'd called 9-1-1? Did he hate her for the way she'd reacted to hearing the truth about him? Did he know she didn't mean it when she'd told him she didn't want him around?

She stood for what seemed like hours wrapped in Ten's arms, then watched the fire truck pull away. Ten took care of talking to the fire captain and the officers on scene, leaving her side only long enough to do that. Once finished, he led her to his truck, lifting her into the front seat when her feet didn't want to move. "C'mon. You'll stay with me tonight."

"My things—"

"I'll get what's in your Jeep. You stay here," he said, and shut the door.

She watched him walk to where she'd parked, watched him reach into the back for her laptop and knife and wallet. He pulled her keys from the ignition and motioned Magoo out. The dog followed, and when he opened the passenger-side door, Magoo jumped in beside her.

She wrapped her arms around his neck and mouthed *thank you* to Ten as he slid her laptop beneath the seat. He nodded, shut the door, then came back to climb behind the wheel. As they drove away, Kaylie closed her eyes, not wanting to see her house, dark and all alone in the middle of the night.

Two Owls' Brownie Bouquet

april showers bring flowers for may

1¼ cups flour
1 teaspoon salt
8 ounces unsalted butter
2 ounces bittersweet chocolate
4 ounces unsweetened chocolate
1 teaspoon vanilla
2 cups sugar
4 large eggs

Preheat oven to 350°F. Grease or spray with cooking oil and flour (or line with aluminum foil) an 8 x 8–inch baking pan.

Sift the flour with the salt into a bowl and set aside. Melt the butter and the chocolate in a double boiler (or in a microwave), stirring often so as not to burn the chocolate. Mix in the vanilla and 1 cup of the sugar and stir until smooth. In another bowl, stir the eggs into the remaining cup of sugar. Mix half of the sugar-egg mixture into the chocolate batter. Use an electric mixer to whip the remaining sugar-egg mixture, 2–3 minutes, until thick and pale. Slowly fold the whipped mixture into the chocolate batter. Add the flour mixture and stir gently until blended.

Pour the batter into the prepared baking pan. Bake 30–35 minutes, or until an inserted tester comes out mostly clean. Cool completely before cutting.

CHAPTER THIRTY-NINE

Creeping out of Ten's bed before dawn, Kaylie told Magoo to stay put and set off on her own for the house. She'd seen it in the dark of the wee hours, lit by flames and spinning red-and-blue beacons, smoky and wet and sad, but she needed to see it at first light.

To watch the sun rise behind it, the yellow-white beams winnowing through the trees to touch what remained of the new shutters. To dry up the ashy water puddled black in the yard. To show her the extent of the physical damage, not just what she'd imagined last night. She needed to be alone and measure that loss against the one charred and dark, deep in her chest.

She drove past her Jeep where it sat on Chances, parking at the very end of the driveway, and climbed onto the hood of Ten's work truck she'd borrowed, absorbing, grieving, trying to find solid ground. Trying to find acceptance. Less than three months ago she'd stood in this yard and held the keys in her hand for the very first time. Her keys. Her house. Her ten-year dream of returning fulfilled.

This house had been her whole life. The richest love she'd ever known, and absolute joy, and keening, wretched sorrow. She owed her very being to Winton and May Wise. Their nurturing had come without effort, as sure and true as summer sun, brown leaves of autumn, bare blue winter, and new spring.

She wondered if she'd lost the pictures of the seasons she'd decided on as dining room accents. She'd moved them to the parlor for the trial run, having no time to hang them before inviting her friends to eat. She wondered about her furniture stored on the second floor, if the wingback chair was gone, or the afghan. All of the café's linens would be ruined by the smoke, if not the flames. And the windows' lace panels, too. But maybe the front door's stained glass had survived. She'd have to get closer—

At the sound of an approaching truck, she turned, smiling to herself at the sight of Ten. She hadn't left him a note—he would know where to find her—having planned to be back before he got out of bed. She'd wanted to shed this sorrow with her clothes when she climbed in beside him. She'd wanted him to make her, if only for those moments beneath his body, forget.

He walked toward her, holding up her phone. "You forgot this."

"No, I didn't," she told him, taking it from his hand when he drew close. "I needed to be alone. I needed peace and quiet."

"Don't do that again. Leave it in your pocket if you don't want to talk, or turn it off, or whatever, but take it with you. You could have a flat, or an accident, or get—"

She cupped her palm over his mouth. "Did you tell Magoo you'd be back?"

He nodded and kissed her palm. "He's settled in with fresh water and the mess he made clawing around in the blankets I laid out for him."

"He has to have his bed just right."

"Reminds me of someone else who likes more than her share of the covers."

"I do not," she said, leaning into him when he sat beside her, hooking her arm through his. She loved that he'd taken her home.

Later, after the sun hit the ugly spoils of the third floor where it was wet like an oozing gash, he asked, "Do you think you'll rebuild?"

She hated that her house would have a scar. "I hope I don't have to start from the ground up, but it looks pretty bad. I'll have to see what the insurance people say. Then get a contractor inside to determine the extent of the damage."

"I happen to know one."

"I thought you might."

They were silent for a long time after that. Until Kaylie couldn't be silent anymore. "I should never have rushed into this. I should've taken more time. Hired an inspector who would find the termite damage. And the water damage. And the electrical—"

"This isn't your fault, Kaylie," he said, pressing her hand between his. "If anyone's to blame, it's me."

"It is not! I told you that last night."

He ignored her and went on. "I hadn't had time to go through the attic. I should have. I know Will was up there a lot, but if I'd looked specifically—"

"Listen to me." As much as she loved him, it wasn't hard to guess where this guilt trip was coming from. "You think you failed me. You didn't. You think you would've seen whatever this was. Maybe you would have. But maybe not." She took a deep breath and hoped she was right. "Just like you think if Robby Hunt hadn't stayed with you that night, he wouldn't have assaulted Indiana, and Dakota would never have served time."

"That's hardly—"

"I'm not done. Robby could've assaulted Indiana when you weren't there to stop him. And she might never have told you, to protect you, to protect Dakota. Whenever, wherever, the fault would've been Robby's. Not yours. Never yours. I know your sister would agree with me. And I have a feeling your brother would, too."

He stared down at their joined hands, brooding, sober. "My head wants to believe you. But my heart…"

"I know," she said, and didn't say anything more.

"How did you get to be so smart?"

She wanted to be flip, to tease him, but her path to this place had not come easily. "If I was smart, I would've told you sooner that I love you. Because I meant what I said on the phone last night. I love you, Tennessee Keller. I love you with all my heart."

"I love you, baby. I had wanted to tell you long before that, but I could never find the right time."

"It was the perfect time. It was when I most needed to hear it. And when I most needed to say it. Because it was when I most needed you."

Ten wrapped his arm around her and drew her close, resting his chin on her head, holding her hands in his lap. Kaylie thought she'd be perfectly happy if she never moved again, and they were still sitting there, still happy, several minutes later when Luna's car pulled to a stop behind Ten's truck.

Ten glanced over his shoulder, then down at her, nudging her off the hood. "Go on. Talk to Luna. I'll be here."

She kissed him before she hopped down, opening her arms for her friend as they reached the end of the driveway together. Luna rushed forward and held her and rocked her and cried. "This is all my fault," she said, while still in Kaylie's embrace, pulling back to wipe the tears from her cheeks.

Kaylie understood Luna's guilt, but not over the fire. "Of course it's not your fault. The fire department is pretty sure it was a wire and a very sorry squirrel."

Luna gave a sniveling laugh. "Not the fire. My ruining things between us."

"You didn't ruin things between us," Kaylie said, realizing how profoundly she meant every word. "You were honoring your friendship with Mitch."

"But not my friendship with you," Luna said, and squeezed Kaylie's hand.

Kaylie squeezed back, forgiving. "You would have. I know that. You would've told me when you could."

"I wanted to tell you. I knew I needed to. But I had to tell Mitch first. I've known him my whole life. He was so devastated to lose you."

"Luna, it's okay. I understand totally why you had to tell Mitch. I would've done the same thing," Kaylie said, giving voice to a truth she'd come to accept while processing the secret the three people closest to her had kept. "And I think I needed to hear it from him. Not you. Not even Ten. Hearing it from Mitch…it was the best way."

"Ten did that, you know. Had Mitch drive you to Austin."

She nodded. It was who Ten was. He would have insisted a wrong be made right. That tenet was the cornerstone of his life. And then she remembered… "I lost the scarf. I'm so sorry."

"Don't be," Luna said, actually looking relieved. "I'm glad it's gone."

"What?"

But Luna was nodding. "It wasn't right. And it wasn't salad. It was sadness. Some of the greens edging toward blue. I could see it. It was my punishment, but you wouldn't have to know."

And this was why Luna's weaving was brilliant. She put herself into her art, while Kaylie baked brownies…and ate her creative efforts. "Then I'm glad it's gone. I don't want a scarf that makes you sad. I want the scarf we talked about in Gruene. The scarf that makes me think of that day. And of Ten."

"Ten?"

"The *dulce de leche* of his hair. And the coconut sprinkles where he doesn't know he has gray. And the pecans. His eyes are that color of brown. And the cayenne…" She stopped, shivered. "You were right about him being hot."

Luna's face broke into a huge smile. "So when I thought you were coming up with a recipe for brownies, you were coming up with a recipe for Ten?"

"I was," she said, and she didn't even blush.

"I'm glad, Kaylie. I'm really glad. You two are perfect as one." Luna gave her a quick hug. "I'm going to go. You've got a lot to deal with here and I don't want to get in your way."

"You'll never be in the way. We're friends."

"And I'm so glad we are," Luna said, smiling as she ran back to her car.

Kaylie had just returned to Ten, waving Luna on her way, when Mitch's truck turned off Second onto Chances.

"Crap on a cracker," Ten muttered, more to himself than to her.

"Hey, you." She shoved him, but playfully. "That's not very nice."

"I'm not a very nice man," he said, crossing his arms and glaring down.

"You're the nicest man I know. Which is why you're going to wait here while I talk to Mitch."

"If you say so."

"I do. And don't be grumpy about it."

"I'm allowed to be grumpy. You just lost your house."

"But that's not what you're being grumpy about."

He twisted his mouth before saying, "I'm grumpy because I don't like that he lied to you."

"Luna lied, too, and you weren't grumpy about her."

He didn't have anything to say to that. So she rose up on her tiptoes and kissed his cheek. "Let me do this, and then we can go talk to my insurance guy. See how long it's going to be before I can get a check."

"Am I sensing some impatience here?"

"You're sensing a lot. If I know what's ahead, the crash won't be so bad when it comes."

"I was wondering about that, too."

She took a deep breath, reached out, and squeezed his arm. "I'm trusting you'll be here to catch me when I fall?"

The look in his eyes took her breath away. "I'll be here always."

CHAPTER FORTY

He'd tried to stay away. He'd really tried. Last night he'd been on his way home from Bent Bailey's Bar, having eaten a late burger with Morris Dexter, when he'd seen the ladder truck headed down Second Street, sirens blaring, lights cutting swaths of color through the night. His gut had tumbled, his heart pounding furiously through the U-turn he'd taken on two wheels.

He'd detoured across town to Chances Avenue just in case the alarm had indeed come from Kaylie's, not wanting to hit the blockade meant to keep onlookers away. His father's intuition was telling him that it had. The fact that he hadn't been a parent to her didn't matter. His little girl was in trouble, and he couldn't stay away. Not then. Not now. He'd had to come back, see what she'd lost, if the damage was irreparable. Find out if she was done with Hope Springs and moving on. Moving out of his life.

Last night, when he'd pulled up with the other cars behind her Jeep and parked at the end of the long line, he'd seen her in Ten Keller's arms and realized she didn't need him at all. In trouble or not, she was all grown up, and he was just excess baggage.

He'd stayed anyway, watching the firefighters battle the third-floor blaze. He knew from the hours he'd spent in the house that those windows had been in her bedroom. The thought of her asleep, waking to smoke, all alone…

Unless she hadn't been alone. Unless Ten Keller had been with her.

Looking at the two of them now, he thought that might've been the case. And his personal issues with the other man aside, he couldn't deny Ten cared for Kaylie. After seeing them together the last few weeks, he'd easily come to that conclusion. And he liked that it wasn't a case of lust. Or lust only, because any relationship worth its salt came heavily seasoned with physical longing. But Ten's attentiveness went beyond sharing Kaylie's bed. And the look in her eyes when she took him in said everything Mitch needed to know about her feelings.

It made him happy, knowing she'd found someone. That after all this time, she wouldn't be alone. It didn't do anything to ease his guilt over abandoning her in the first place, but he could live with himself if she was well settled, and happy. And maybe one day she'd forgive him. Maybe one day they could share a cup of coffee and she could feed his father's hunger with tidbits of her life. Maybe. One day.

Hands in his pockets, his throat and nostrils raw from breathing the sour air, he kicked at a chunk of charred two-by-four that had somehow wound up in the street. When he looked up again, Kaylie was walking toward him. He rubbed a hand over his bristled hair, stuffed it in his pocket again, tried to smile but it came out stiff, so he dropped it. He wasn't feeling much like smiling anyway.

"I'm sorry I couldn't talk to you last night," she said, her hands in her pockets, too. "I was pretty much a basket case."

So she'd seen him. Noticed him there. Somehow that helped. "How're you doing now?"

She shrugged. "I keep laughing. It seems so inappropriate. I guess it's shock, and when it wears off I'll fall hard. But I really am sorry about last night."

"Don't apologize. I wouldn't have expected you to be anything but a basket case." He paused, uncertain at first where to go, choosing the straightest route in the end. No detours. No beating around the bush. He wasn't here for any of that. "I wasn't sure you'd want to talk to me anyway."

She was slow to answer, as if weighing her words, measuring them against all he'd done, past and present. Against this moment and where they would go from here. "I do. But I think we're going to need a lot more time than we have right now."

"Yeah." It was all he could say because of the hope suffocating him.

"Listen." Her gaze fell to the driveway, her shoulders hunched. She turned both feet out, standing on the edges. Turned them back. "I wasn't able to save the letters. I grabbed Magoo and my laptop and that was about it."

"It's okay—"

"No. It's not," she said, her head coming up. "I hadn't read them yet. I couldn't. I was waiting…I don't know why I was waiting, but I was going to read them. I wanted to read them. Desperately. But now I can't," she said, catching back a sharp inhalation. "And I hate that more than you can know."

He wanted to go to her and soothe her and he had no right. "Kaylie, it's okay. They weren't important."

"They were important to me. They were all I had of you," she said, and on those words, her voice broke. Tears welled, spilling, and she sniffed and swiped the back of her hand beneath her nose.

He dug into his pocket for the handkerchief he always carried and offered it to her. She took it, dabbed gently at the damp skin beneath her eyes, then her nose, folded it into a tiny square and rolled her palm around it.

"They were just pieces of paper." He tapped a finger to his temple. "Everything I put down is still up here."

Her gaze searched his face, imploring, that of a little girl looking to understand something too big for her reach. "Tell me what was in them. I want to know what I missed, what you were thinking."

His own throat worked, aching. He squeezed his eyes shut and rubbed over them with a finger and thumb. She'd said they didn't have time for all the things needing to be said. She was right. So he chose just a few. Words he hoped would allow her to forgive him. Aid him in forgiving himself.

"I wrote some late at night in the barracks. In Germany. In Kuwait." He shrugged. "Other places. I told you how hot it was, and how the sand itched in my cammies like crazy. How glad I was you were inside where it was cool and your skin wouldn't get burned. How I wondered if, when you did go outside, you freckled."

She scrunched up her face. "As you can see..."

He kept himself from reaching out and drawing his finger down her nose. It wasn't easy. He'd done it so many times when she'd been a child. And she'd wrinkled up like she was doing now. He wondered if she remembered. If any part of her was waiting for that teasing touch that had always made her laugh—

"What else?"

There were so many things. "Some guys and I had leave during Oktoberfest once. We ate until we were sick, and drank until we were sicker. Never knew I could down that much beer," he said, grimacing at the memory of his stomach roiling. "There was this little girl, no more than seven or eight, wearing a dirndl like her mom. Perfect little fräulein. She was sitting in a corner, coloring, while her mom slung steins. I remembered how you and I would sprawl out on the floor in your room, a box of crayons spilled between us. You always claimed the pages with ponies and puppies—"

"And I always colored them pink."

He nodded. "She was coloring cats. Blue. I sat across from her and picked up a pink crayon. She looked at me and turned her book so I could color the dogs," he said, watching Kaylie's throat work as she swallowed. "She didn't speak English, but I told her all about you anyway. How you liked pink. And puppies. How your mother tried to braid your hair, too, but you liked it in your face. You said it felt like pony hair."

The wind grabbed at her ponytail then, tugging loose hairs she swiped back and tucked behind her ear. He made a fist to keep from helping her. "It still looks like pony hair. It's beautiful."

"It will look a lot better once I replace my brush and blow dryer. Ten's comb—" She stopped herself, as if admitting to him, her father, where she'd spent last night might meet with his disapproval. His heart grew two sizes, and he found himself smiling when she asked, "What else?"

Breathing deeply, he glanced over her head toward the black and blue of her house. "After my discharge, before Harry convinced me to settle here, I rented a room in a bed-and-breakfast for a while. A friend of Harry's owned it, and she needed the booking, but still cut me a really nice deal. It was big house like yours, but white. And two stories. I had a corner room upstairs. Big dormer windows. Huge canopy bed. Hand-knotted rugs. Doll would love it."

A smile and a nod. "Sounds just like her, but it doesn't sound like you."

"It wasn't me. But I didn't even know who I was then. What I was going to do. Where I was going to go. Christmas rolled around, and I was still there. I'd go to work with Harry at the farm, this was before the Gristmill, then come back and spend the night in the window seat, listening to your favorite cartoons on TV. The Grinch and Charlie Brown and Frosty. Mr. Magoo. I figure that's where your dog got his name."

"It is. I got him from a shelter when he was about six weeks old. He had the ugliest scrunched-up face."

"I wrote to you a lot when I was there. When I'd been overseas, the letters were as much for me as anything. I wanted to save them and read them to you when I got home. But it was different, writing to you when I was back and didn't know where you were." She thought she'd been a basket case last night; she should've seen him then. "It's probably a good thing they burned. A lot of crap in there I would just as soon you not know. A lot I would've never said to you in person. Probably wouldn't say now."

Her face screwed up in confusion. "But you already said it to me. You wrote it down."

"I should've said it into the bottom of a bottle and left it at that."

"Mitch—"

"Like I said, the letters aren't gone. The exact words, maybe, but all the things I wanted to share with you, all of that's still upstairs." He jammed his hands to his hips, done with the past, putting it away. Either they moved on from here, or they didn't.

Silence fell between them then, comfortable rather than strained. Kaylie was the one to finally break it. "I'm glad. I would hate not to hear your stories. And I'd like to hear more. Soon?" She gestured over her shoulder to where Ten waited. "Right now I've got to go. I've got a meeting with my insurance agent in Austin."

"Sure. You need someone to watch Magoo?"

He could tell by the light in her eyes that she loved that he'd made the offer. "He's at Ten's place. We'll be back before supper. But thank you. For thinking of him."

He nodded. "Walk with me to my truck?"

She fell into step beside him, standing back when he opened the door. He thought for a moment about getting in, driving off, waiting until a better time to show her what he'd come here for. But he had now. He might not have later. And so he reached across the seat for the cigar box.

"I found this in my things the other day. When you were born, a bunch of guys I knew gave me these. I know you wanted a box like this for your café. If you can use it, it's yours." He handed it to her without looking up, watched her trembling fingers as she reached out.

She took the yellowed box from his hands, her throat working. He saw it through her eyes, the edges frayed, the label rubbed and worn. He'd wiped it down the best he could, but he hadn't wanted to get it wet, and he knew it still smelled of musty tobacco. He never had smoked but the one. The rest he'd kept.

When he'd returned to find his possessions in storage, he'd hunted through Dawn's mess until he had his hands on the box. And then he'd sobbed, remembering his little girl being born, regretting his mistakes that had cost him everything.

"Oh, Mitch," she said, coming to him, the box crushed between them, the fabric of his shirt wadded in her free hand, her tears soaking through to his chest. "Oh, Daddy."

Mitch nearly crumpled where he stood. It had been so terribly long since he'd heard those words. A lifetime. Forever. It had been even longer since he'd held her while she cried. And she hadn't felt like this then, grown-up and a woman, independent. She'd needed him then. To soothe her bruises. To tell her everything was going to be all right. She didn't need him now.

But dear God, did he ever need her, his tears making a soggy mess of his face and her soft pony hair as he let go of the weight of the past. "Can you ever forgive me, Kaylie? For leaving you alone?"

"You didn't leave me alone. You left me with my mother."

He shook his head. "I knew what she was like. I knew she'd go back to using. She didn't have it in her to stay sober. I wanted away from her. But I wasn't thinking. I should've made arrangements for you in case something happened. I wasn't surprised that something did. Just what it was."

"Why were you with her? If you didn't love her?"

"I thought I did. I was a kid, what did I know? We had a good time together. We partied, hung out."

"Slept together."

"Yeah."

"I wasn't planned, was I?"

This was one thing she needed to know. "Don't think you weren't wanted. You were always wanted. By both of us. We loved you to death. We just didn't know how to love ourselves."

She wiped her eyes as she stepped away. "Do you realize how little I know about you? Other than what I've learned from Luna, and from working with you. And now these stories. I want to know the rest. I want to know it all."

"I'm not sure the rest is worth knowing."

"It is. And I want you to tell me everything. And I still want you to cook for me. If I can get the house rebuilt. And even if I can't..."

He couldn't stop himself. He reached out and brushed back her hair. "I'll come cook for you anytime, daughter. You tell me what you want, and I'll be there in a heartbeat."

"Will you come cook for me at Ten's? The next time you have a night off?"

"You sure he'll let me through the door?" he asked, brow raised.

She bobbed her head. "I'm sure."

"Then I'll see you Wednesday night, punkin," he said, waiting to see if she remembered their old routine.

"You will if you're lucky, Daddy," she replied, and his heart, nearly too big for his chest, took flight.

CHAPTER FORTY-ONE

It had been a week since the fire had burned through the bedroom where she and Magoo had slept, yet walking the perimeter of the grounds this evening, Kaylie swore she could still feel the heat. It was all in her imagination, of course, but she thought it would be a long time before she could shake off the warmth. If not for her dog…

She dropped cross-legged to the ground near her garden, Magoo in front of her, panting as he waited for permission to roam. After a hug and a crinkle of her nose against his, she gave it, though reluctantly, and watched her knight in shining armor race through the underbrush awaiting the landscaper's scythe.

Magoo would never know what he had given her. It was so much more than she could put into words, but since he was a dog, she didn't have to. That made her smile. Then it made her laugh. And oh, it felt good to laugh, to fall to her back and look up at the sky, cut into blue puzzle pieces by the leaves of the trees. Closing her eyes, she listened to the sough of the branches overhead, the chatter of squirrels, Magoo's bark in answer, the trills and the coos and the chirps of the birds…

"Kaylie?"

"Hmm?"

"Are you asleep?"

She opened one eye, then the other, and smiled up at the man standing over her. The man to whom she'd given her body and heart. "When did you get to be so tall?"

"When you lie down for a nap," Ten said, crossing his legs and folding himself to the ground beside her, pulling her to sit when she reached out a hand. "I'm glad I stopped. I almost went straight home. I would've hated to have to drive back to wake you up."

Until the insurance was settled and they knew exactly where they stood with the house, Ten, along with Will, had taken a short-term job in San Marcos. Kaylie missed having him around during the day. "I might've beaten you home if I hadn't fallen asleep. But I learned my lesson." She dug into her pocket for her phone. "See? And it's even turned on."

"Nice to see my threat worked."

"Good guys don't make threats."

"Huh. Does that make me bad?"

"I don't know," she said, leaning toward him. "Let's find out."

Smiling, he cupped her cheek and brought his mouth to hers, his lips parting, his tongue sweet. She smiled, too, kissing him back, loving him back, until they were both grinning. Then she pulled away with a sigh, resting her head on his shoulder. "I haven't mentioned this to Mitch, but I was thinking of changing my last name to Pepper."

"I bet he'd love that," Ten said.

She was so glad the two men in her life were becoming friends. "I feel so dumb having changed it to Flynn, but when I was five, Ernest was so good to me, like Santa Claus, with his white beard and big belly. I had no idea that he was more than a friend to my folks."

"He was a friend to you when you needed one. Your taking his name is about that, not his relationship with your parents. From what you've said, it sounds like he loved you a lot."

"I guess. But I think Kaylie Pepper sounds nice."

"It does," he said, reaching for her hand. "But not as nice as Kaylie Keller."

She couldn't say anything. She couldn't even breathe. All she could do was stare at her hand in his, her fingers folded in his, his so much larger and so gentle and always so very sure.

"I love you, Kaylie. I want to spend the rest of my life with you. I don't care if we do it here, or if we go to Austin, or if you want to start over in Nova Scotia. I want you to be my wife."

"Oh, Ten," she said, happiness bubbling up. "Nova Scotia is way too cold."

"I know it's out of the blue." He ignored her comment and hurried on, as if afraid his proposal had frightened her, as if fearing her response was meant to laugh off what he'd said. "And I know you didn't come to Hope Springs looking to complicate your life even further—"

"Tennessee Keller! You are not a complication." She turned to him, took his face in her hands. "You could never be a complication. I love you, too. So very, *very* much. Don't ever think otherwise. Promise me."

"We don't have to rush," he told her. "In fact, we can wait as long as you want—"

"I don't want to wait," she said, and when he frowned, she reassured him. "I've put off too much of my life already, waiting on one thing or another while I figured out who I was and where I came from, what I wanted. I'm tired of waiting. I want everything now."

"Don't big weddings take a lot of time to plan?"

"Do you need a big wedding?"

"No, but I thought you would."

She laughed, so happy she couldn't stand it. "Maybe we do need to wait, since you don't seem to know me at all."

"I thought all women wanted big fancy weddings," he said as he got to his feet.

She took his offered hand and let him pull her to hers. "No, but all women want their father to walk them down the aisle."

"I think I know a guy who can do that."

"You know a lot of guys," she said, wrapping her arms around his neck.

He rested his forehead against hers. "It's my job."

"I thought that was being a man and knowing everything."

"There is that. But there's one thing I don't know."

"Which is?"

"Your answer."

"What was the question again?" she asked, giddy and floating and in love.

Holding her hands in his, he dropped to one knee, his expression solemn and true. "Kaylie Flynn. I love you. Will you be mine?"

She already was, but she knew that wasn't what he was waiting to hear. "Tennessee Keller. Nothing in the world would make me happier than being your wife."

And from somewhere behind her, in one of the lot's distant oaks, came the hoot of one owl, carried to her on the wind, and answered softly moments later by another.

ACKNOWLEDGMENTS

The Second Chance Café, aka Two Owls Café, is based on a restaurant that friends from work and I used to frequent. It was lunch only. There was a single entrée. And the honor-system cigar box did exist. Truth is stranger than fiction.

Thanks to Jill for her help with general contracting, Sheila for her help with craft fairs, and Sasha for his help with that thing he does in Round Rock. (And, yes, I'm being cagey so as to avoid spoilers.) Thanks to Bekke for the lavender oil and magnets, to Robyn for the photos, and for Maya.

Thanks to Megan F., Margaret M., Stephanie F., Helen-Kay D., Jill S., Laurie D., and Sarah W. for early reads as I shaped this story. (Apologies if I missed anyone; my brain is a sieve!) Once upon a time I had a critique group. Now I have the whole Internet.

Thanks to the professional chefs and hobbyist cooks for the wealth of recipe ideas I tweaked and adjusted for the Two Owls Café menu. Boy, the things I have learned about brownies!

I owe big hugs to Laura Bradford for finding Ten and Kaylie a home, to Lindsay Guzzardo for giving Ten and Kaylie that home, and to Tiffany Yates Martin for making Ten and Kaylie's home a showpiece.

As always, thank you to Walt for your love and all that means. This time, too, for buying me a Mini, then driving me in it to Gruene, and lunch at the Gristmill, and cold water at Gruene Hall. You make every bit of the sweat worth it.

Read on for a sneak peek of Alison Kent's next heartwarming romance

Beneath the Patchwork Moon

Available September 2013 on Amazon.com

The house sat forlorn as it had for ten years, mourning the family who had left it abandoned. Luna Meadows missed them, too. Day in and day out, beneath moonlight and sunlight, from behind painful scars. She missed them with more longing than she'd felt for anything else in the whole of her twenty-eight years. She missed them as if they'd been her own. In many ways, they had been.

Sitting on the hood of her car, a photo of the friend who'd lived here pressed between her palms, she strained to hear the voices that had once filled the rooms inside. With her eyes closed, she pictured the four youngest Caffey children running circles around the legs of the two older, the parents of the six siblings laughing the loudest of all. Yet Luna had only the memories. The sounds had turned to silence, and sadness was all that remained.

Sierra Caffey's family had been one of the joys of being the girl's best friend. She and Luna had bonded their first week as high school freshmen, Sierra new to the private school Luna had attended all along. Even the accident that had stolen Sierra days into their senior year hadn't diminished the connection. Luna had kept her friend close for a decade, bearing the burden of a truth Sierra had taken to her grave.

It was a truth no one needed to know.

It was a truth no one else did.

Pushing off her car, she walked up the pebbled path to the porch where the swing still hung from ceiling chains, where the two big rockers and the table between had weathered to the gray of old age. The lawn, in the past always verdant, was dried to straw, and littered with leaves and acorns left to rot. The dark wood of the structure, the brown of burnt umber, was a victim of creeping moss and clinging mold and ground cover crawling above its station.

The Caffeys had lived on five acres at the far edge of Hope Springs, Texas. Sierra's mother had belonged to many of the same craft guilds as Luna's. But while Julietta Meadows spun and dyed wool for weaving, at first her own and then later, after the accident that had taken Sierra's life, Luna's, Carlita Caffey had been known for the precision of her quilts' tiny stitches, as well as the intricate tops patched together as if the fabrics had always been one.

Not a single night had passed with Luna sleeping under this roof when the mother of the Caffey brood hadn't spent the evening with a quilt hoop in her lap. Luna knew this because she'd helped Sierra and Teresa and Isidora clean the kitchen after supper, sneaking peeks at their mother, who'd kept her head down, her eyes on her needle. In the same way Luna's mother had taught her about weaving, working silently as Luna watched her shuttle fly, Sierra's mother had shown Luna how to patch together stories with colors and patterns and pieces of cloth while never saying a word.

Her key ring in her hand, Luna searched out the one that fit the front door and let herself into the house. The interior was dark and stale, the living room lit only by the beams of light able to cut through the shade trees and the windows smeared with the dirt of time. The lamps had long since gone dark. There were no bursts of illumination shining into the hallway from beneath closed bedroom doors, no glow from the kitchen as Angelo, the oldest Caffey child, stood in front of the open refrigerator searching for something to eat.

Angelo. Angel. Luna's first love. A one-sided love, but no less true, and her heart no less broken for his indifference. While Sierra had attended the St. Thomas School on a music scholarship, Angelo had played quarterback for the Hope Springs Bulldogs. For two years, Luna hadn't missed a game, begging rides from her father to those across town, even those across the state during play-offs. Harry Meadows loved his football, and loved pretending that his daughter loved it, too. Doing so made it easier for him to ignore the fact that she had eyes for only one player and no interest in the game.

Losing Sierra had been devastating, but losing Angelo to college, and later to the family's move from Hope Springs, had crushed her. It shouldn't have. They had nothing in common but his sister. He knew of her longing, of that she was self-consciously certain, but he was two years older and his social circle rich with friends from his much larger school. Luna and Sierra had a smaller circle, fewer friends, making the bond they shared vital to both.

It was going to be hard to see this house destroyed, Luna mused, regret tightening her chest as she walked from the living room into the dreary kitchen. But the structure wasn't large enough to accommodate the new education center planned for the site, a center designed to fill the void left by funding cuts to the school district's arts program.

Where other potential buyers had failed, the local nonprofit behind the venture had convinced the Caffeys to sell the property. The Arts of Hope Springs planned to name the center in honor of the Caffeys' daughter and Oscar Gatlin, the boy who'd suffered a traumatic brain injury in the accident that had claimed Sierra's life. Of course neither family had any idea Luna was the one who'd established the nonprofit, or whose idea it was to build the Caffey Gatlin Academy.

Funny how it had taken a perfect storm of events for her to decide to do more with her life than weave the scarves that had made her a minor fashion star and a major amount of money. The last four months had been so busy, in fact, that she'd done almost no weaving at all, and that wasn't good. She needed to get back to the projects she'd started for the center's initial fund-raising auction, but first things first. Today was about finding the box of Sierra's things she'd come here for.

Sierra had hidden it as well as her larger secrets, entrusting Luna with those but never sharing what she'd done with the box. Luna had looked for it from time to time, checking the most obvious places, but never with the urgency now driving her. Knowing what was inside, she couldn't let it fall into someone else's hands, and construction was just weeks from breaking ground.

She tucked Sierra's photo into her back pocket, tucked her keys into her front, gathered up her hair and knotted it at her nape. She doubted a search of the kitchen would be worth her time, but pulled a chair toward the refrigerator anyway, no stone left unturned and all that. Stepping onto the seat, she opened the first of the highest cabinets, wishing for a flashlight as she reached around inside. She'd definitely bring one next time.

And there would be a next time, and a next, and probably a next. The rambling two-story farm house was so big it had nooks and crannies in its nooks and crannies. A thorough search would take days, if not weeks—something she should've considered sooner, having been here so often in the past. From now on she'd come prepared, she mused, and then she went still, cocking her head at the sound of footsteps climbing the steps to the back porch.

She didn't need permission to be inside. She was, essentially, the owner now. But few people knew that. No one knew she was here, and no one else had reason to be. She eased from the chair, her second foot touching the floor as the kitchen door opened into the room and a man moved to fill the entrance. He stood still as he took her in, not threatening, but waiting, as if she wasn't who he'd expected to find. His face was shadowed, his body large, and her heart thundered in her chest and her ears.

She thought she'd seen knives in the block beside the stove, but not wanting to lose the advantage of surprise, reached into her pocket instead. Just as she wrapped her hand around her key ring, the keys jutting from between her closed fingers like spikes, he stepped over the threshold, ducking beneath the door's facing, then straightening to stand. The light he'd been blocking followed him in.

In that moment, recognition dawned, and her stomach tumbled to the floor, unraveling toward him like a spool of thread. "Angelo?"

"Hello, Luna," he said, his voice deep and sure and aged like fine wine.

After all these years. She swallowed around the lump in her throat and drank him in. His black hair was long, brushed away from his face, his strong jaw darkened with several days' growth of beard. His nose was blade-straight and narrow, his lips pulled into a smirk and beautifully full. His body wore ten years of use that showed on his arms in muscles and scars. His hands were a mess of healed cuts.

"I didn't know anyone was here," she said, ignoring the urge to go to him, to hold him, to touch him, to feel him along with her past. "You scared me."

"Wouldn't want that now, would we?" He closed the door, shutting out what light had been shining through. Shutting them in the room that was full of old pain and Sierra and that very sad silence.

She wanted him to reach back and fling the door open. She wanted him not to know how nervous she was. She wanted to ask him a thousand questions. She wanted him to leave. She wanted him to stay forever. "What are you doing here?"

"No, baby," he said, stepping closer to where she stood, and smelling of sunshine and sawdust and madness. "My house. I ask the questions."

ABOUT THE AUTHOR

Photo by Robyn Arouty

Alison Kent is the author of more than fifty published works, including her debut novel, *Call Me*, which she sold live on CBS's *48 Hours*, in an episode called "Isn't It Romantic?" Her novels *A Long, Hard Ride* and *Striptease* were both finalists for the *Romantic Times* Reviewer's Choice Award, while *The Beach Alibi* was honored by the national Quill Awards and *No Limits* was selected by *Cosmopolitan* as a Red Hot Read. The author of *The Complete Idiot's Guide to Writing Erotic Romance* and a veteran blogger, Alison decided long ago that if there's a better career than writing, she doesn't want to know about it. She lives in her native Texas with her geologist husband and a passel of pets.